# PAINT THE HORSE BLUE

*A Brush With Tragedy*

# PAINT THE HORSE BLUE

# MARK GRICE

## A NOVEL

ARCHWAY
PUBLISHING

Archway Publishing books may be ordered through booksellers or by contacting:

Archway Publishing
1663 Liberty Drive
Bloomington, IN 47403
www.archwaypublishing.com
1 (888) 242-5904

ISBN: 978-1-4808-7485-5 (sc)
ISBN: 978-1-4808-7483-1 (hc)
ISBN: 978-1-4808-7484-8 (e)

Library of Congress Control Number: 2019935330

Print information available on the last page.

Archway Publishing rev. date: 4/5/2019

# 1

## SPRING 2019

**It was a mindless task, the perfect job to do while** meditating. It was a chance to take in the fresh air, the sunshine, and the signs of spring's renewal, and she had done it countless times before. Today, however, her mind was anything but calm and meditative, and the beauty of the day felt like a slap in the face—an insult.

Kella Major eased the tractor around the sharp corner of her largest pasture and started another row back toward the house and farm buildings. She had a set of harrows hooked on behind, and she was spending the afternoon harrowing the field. There were two reasons to be doing this. First, it was an excellent horse pasture management practice. Breaking up the clods of manure that had accumulated as horses grazed in the fall and scraped through the snow for the winter was a great way to fertilize the soil and encourage the growth of new grass that the horses could enjoy for another season. Years ago, her father baled hay on this particular part of the farm, but as their horse business expanded, it was used for the horses that could live outside all year. They had access to a water trough, a shelter that they rarely used, and supplemental large bales of hay in the winter, but the wear and tear on the soil

1

was beginning to take its toll. The best thing she could do, short of hiring someone to do a reseeding and fertilizing, was to give it a good harrowing.

It was late May in central Ontario, and even though the winter had been harsh and dragged on forever, this really could have been done a few weeks ago. But today was the day. Mindlessly spiraling around and around the ten-acre field in smaller and smaller circles, each time she made the turn at the back and faced back toward her house, her anxiety level rose, and she felt an ache in the pit of her stomach. She was dressed in a flimsy tank top and cutoff jeans, with sturdy Blundstone boots. Her blonde hair was pulled back in a ponytail and tucked under a rhinestone-embellished ballcap. She had too much to do in the morning to worry about makeup, and she took some consolation in the fact that this was a great way to work on her tan. At thirty-four years old, she was fit and lean with the sinewy muscles built by riding horses, cleaning stalls, lifting bales of hay, and emptying heavy bags of horse feed—not from working out at a gym. Circling the field and exposing herself to every angle of the sun gave her an all-over tan, as if on a rotisserie. Her joy at this opportunity was short-lived.

The second reason to attend to this task on this particular day was that she needed to get out of the way. She needed to make herself scarce on her own property. She could have driven into town and killed some time in the local coffee shop, but she was tired of running into people she knew and answering their endless questions about her life and her plans. Yes, she could have left, but her nature made her stay. Was it pride, curiosity, or stubbornness? She didn't know, but she'd be damned if she was going to be leaving her own place on a day like this.

She had spent the morning prepping the rest of the farm as best she could. She turned out the horses in various paddocks as soon as they had eaten, and she was taking advantage of the grass to make up for the shortfalls in her current feed program. She had thoroughly cleaned the stalls and used up most of the last of the pine shavings to bed the stalls and add a fresh scent to the air. She added a few glugs of pine soap to a watering can filled with hot water and sprinkled the barn floor before sweeping up. This kept the dust down and made the stable smell amazing. She knocked down some cobwebs with a broom, did some raking outside the door, and made sure the tack was hung up neatly in the tack room. Saddles and saddle pads, bridles and accessories were all stored just the way her father had taught her. She wanted the farm to look perfect today—or at least as good as possible. In her house, she had made the beds, wiped the counters, put away the breakfast dishes, and lit a scented candle. She slid open a couple of windows to let some fresh air blow in through the screens. *What am I doing?* she kept asking herself. *Is this really necessary?* she wondered. *How has it come to this?*

She rounded the end of the field again and saw another shiny car come down the driveway. It pulled up to the side of the house and parked next to the others. Out stepped a middle-aged woman, immaculately groomed and wearing a white skirt and strappy heels. She picked her way across the gravel and up the steps and let herself into the house. As Kella drove closer, she saw a short, heavy man in a gray suit step out of the house with a bottle of water in his hand. He slowed to glance toward the barns, and before he got back in his Lincoln, he took out his phone and aimed it at the house to take a picture.

Mercifully, Kella rounded another corner and started a smaller lap, taking her to the south and away from her house. *What idiots!* she thought as she pounded a fist on the steering wheel. She took a second to peel the strap of her top off her shoulder and gauge the progress of her suntan. Her exposed skin was beginning to redden, but a little sunburn was the least of her problems.

3

Today was the agents' open house for her property. Her Realtor had suggested it as a great way to give local agents a feel for the place so they could add it to their list of possibilities for potential buyers. She had also said that buyers could come from anywhere once it was listed online. It wasn't unusual for foreign buyers to be snapping up properties within commuting distance of Toronto, and whether or not it would be maintained as a horse farm remained to be seen.

Kella's perspective of the place was biased. It had been her life-long center of the universe. She had grown up here, moved away, come back, and thought she would stay forever.

She knew there was a great hill behind the house for tobogganing in the winter. She knew that in the summer, along the edge of the woodlot, you could pick as many wild raspberries as you could hold in your hand or stuff in your mouth before the mosquitoes made it unbearable. She loved to see the wildlife that also made it their home—the whitetail deer, foxes, coyotes, wild turkeys, Canada geese, raccoons, and squirrels. Brook trout filtered into the pond from the stream that slashed across the corner of the property, and years ago, her dad baited hooks with moths that they gathered from the windowsills in the barn, to let her catch fish and collect them in a bucket before releasing them to catch another day.

On magical autumn evenings in the past, she had sat on the grass on top of the highest hill and looked north to witness the colorful spectacle of the northern lights. She had walked in and out of the laneway countless times to catch the school bus as a child or to get the mail from the mailbox. She had waited at the road for the school bus in a pickup truck with her daughter, Corby, on the coldest days and waited for her again to get off the bus and give her a ride back to the house—just like her dad had done with her. It was the only real home she had known, and now she was selling it.

Her anger continued to build with each lap of the field. Every car that came and left, every person trotting into the house and out again was like salt in a wound. Her fashionably dressed agent had set out some cookies on a platter and some bottles of water next to the feature sheets that outlined the details of the house and property. Business cards from each visitor were collecting in a pile on the kitchen counter, each one with a grinning headshot and promises of top dollar for the sellers and great value for the buyers. Kella felt exposed and vulnerable. She felt as though an incision had been made in her torso and she had been opened up and laid out on display. All of her flaws and imperfections, her failures and missed opportunities, were revealed for the judgment of others. All of these strangers were snooping through her house, and while she knew that their presence was the point of the exercise, what bothered her most was that none of them, not one, had gone out to the barn. Nobody had appreciated all the work she had done all morning. Nobody caught a whiff of the stable. Nobody poked their head into the workshop. Nobody would know about the trout or the raspberries.

Mercifully, the time frame for the event had expired, and the only car remaining next to the house was that of Kella's agent. She had greeted each arrival and proudly gloated over her latest listing. She was carrying a half a case of water back out to her car when she spotted Kella and waved her over. Kella pulled up to the nearest fence and pulled the toggle to shut off the tractor; the knocking and wheezing of the diesel engine fell silent.

Major Meadows is an established equine facility situated on one hundred acres of rolling farmland near the small town of Duckville, Ontario. It is a region known for its dairy cows and horse farms, with increasing encroachment by greedy developers creating dense housing within commuting distance to the Greater Toronto Area. The farm features a century farmhouse with an attached, fully contained farm manager's apartment. Outbuildings include a drive shed and workshop, a twenty-stall stable in a converted bank barn with a large addition, and an indoor riding arena with a small viewing lounge. Numerous board-fenced paddocks crisscross the rest of the property and a covered shelter for some retired horses and broodmares that basically live outside all year. There are also two large outdoor sand rings, one of which usually has a simple course of jumps in place. A round pen that is sixty feet in diameter with high, solid wooden walls is positioned next to the parking area.

Kella Major, with the help of her father, Danby, ran a nice little horse boarding business, with a few clients taking riding lessons and going to a few horse shows each summer. It wasn't quite the first-class facility that she wished it was, and therefore the high-end clients in the show-jumping world had passed her by, and she had to be content with taking in retired Thoroughbred racehorses from nearby Woodbine Racetrack and turning them into usable mounts for the schooling-level show riders. Some of her clients were just boarders with their pet horses that they rode a few times a month, while others had dreams of moving up in the horse show world, just as Kella once did.

Kella's father, Danby, was already an established Quarter Horse trainer when Kella was born. He had grown up when the Quarter Horse industry was in its infancy in Ontario, with more and more top Western horses being imported from the States. He had done it all in his career as a professional horseman, from the rodeo arena to the show ring, buying, selling, and exhibiting champions in a variety of Western events. He had stood stallions on the farm and bred his broodmares to raise some top horses in his day, but his day was past. The industry had evolved years ago, and his old-school ways were yesterday's news. His style of horses and his training methods were no longer fashionable, and even though he always said that he had likely forgotten more about horses than any of today's crop of trainers ever knew, he was a relic, a dinosaur, and he knew it.

Kella had been raised with an appreciation for anything that horses could do, but once she started turning the Western trail course obstacles into jumps for her pony, Danby knew there would be no stopping her. As his star was fading on the Quarter Horse show circuit, hers was rising in the hunter/jumper world. She started with the Quarter Horses that her dad said were too tall and "Thoroughbredy" and turned them into successful hunters over fences. She had all the qualities of a rider—quiet hands, a strong seat on a horse, a good eye, and nerves of steel. Her local success did not go unnoticed, and as a teen, she wrangled her father's wide connections into intern positions with some of the top show-jumping stables in the province. She was offered horses to develop into more valuable prospects, and she was a sought-after catch rider at the shows who could get on any horse and within minutes guide it over a course of jumps more smoothly and with less apparent effort than its regular rider had ever done. By the time she finished high school, the tack room at Major Meadows had more English saddles than Western saddles, and the transformation from a Western training center to an elite equestrian facility was underway. Danby could not have been prouder. He adapted to his new role as mentor, manager, truck driver, and handyman, while Kella took the reins as the star attraction.

Kella's mother, Donna, was also pleased, and while she never had taken an active role in the horse activities, she considered herself more like British royalty and less cowgirl. Donna had a job as an assistant bank manager in Duckville, and as the city got closer and closer to the farm, she gravitated toward it. The devilishly handsome cowboy that she married now resembled a character from the old *Hee Haw* TV show, and she resented his corny country ways. She started taking vacations that were of no interest to him. There were mysterious trips to the city to unexplained destinations, and eventually, to nobody's surprise, she asked for a divorce. Keeping the farm for Kella and away from Donna saddled Danby with a second mortgage, but business was good, and he never looked back.

Kella was taking the farm to a level that Danby never could. She was teaching riding lessons to beginners and coaching show riders. She was training clients' horses for show or sale and was on the path of success. Realizing that their business was now outgrowing their quaint facility, Danby bit the bullet and built an addition with ten more stalls and a much-needed indoor arena. Times were good, the money was flowing, and Major Meadows was hitting its stride.

If you ask a father why he got his daughter into horses, he might talk about the responsibility it teaches them, the fresh air and exercise, the wholesome environment, the compassion they sense for an animal, and the work ethic they develop, but if you dig deeper, they'll admit it's a great way to keep them away from boys. Girls outnumber boys in almost every segment of the show horse industry, and nowhere more so than in the hunter/jumper world.

For Danby, this happenstantial strategy had been working in his favor. While there was no shortage of boys poking around Kella during her high school days, the opportunities for her to find her soul mate on the horse show circuit were few and far between.

This changed, however, when she was invited to a Sunday brunch with her mother at Fox Cover Golf and Country Club. Donna didn't golf herself but maintained her social membership status to partake in the amenities and functions at the club. Kella arrived in a simple floral sundress that made her look as delicious as the buffet, and her entrance was not unnoticed by a young man named Reese McLaren. "Well, you clean up nicely, don't you?" Donna said as a sarcastic greeting and kissed her daughter on the cheek. "The McLarens have invited us to join them at their regular table today. Follow me."

Kella and Donna stood at the edge of the McLaren family table as Mr. Corwin McLaren rose to welcome them and make the introductions. Reese was standing too, and as his luck would have it, the seat next to him was empty. He pulled it back from the table and guided Kella into it as he shook her hand.

Reese was twenty-four at the time and, having finished university, was working in his father's insurance business. Kella was just twenty, and since she had basically stayed home since high school, she felt considerably overmatched by this accomplished young man. Conversation around the table seemed to focus on Reese's golf tournament accomplishments, with Donna trying to one-up the McLarens with layman accounts of Kella's equestrienne success.

By the time Kella and Reese made their way back to the splendid buffet for dessert, she was beginning to sense this had been a setup, but she was enjoying it. They each picked out a few of the items from the baked goods selection and decided to share with each other when they got back to the table. Not surprisingly, in the days and weeks to follow, the two began seeing each other on a regular basis. It didn't matter at the time that Kella had never swung a golf club or that Reese was allergic to horses; they found a middle ground, and Kella was head over heels in her first grown-up relationship.

Donna's delight was slightly outdone by Danby's distain. While he hadn't been looking for a partner for Kella, he certainly didn't expect it to be someone like Reese. "It wouldn't kill him to help with the chores once in a while," he'd say when Kella told him that Reese was coming over for dinner again. "I don't care if he's allergic to horses, as you say; he's sure not allergic to grass. There's plenty to do outdoors if he wants to make himself useful."

Their courtship seemed brief to some before their hasty wedding at the club where they met. The wedding photos show Donna and Danby flanking the young bride and groom, and although Danby was cordial and composed, the expression on his face couldn't hide his discomfort with the situation.

The newlyweds set up home in a rented two-bedroom townhouse in Brampton, about a half-hour drive away from the farm but just ten minutes from C. McLaren & Son Insurance. Kella started commuting back and forth to keep things going at the farm with her dad, until five and a half months after the wedding when their daughter, Corby, was born.

As wildly predicted by Danby, this put a lot of pressure on him to keep the farm running smoothly with less and less help from Kella. There were part-time helpers and working students with boarders pitching in once and a while to pick up the slack, but the long days that father and daughter had spent working together were at an end. Kella's attention to the horses and clients was understandably limited as the young mother cared for baby Corby.

Corby of course was the apple of her Poppa's eye. To see a weathered cowboy with his rough and callused hands, sitting on a hay bale and holding a bottle to a baby's mouth, while the baby's mother worked with a horse was a delight to the barn visitors. What made her even more endearing to Danby was the physical resemblance to him and Kella. "She's got the Major nose," he'd declare as he pointed to the wide bridge of the nose that he and Kella shared. It wasn't long, however, before the commute back and forth to the barn with a baby in tow took its toll on Kella and Reese's marriage. Reese expected weekends at Fox Cover, and Kella was more likely heading to another horse show. He resented the "horsey smell" on her clothes, in their car, and in her hair at the end of the day. Their worlds were growing further apart, and finally their differences were irreconcilable according to the court.

Less than two years after her country club wedding, Kella moved back to the country with her dad and her child. The manager's apartment attached to the main house was vacant at the time, so Danby chose to move there and give Kella and Corby some privacy. He remained available for babysitting duties and usually joined them for breakfast and dinner. He left his den intact in the main house but spent little time in there once he was settled into his modest apartment. They'd meet in the barn at seven each morning, and Kella would have Corby stuffed into a stroller or sometimes in a wheelbarrow. Usually Danby already had the feeding well underway, and she would bring him a cup of black coffee in a travel mug. Once the horses were fed, they would go back to her kitchen for breakfast and to discuss the plans for the day. Reese picked up Corby every other weekend, but their schedule was flexible, and Reese's mother was happy to take her if Kella was going to be out of town with the horses. Donna, on the other hand, was anything but a doting grandmother. She posted profile pictures of herself holding Corby on her new Facebook page and claimed the "glamother" moniker, but the reality was she didn't have much time for a toddler. She had gotten that urge out of her system two decades ago.

# 3

## AUGUST 2018

Thirteen-year-old Corby had just been dropped off at the farm by a teammate's mother after her rep hockey team practice. In spite of her mother and grandfather's best intentions, horses weren't her thing. Danby had put her on a pony before she was out of diapers, and Kella and Corby were adorable in the lead line classes when she was a preschooler, but the horse bug never bit. The in-laws didn't mind at all, but they never expected to see the McLaren name again on the back of a hockey sweater. Corby took to hockey with great enthusiasm.

Each winter, her Poppa shoveled off the ice on the pond and built her a little rink. He would strap on his old skates, and the two of them would pass pucks back and forth. Colby's Golden Retriever, Cider, dug the pucks out of the snowbanks for them if they overshot the ice, and all the extra ice time she got put her miles ahead of other girls her age. She and Danby watched the Toronto Maple Leafs game every Saturday night, and she was thrilled when she was finally old enough to stay up to watch the third period, overtime, or even a shootout. Occasionally he would take her to playoff games when the local Duckville Devils Junior B hockey team was in the hunt for a championship, and to see the same arena that she played in packed to capacity with screaming fans inspired her even more.

Corby greeted Cider and checked into the barn where she knew she would find her mother and grandfather on this hot August afternoon. She had seen the familiar truck of their blacksmith, Alfonso Rhodes, parked close to the barn, so she knew he would be working on a horse inside, and she looked forward to seeing him. "How's our little hockey star?" he said without missing a beat as he hammered a red-hot horseshoe that was balancing on his anvil.

Corby tried to time her answer between the blows to make sure she was heard. "I'm going … to be playing center … this season," she said proudly as she took a broom and swept some of the hoof clippings out of his way. Corby may not have been into riding, but according to Danby and Kella, that was not going to excuse her from being part of the family business in any way she could, and her work ethic they established on the farm carried over to her schoolwork and on the ice.

"I'm not surprised!" shouted Alfonso. " I bet the Leafs will be wanting to draft you pretty soon!" Corby giggled, and Cider grabbed a chunk of horse hoof from the sweepings and trotted out the door to settle down and give it a good chewing.

Danby was around the corner of the barn on the tractor, using the loader bucket to push back the manure into a more organized pile. He reversed far enough to catch a glimpse of Corby through the barn door, then put the machine in neutral, engaged the parking brake, and went to get Corby.

As he greeted her with a hug, she felt the warm dampness of his shirt against her. "I need ya to come help me with something," he said as he started back to the tractor. Corby followed without question and hopped up in her familiar place next to him, one hand on the back of his tanned neck and the other gripping the tractor fender. "There's a gate that's popped off the hinge pins, and it takes two of us to set it back on," he shouted over the noise of the engine, but she couldn't make out exactly what he said. It didn't matter. She was up for anything. They headed down a grassy lane between the back paddocks to tackle the gate project. Cider, sensing adventure, jogged along behind.

Kella was finishing up the second riding lesson with one of her beginner students. The young girl's mother was watching the lesson from a lawn chair under a tree next to the outdoor sand arena. She was using her cell phone to take some photos and videos and was prematurely posting them straight to Instagram (#futureolympian).

The young girl gave the horse a pat on the neck and dismounted, while her mother rushed to her side in her flip-flops to help her take off her helmet and hand her a water bottle. Kella stuffed the two twenty-dollar bills the mom gave her into her breeches and made her way back to the stable with the horse. Mother and daughter got into their SUV, cranked up the air-conditioning, and made their way out the laneway, stopping to take a picture through the window of some horse grazing in another pasture.

Kella led Banjo, or "Jo" as he was usually called, into the barn where Alphonso was working. She could smell the scorched hoof aroma as Alphonso expertly aligned a hot shoe against a horse's foot to check for a perfect fit before nailing it in place.

"I think Jo is going to need a hind set after all," Kella called to Alphonso as she hooked him into the crossties and began to take off his saddle. "He seems to be stepping a bit short behind." She took a fat sponge out of a nearby water bucket and gave the gelding's back a cool wipe. Banjo was supposed to be Corby's horse, and technically he still was, but with his reliable disposition and durability, he had long ago been relegated to the title of school horse. He was a valuable part of the team at Major Meadows, and Kella had to balance the expense of keeping shoes on all four of

his feet against the cost of him being too sore to work. "Did you
see which way Corby went?" she asked as Alfonso clinched the last
nail into the horse's hoof.

"I think she went with your dad somewhere," he answered.

"Can you add Jo to your list for next time for a new set on the
back?" asked Kella.

"Say, darling, I've been meaning to tell you something." He
paused and mopped his face with a bandana out of his back pocket.

"What's up?" she inquired.

"Okay, so here's the deal. My wife took her retirement from
teaching school at the start of the summer, and she's been bugging
me to retire too."

Kella had no response. The last thing she needed was to be
breaking in a new blacksmith. Alfonso had been part of the program as long as she could remember. He and her father went way
back.

He continued. "We are thinking of slowing down and maybe
doing some furniture refinishing, maybe have a little antique shop
on the side or something. I don't know. All I know is that my knees
and my back are saying enough is enough. I'm not going to leave
you hanging. Don't worry. My son has moved back from the States,
and he's been shoeing down there on and off for ten years or so.
I'm going to let him take over my clients here. With their approval
of course. So don't be surprised if Damien comes next time. He'll
take care of Banjo—don't you worry. He's got a lot of skills and a
whole lot more energy than his old man!"

"Have you told Dad?" she asked.

"I may have hinted about needing a change a while back but
no—not in so many words," he said, looking at the floor. Alphonso
was practically an uncle to Kella, and she didn't look forward to
any changes. Her dad wouldn't be happy with a rookie doing the
horses, even if he did have ten years of experience.

Alfonso was already packing up his tools, as he could hear the tractor coming back and getting louder. "I stuck your bill on the corkboard," he said as he was getting into his truck. He clearly didn't want to be around when Danby got the news.

A cloud of dust followed Alfonso Rhodes's truck out the lane. Kella picked up the trimmed, sharp ends of steel horseshoe nails from the floor before sweeping the remaining dirt and trimmings into a nearby stall.

Corby grabbed a broom, turned it upside down, and was stick-handling an empty little cardboard box that Alfonso had left behind. She raised the broom to take a slap shot and fired it against the wall of the barn, causing Banjo, who was still waiting in the crossties, to toss his head and scoot back. "Corby!" Kella scolded. "How many times have I told you this isn't a hockey arena!"

"I know, I know!" Corby responded as she gave the box a little hacky sack kick into the garbage can. Cider made a half-hearted lunge for the box as it arced through the air. The Golden Retriever had been bought as a puppy when Corby was five years old. She was named for her color, but Danby always laughed at his own "dad joke" when he told people, "Just look for Corby. and you'll find the dog be Cider … Get it? Cider?" Truth was the dog spent as much time following Kella or Danby around when Corby was in school, and she spent occasional nights keeping Danby company in his little apartment.

"Can you put Banjo in his stall?" Kella asked even though they both knew it wasn't optional. "What did you do with your hockey equipment when you got home?" Not waiting for a reply, Kella continued. "Why don't you just lay it out on the porch to air out a bit until tonight so it doesn't skink up the mudroom any worse?"

"Okay," said Corby, replying to both requests.

Kella had one more horse to deal with before finishing up in the barn for the day. Danby was parking the tractor and started to bring in a few horses that had spent the day outdoors but would get their evening feed inside and spend the night in a stall.

Millennium Blue Jay, or "Millie" as she was called as a barn name, was a sixteen-hand, three-year-old Thoroughbred mare that had been started at a neighboring racing stable but had shown little aptitude for the track. She had been picked up in a claiming race in the spring for $5,000, and her new owners had brought her directly to Kella, hoping to make her a Children's Hunter division contender for their thirteen-year-old daughter. Kella could only roll her eyes at the absurdity of that possibility, but she would always give the horse the benefit of the doubt. A green horse with a green rider was never a good combination. Millie was an anomaly because she was actually starting to prove the owners right and Kella wrong. While she never expressed her misgivings directly to them, saving those conversations for dinnertime musings with her father, she tried to remain positive and keep the horse in training as long as possible to provide herself with a steady income.

"You might want to lunge her before you get on!" Danby called to her. He sensed that she still looked a bit frisky as Kella was leading her out to the riding ring. Kella picked up a lunge line that was coiled up next to the gate and snapped the end to a halter that she had attached over the bridle. She clipped the reins through a small ring on the pommel and ran the stirrups tightly up the leathers on both sides of the saddle so that they wouldn't be swinging wildly. Her hands did all these tasks with muscle memory that came from a lifetime of repetition—the endless adjustments of leather straps, buckles, and clips that every horse trainer can do blindfolded. She quietly grabbed a long whip that was leaning against the fence and smoothly uncoiled the line, then clucked to the horse as she jogged out into an ever-growing circle until the lunge line was fully extended. Millie extended into a brisk trot, and Kella held the whip in her opposite hand. It acted as an extension of her arm, keeping the horse at a consistent distance and pace.

After several laps at the trot, Kella raised her whip and took a more aggressive step toward the mare as she made a smooching sound with her lips. Immediately the horse picked up the cue to canter and gave a scoot, a fart, and a buck that almost tugged Kella off her feet. The next few laps were at what felt like racetrack speed, and the Thoroughbred's lineage was showing itself again.

"I told you so!" shouted Danby, who had taken a position with his arms resting against the fence as he was making his way to another paddock to retrieve the next horse. "I don't think you'll ever be able to just get on her and go," he said. "She sure ain't no Banjo!" He laughed and left Kella to manage on her own.

After a while, the bay mare settled into a quiet rhythm of cantering. Kella buckled up her helmet and led the horse to the mounting block in the corner of the sand arena. Millie stood quietly to be mounted, but Kella realized quickly that she hadn't put any fly repellent on her, and the late-summer horseflies were out for blood. She decided to carry on anyway, and after working the horse at the walk, trot, and canter, she took her over some poles that were laid out on the ground and spaced properly to accommodate a horse's stride. The first time through the poles, the horse slowed, snorted, then quickened, and her hooves ticked against the poles. After a few more attempts, Millie got the hang of it and was able to maintain a steady pace through the poles without touching any. Kella decided to end the session on a good note before the flies drove either of them crazy. She gave Millie a vigorous rub on the neck, hopped down off the saddle, and took her back to the barn.

**4**

A week had passed since Kella got the word from her farrier Alfonso that he was finally retiring and turning over his shoeing business to his son, Damien. She still hadn't mustered up the nerve to break the news to her father, hoping that the two men would run into each other in town and have that conversation on their own. Then her dad would tell her, and she could act surprised. She had received a text midmorning from an unknown number that read: "This is Damien Rhodes. Alfonso's son. Dad said you needed back shoes put on your gelding. 3:30 ok?"

Kella responded: "Yes thanx I'll have him in the barn for you. :)"

Kella saved the number in her phone with Damien's name.

She was relieved that Danby had a doctor's appointment in Brampton that afternoon and wouldn't be around. Sooner or later, he had to know, but the later the better.

Danby avoided doctors' offices like most men of his generation. Without a wife to prod him with "You really should get that looked at" or "I've made an appointment for you on such and such a date," Danby was on his own to manage his health care, relying on the occasional nudge from Kella to spur him into action. What made matters worse was that his longtime family doctor had recently moved his small, antiquated practice into a partnership with several other specialists in a brand-new medical center attached to a large indoor mall. Then to Danby's surprise, he retired and passed on his patients to a young female doctor named Fahmida.

Exiting her office with a brand-new prescription for his high blood pressure, he could only laugh at the changes he had experienced in his seventy years. He decided to delay heading back to the farm for a while, enjoying the cool, air-conditioned atmosphere in the mall. His cowboy boots ambled across the tiled floors with a clickety-clack sound that made him feel quite conspicuous. He glanced at the mannequins in the storefronts, trying to figure out if the clothes were for men or women. Soon he was confronted by a young lady at a kiosk with a Russian accent, asking him what sort of skin care products he used. He spent a few minutes with her and politely allowed her to rub some lotion on his gnarly hands. When she finally told him the special price for the little jar was just forty-nine dollars, he retracted his hand like the head of a snapping turtle. He strolled into a Starbucks to get a cup of coffee and stared at the menu board before his turn in line, trying to find something familiar.

"What can I get started for you?" offered the tattooed lady with the nose ring.

"Just a coffee please," replied Danby, realizing this might be an inadequate response.

"Blond, medium, or dark roast?" the barista shot back.

"Just a medium, I guess."

"And what size, sir?"

"Um … medium is fine."

"We have tall, grande, venti, and trenta."

*Oh, for crying out loud*, he thought. *How has this become so goddamn complicated?* "So what's the smallest?" he asked.

"That would be tall," she said as she glanced at the growing line behind him.

"That's fine, whatever," he said as he considered the absurdity.

"And do you need room?" she continued.

"Oh, I'll probably just sit over here if that's okay," he said sheepishly, pointing to an empty table.

"Do you need room for dairy?"

"For what? Oh, you mean cream? No, just black is good—thanks."

The girl held up a cup and a black marker as Danby laid a five-dollar bill on the counter. "Can I get your name?" she asked.

"Danby Major," he stated, determined to comply with any further requests and avoid more embarrassment. As he took a seat in a brown leather chair, he looked at his cup. Next to a happy face were the loopy, cursive letters: Danny.

Kella was sweeping up in the barn when the grumble of Alfonso's truck came to a stop outside. The engine turned off, but Eminem was still blaring from the speakers through the open windows until the driver door squeaked open. Kella knew for certain that this must be Damien.

Her recollections of Damien were distant. He had started at the same high school the year after she graduated. She remembered vague reports from Alfonso about him being a good athlete, and he played for the Duckville Devils Junior B hockey team. She knew he had gone to the horseshoeing school in Oklahoma to get his certification, but that was where the trail went cold. He hadn't come up in conversation with Alfonso again, and she had more or less forgotten that he existed.

When he stepped into the barn, he approached her confidently and shook her hand. "I'm Damien. You must be Kella," he said.

Before she could answer, she thought, *My, my, my, aren't you all grown up!* "Yes, thanks for coming. Banjo's over here. I'll get a halter on him and put him in these crossties."

"Okay, I'll get my gear set up," said Damien as he went back to his truck.

Kella stood by Banjo and observed Damien as he went back and forth to the truck. Setting up his anvil outside, he fired up the little forge. He was dressed in Wrangler jeans, construction boots, and a tight black T-shirt with Nirvana across the front in faded gold letters. His arms and face were tanned, and he had the same olive skin and swarthy look of his father. His dirty ball cap had a United States Equestrian Team patch on the front, and it covered his black, wavy hair.

He asked Kella if she could walk the horse up the barn aisle and back a couple times so he could study how he moved and decide how best to approach the shoeing. The second time down the aisle, he already had all the information he needed, so he took the moment to appreciate how nicely Kella fit into her jeans. "Has he been forging at all?" he asked. Forging was when a horse clipped the back of his front feet with the front of his back feet at the trot.

"Not that I've noticed," said Kella. "I just think he needs a bit of support behind to keep his soles off the ground."

Damien went straight to work on the gelding's left hind foot, paring it down with a hoof knife and using the rasp to file it flat. He had a blank steel shoe heating up in the forge, and he quickly but carefully held the hot shoe against the hoof with a pair of tongs, blowing the smoke out of the way so that he could examine the fit. Back in the forge to reheat it and then onto the anvil for a few blows to adjust the shape to a custom fit for Banjo. Kella had seen Alfonso go through this routine hundreds of times, so the technical aspect didn't hold her attention as much as the man himself. She was admiring his arms and watched as the veins filled in his forearms when he bent over to work on the foot. The heat from the forge made his skin glisten, and a bead of sweat formed on the end of his nose as he labored. His shirt was sticking to his athletic frame and revealed his hard shoulders and defined muscles on his back.

*Maybe this change isn't going to be so bad after all*, she thought. "So you're back up here to stay?" she asked.

"Looks that way," he replied. "It was just getting too complicated for me to be working in the States anymore, if you know what I mean. I sold my tools down there before I drove back. Crossing the border is sketchy enough these days without a trunk full of gear. The timing seemed right with my dad wanting to slow down and that. I'm really hoping to be able to pick up where he left off." Damien deftly tacked the shoe into place and set the foot up onto his knee to clinch each nail over in the front. He slid a rasp out of his leather apron and smoothed off the front of the hoof, giving it a perfect alignment with the shoe. He was repeating the process with the back right hoof when Corby came through the door.

"Come here! I want you to meet someone," Kella called from the other end of the stable. Corby came around the corner expecting to see Alfonso. "Corby, this is Alfonso's son, Damien."

"Hi," said Corby shyly.

"Hey, Corby," said Damien as he wiped his sweaty hand on his thigh before offering it to Corby to shake.

"Damien used to play for the Devils," said Kella.

Damien's smile left his face, but Corby lit up. "You did? What position? I play center. I play rep hockey. Girls' hockey. Do you still play? Did you get drafted?" inquired Corby in rapid fire succession.

Damien turned back to his work. "No, I don't play anymore. Never got drafted. I played defense," he said quietly.

"What's your favorite team? Mine's the Leafs—and Duckville Devils of course. My friend's brother plays for them. The Devils, not the Leafs!" said Corby, and she and Kella laughed at that.

"Washington Capitals, I guess. They just won the cup," said

Damien. "I was living in Virginia for a while. They were all I heard about down there."

Corby rubbed Banjo's forehead, while Damien continued on the second shoe. She continued to try to coax a conversation about hockey out of him, but Damien kept his answers brief and stayed focused on the task. He wanted to make a good first impression on Kella and didn't need Corby's hockey talk to distract him into making a mistake. One gouge of the hoof knife, one too many strokes of the rasp, one nail out of place, and Banjo would limp away—and so would Damien's chances of staying on as the regular shoer for Major Meadows.

Kella had seen more than enough to be convinced, but she didn't need him to know that just yet. He was still going to have to get past Danby. She looked down the laneway, hoping to not see his pickup truck just yet.

Kella sent Corby out to start bringing in some of the quieter old horses that she could easily handle. Damien was finishing up the right foot and said to Kella, "If you don't mind, I'm going to paint some Venice Turpentine on the bottom of his soles. It'll toughen them up a bit."

"Sure," said Kella, "sounds good to me. Let me go to the house and get you some cash."

"Do you need a receipt?" asked Damien. "I don't have my bookwork in order yet. I can just write something on a piece of paper if that's okay."

"It's no problem. He's my horse. I'll just get you the cash."

"Fifty is fine," said Damien.

Kella returned with three twenty-dollar bills and insisted she didn't need the change.

She lingered as he was packing up and watched him put the tools back in order in Alfonso's truck. Then he reached into the truck behind the driver's seat and pulled out a fresh T-shirt bragging

Virginia Is For Lovers across the front. Kella tried to come up with something important to say as Damien peeled off his dirty shirt, dipped it in a bucket of water that he had been cooling horseshoes in, and then wiped his face and his neck with it. He was impressively fit—though not surprisingly, considering his athletic past and physical line of work. His tanned arms contrasted sharply with his pale torso.

"Excuse the farmer tan," he said, catching her staring blankly as he pulled on the clean shirt.

Again Kella looked frantically down the laneway, hoping not to see her dad pulling in. "Oh no, that's … quite okay," she said, desperately searching for something more clever.

"So, I guess I'll see you again?" he said, hoping for some confirmation that at least the trial was going to continue.

"For sure," said Kella. "I've got your number now, so I'll text you when I need you. Next time, I'll try to have a few more lined up at the same time to make it worth your while."

"Awesome. Thanks again," said Damien.

Alfonso's truck had just disappeared up the road to the north as Danby's pickup arrived from the south.

*Phew!* thought Kella. *That was too close!*

Danby came straight out to the barn and grabbed two horses from the nearest paddock to bring them in. Kella was scooping feed into feed bins, and Corby was filling water buckets.

Danby noticed Cider gnawing on some hoof clippings. "What horse got trimmed today?" he asked.

"Banjo got hind shoes on," Kella replied and quickly changed the subject before Corby got a chance to say anything about Damien.

After dinner, Danby was reading a *Toronto Star* newspaper he had picked up at the mall, and Corby was playing NHL 18 on her Xbox. Kella decided it was as good a time as any to tell her dad.

"Alfonso's son, Damien, came today to do Banjo. He's going to be taking over now that Alf is retiring."

Danby paused and replayed what he had just heard. "What's that?" he said.

"Damien is taking over for Alfonso now."

"Damien Rhodes was here today?"

"Yes," said Kella as she put the last dish in the dishwasher.

Danby checked to make sure Corby had her headphones on. "I don't want that kid around here. He's nothin' but trouble."

"He's not a kid anymore, Dad. What do you mean trouble? He seems pretty nice to me, and Corby sure liked him. He did a great job on Banjo," said Kella.

Danby checked on Corby again, then lowered his voice and said, "Well you might think differently if you knew that he killed someone."

The Duckville Devils Junior B hockey team had been the talk of the town for more than fifteen years. The franchise struggled to keep any following for several seasons, and sponsors came and went until Richard Morden stepped up and took over the team. Richard owned the *Duckville Dispatch* weekly newspaper and Morden's Modern Printing Inc. Soon after he acquired the team previously known as the Huntsmen, he changed the name to the Devils. The name came from the tradition in the print industry of calling the apprentices devils—the ones who set the pieces of lead type into trays to form words and sentences, which would then be coated with ink and pressed onto paper. The workers inevitably would get covered in ink and "look like the devil"; thus the term *printer's devil* was coined.

Under Morden's ownership, the team shot to prominence in the community, largely because he could tout their exploits on the front page of the *Duckville Dispatch* anytime he wanted. Crowds in the early-season games were understandably limited, but after Christmas and once the push for the playoffs was underway, the *Dispatch* would whip the town into a frenzy over the excitement of each game and write about the players as though they were each the next Wayne Gretzky. Excuses and justifications were invented for the losses, but the wins were celebrated. The brainwashed community responded with their attendance and support. Better players from out of town were brought in and billeted in local homes and attended the local high school. The Duckville Devils were known as the "Hottest Thing in Town!"

Damien Rhodes was in his third season with the team as a defenseman. Rhodes was a fan favorite for two reasons. First, because he was a local. He had grown up in the school system and was a popular multi-port athlete in high school. Second, he was known unofficially as the team's enforcer. He wasn't the biggest player on the team, but what he lacked in size, he made up for in ferocity. He held the team record for penalty minutes, and on more than one occasion, he faced suspensions by the league for fighting and questionable on-ice tactics. Opposing teams feared him, and he embraced his role as the one who would stick up for his teammates if any of them received rough treatment from an opponent.

Damien was out of high school and putting college plans on hold to continue playing hockey, hoping to get noticed so that he could move up to a higher league. Those opportunities were fading as his type of player was being replaced by the skilled players, while the next generation of fans and officials were losing their appetites for fighting in hockey. In the meantime, he was working full-time for Morden's Modern Printing Inc., packing and stacking boxes of paper and supplies. Richard Morden was always able to employ two or three players and was generous with the flexibility of their schedules during the hockey season.

The 2006–2007 season went well for the Devils. They finished second in the league overall and were poised for a great playoff run. The *Dispatch* continued to flood the pages with reports of the team's heroics, and the fans filled the arena for every home game. Some wore clipped-on red devil horns, and others brought plastic devil's pitchforks emblazoned with the team name on them, waving them enthusiastically with every goal.

The team powered through the first two rounds of the playoffs before they faced their most intimidating rivals, the Beaverwood Loggers, in the finals. Beaverwood had finished first overall in the regular season and had a winning record against the Devils, but the *Dispatch* downplayed their prowess with an expected bias.

It was early April, and the best-of-seven series was tied at two games apiece when the Loggers faced off against the Devils in their home arena. The *Dispatch* had the town in a fury over the team and had published a weekend special edition to keep up with the play-off fever. The boys enjoyed celebrity status at school, were usually treated to meals in the local diner, and received employee pricing at Donovan's Sporting Goods. The stands on this night were a sea of red, with fans decked out in all of their Duckville Devils gear. Kids in replica red team sweaters, grandmothers in red scarves, farmers in their red ball caps, and Richard Morden in his glory. Two more wins, and they would take the championship, and a banner would be raised to the rafters of the arena for an eternity.

The first two periods went back and forth, with the teams trading shots and blows like modern-day gladiators. At the start of the third period, the game was tied 2–2, and the fans were anticipating a heated finish. Beaverwood fans congregated in the open seats behind their team bench and waved their blow-up axes to cheer on their team. There were always a few fans who took the rivalry too far, and the jeering would turn to name-calling and profanities, but in general, the two sides respected the boundaries, and an outright riot was not expected.

Damien received a penalty for roughing in the first period when he took too many liberties with the opposing goalie after the whistle had blown. He was swarmed by the Loggers and knocked at least two down before the referees separated them and sent him to the penalty box. In the second period, he took a two-minute charging penalty when he drove the Loggers' top scorer into the boards with such force that the impact popped the clear Lexan panel out of the stanchions, and the game was delayed while the arena maintenance staff repaired it.

Five minutes into the third period, with the game still tied, Damien looked for the opportunity to ignite his team and his fans with a fight. He prowled the ice looking for any reason to spark an exchange. When he saw a Logger forward graze the Devils' goalie's head with an elbow as he skated by, Damien pounced on him.

The two players dropped their gloves, unclipped their helmets, and squared off as the fans stood from their seats with a roar. This was the kind of excitement they had come to see. Their stud player, Damien Rhodes, was standing up for his goalie, his team, and his town, and Duckville citizens could not have been prouder. Richard Morden was rubbing his hands together from his box seats.

The referees backed away and kept order among the other players, fearing a bench-clearing brawl. They knew the enforcer's code, and both young men were willing combatants. They would not step in and separate them until one or both went down on the ice.

Damien took off his sweater and circled around his adversary, waving his outstretched arms up and down to stir up his appreciative audience. He slid his elbow pads up his arms and clenched his fists to move in for the first blow.

Representing the Beaverwood Loggers was seventeen-year-old Justin Semper. Justin was big for his age, but his coordination had not kept up with his growth spurt. At six foot two and 195 pounds, he was larger than Damien but not as nimble and not as skilled a fighter. Justin still had a genuine hope of moving up in the league ranks, and Junior A scouts were watching him intently.

Damien's first punch rocked Justin's jaw, and the crowd cheered and pressed tighter against the glass. Justin grabbed Damien by the shoulder pads and started to swing wildly. He landed glancing punches, but Damien was ducking and dodging skillfully, waiting for his next opportunity. As the big boy slowed down, Damien took advantage with a left hand that caught him just above the eye, splitting his eyebrow. Damien continued with a flurry of body blows, reaching up and punching his chin and throat, and they grabbed and punched and spun until Justin lost his footing and stumbled to the ice. Damien was on him instantly, grabbing his neck, and the referees quickly dove in to protect both players from further damage. As the two warriors stood, each side claimed victory, and they clapped and cheered and waved their supporters' paraphernalia while the two were escorted off the ice and banished to their respective dressing rooms. Damien took a moment to pause and raise his arms in victory, clasping his hands over his head. Duckville fans responded with a roar. Teenaged girls swooned, children jumped up and down, and adults clapped proudly for their native son.

The announcer clicked on his microphone and delivered the proclamation that both players had received a ten-minute penalty and a game misconduct, sending both to the dressing rooms for the rest of the game. Both teams continued at even strength, and the fans quickly refocused on the game, with fifteen minutes left in the period.

Alone in the dressing room, Damien took off his equipment and checked his face in the mirror for damages before showering and getting back into his regular clothes. Justin Semper did the same, then took a Band-Aid out of the trainer's first aid kit and covered the cut on his eyebrow, secretly hoping for a scar.

Once dressed, both players stepped out into the hallway behind the stands where the dressing rooms were. The rise and fall of the noise of the crowd muffled their conversation, and everyone else in the building was intently watching, waiting for the next all-important goal.

"You wanna go?" Damien taunted Justin in the hallway.

"I could have kicked your ass if they left us alone. You're all talk, you little prick," Justin replied.

"Hey, if you want another piece of this, I'm right here," said Damien. "If you've got the balls, we can take this outside and see who's the little prick."

Justin was cornered. He'd lost his enthusiasm for the battle now that there weren't any teammates, fans, or scouts watching. Meanwhile, Damien was always itching for a scrap, on the ice, on the basketball court, at work, or in the halls at school. He had a reputation he was proud of. Local boys feared him, and that was the way he liked it. He knew that a lot of girls liked it too. He was confident and cocky, and he backed it up with his fists.

"Let's do this," said Damien as he headed for the exit at the end of the hall. They wouldn't go back out through the front, past the snack bar; they would use the staff door next to the Zamboni machine. Justin followed. The night was cool, and it was already dark outside. A single floodlight lit up mounds of artificial snow that had been piled up by the Zamboni when it scraped the ice between periods. There was a dumpster and some rusty seats that had been removed from the arena long ago and left out back.

Damien didn't have time for small talk and caught Justin off guard with a right hook as he came out the door. Justin rose to the challenge and plowed headlong into Damien, taking him to the ground at the base of the snow pile. Damien fought off the punches and grabbed Justin's right hand, holding it back as he squirmed out from under him and jumped back to his feet. He delivered a vicious kick to Justin's ribs before the younger man could get back up. Damien then jumped him from behind and put the Logger in a chokehold, using all his strength and skills to outmaneuver his large opponent. Damien pulled his own forearm across Justin's throat, cutting off his windpipe and tightening his grip until he felt the boy melt from under him and collapse into the snow. At that moment, he heard a telltale eruption from the arena as the hometown fans celebrated a much-needed goal to take the lead in the game and possibly in the series.

Breathing heavily, Damien considered reentering the arena like nothing had happened, but the door that they had come out of was locked. There was less than a minute left in the game, and he couldn't be seen coming back in through the front of the arena, so he took his keys out of his pocket and headed across the parking lot for his truck.

Justin's body was found later that night by the Zamboni driver, after the game had ended and the elated Duckville crowd had dispersed. An autopsy showed many traumas to his body, and it was determined that he had died from wounds suffered during the hockey fight that had been witnessed by more than five hundred people.

Damien Rhodes was picked up and questioned by the Ontario Provincial Police. Manslaughter charges were laid but later dropped since the fight happened during the hockey game, and Damien was released after spending three weeks in pretrial custody in Maplehurst Correctional Complex.

The Beaverwood Loggers forfeited the remaining games, and the Duckville Devils were named league champions for the 2006–2007 season.

"Why don't I remember anything about this?" Kella asked.

"Because Richard Morden controls the team and the news-paper," said Danby. "He's well connected, and he kept it out of the news. A lot of people that were there think there was more to the fight than what they saw on the ice. Some think Damien beat the boy up outside, but there were no witnesses, and nothing could be proven. Others think the kid just went out the back to get some air and collapsed. Everyone was watching the game at the time."

"That's tragic," said Kella. "Poor Damien. What a thing to live with."

"Poor Damien?" said Danby. "What about the Beaverwood boy? That's who you should be feeling sorry for. That kid had a future. In hockey and in life. Snuffed out. What a waste."

"Well, that was a long time ago. I'm sure he's sorry, and he's grown up now and is making something of his life. No wonder he got so quiet when Corby asked him about the Devils."

"Never played another game in his life as far as I know," Danby said. "Alf sent him to learn the trade in Oklahoma after the incident, and that's about the last I heard about him. He never spoke about him again."

"Well, I'd like to give him a chance," said Kella. "That stuff is long behind him, and he's really good with the shoeing."

"Well, I wouldn't trust him as far as I could throw him," said Danby. "You do what you want, but I'm warning you: he's a bad seed. He's dangerous. Just keep an eye on him."

Kella wanted to change the subject. "So, tell me. How did it go at the doctor's?" she asked.

"Same old, same old. Got a new prescription. I looked around in that mall for a bit. I can't believe that place is so close to here. Didn't see a single person I knew down there. Sure has changed."

"Who did you expect to see?" asked Kella with a laugh.

"I don't know. It's all so foreign to me. I feel like the stranger. Anyway, I'm going to call it a night."

"Goodnight, Dad."

"Goodnight, honey."

Danby put an arm around Corby. "Goodnight, Punkin."

"Goodnight, Poppa."

Danby went back to his own place. He was still feeling restless about the day. He loved to write cowboy poetry and took any opportunity to share his prose with anyone who would sit still long enough to listen. This was much to the embarrassment of Kella and Corby. They would roll their eyes and make a fuss, but deep down, they loved his stories and were proud of him.

He thought about his day, the doctor, the mall, the coffee shop, and how out of place he had felt even though he was less than a half hour from home. This inspired him, and he came up with the idea of a fictitious old cowboy who has to pull up stakes and finally quit ranching and move into town next to some city slickers. He found a pen, set his notebook on his little kitchen table, pulled up a chair, and started writing.

# When a Cowboy Moves to Town
## By Danby Majors

There comes a time in every life to pause and catch your breath,
  To give retirement some thought or work yourself to death.
  A cowboy's plan is rarely set upon a cushy pension,
  And quittin' ranchin's something that no cow puncher would mention.

Still, sometimes a feller's thrown a loop with twists and circumstances,
  And it's time to call an auctioneer, sell out, and take his chances.
  The farm sale is the nearest any living man can come
  To being at his funeral but still breathing when it's done.

His life's work and possessions spread out neatly on the lawn,
  All the livestock and the horses with lot numbers painted on.
  There's nothing sacred, nothing spared when bankers want their share.
  All done, all through, the hammer drops, and no one seems to care.

Now look real close; you'll see a sight if you dare take a peek.
  A single tear rolls slowly down that tough ol' cowboy's cheek.
  Oh sure, his dog's still at his side, he's got his hat and truck,
  But if you're lookin' for the cowboy stuff, you'll find you're outta luck.

All's left is just the memories of the life he used to lead,
    Some trophies and the buckle that he won at the Stampede.
    The wrinkles earned from days outdoors are showing on his face,
    But his Stetson, boots, and spurs are all of a sudden out of place.

He didn't hire a mover just to haul his household stuff.
    Used his friend's gooseneck stock trailer, even though it's kinda rough.
    A little place in town's now where you'll find this feller at.
    It ain't no Ponderosa, just a place to hang his hat.

On one side, there's some youngin's prone to playing music loud.
    On the other, there's some yuppies who just ain't his sort of crowd.
    He's done the introductions, as a good neighbor would do,
    But he doubts he'll get real social b'yond a "Howdy, pard," or two.

In the evenings now, he likes to take a folding chair out back.
    He makes a little fire; he likes to hear the pops and cracks.
    It reminds him of his cowboy days and friends of long ago,
    All the rides, the ropes, the horses, cows, the girls, and rodeos.

And once the flames heat up and send some sparks into the sky,
    He's reminded of the stars he's slept beneath in days gone by.
    His dog is curled up at his feet, but he too is out of sorts.
    With no cows to work, no heels to nip, he whimpers, whines, and snorts.

The younger neighbors spot the fire and decide to come over.
    They bring their beer, guitars, and smokes and even pet old Rover.
    They ask him if he knows some tunes, and next thing that you know,
    They're singing "The Strawberry Roan" and "Ragtime Cowboy Joe."

He shares with them some stories as they start to settle down.
    Now they're quiet, and the fire is the only light in town.
    Its hypnotizing flames and smoke have got all their attention.
    When it's time to split some logs now, you bet everyone will pitch in.

Next day, the folks from th'other side come over to complain.
    Seems the smoke and flames and cowboy songs had caused them some disdain.
    They say, "You haven't got a permit. We'll report if you don't quit."
    But it doesn't faze the cowboy—nope, not even just a bit.

He says, "How 'bout tonight you join us, bring some marshmallows too.
    You might find you like that fire when you see what it can do."
    Well, they stammered, stuttered, grunted at his open invitation.
    Then they turned around and marched home with devout determination.

At sunset, kindling was arranged and matches lit on cue.
    And magnetic flames ignited as he bent real close and blew.
    The hippies hopped the fence again and once more gathered round
    To sing "Don't Fence Me In"; they made a harmonizing sound.

And the next thing that you know, the uptight ones from t'other side
    Were marching cross the lawn; it seems they'd done swallowed their pride.
    They were still dressed kinda fancy in their plaid Bermuda shorts,
    But they brought along refreshments—like a peace offering of sorts.

That night see, something happened that nobody would guessed.
    That cowboy looked around and reckoned he was truly blessed.
    It seems that when you mix the night air with some flames and food and fun,
    You can find a little cowboy inside just 'bout anyone.

The first weekend of September was the Duckville Fall Fair. Kella was up early to load up two horses that two of her students were exhibiting in the Light Horse Show division of the 123-year-old fair.

Corby was enlisted to help load the trailer with everything they would need for the day, and she was excited that she would be able to see some friends there, go on some rides, and also see her project on display in the Homecraft division. There was a category in her age group for a centerpiece for a table, and she had created a hockey themed candle holder.

Kella's student Megan was taking her own horse named Tickety Boo, or just "Boo" for short. Fourteen-year-old Sage was borrowing Banjo for the day and would enter him under his show name, Banjo Pickin Man. Sage and Megan arrived at the farm with Megan's mother to help load the horses and would be following them to the fairgrounds.

Kella had a two-horse, bumper pull trailer hooked up behind her dad's pickup truck. Banjo loaded first without incident. Boo was a bit more hesitant, but with some coaxing from some oats in a bucket, he stepped carefully up the ramp and was secured for the ten-minute ride to the show.

They arrived at the exhibitors' entrance and found a spot to park in a grassy field on the edge of the grounds. Assorted trailers were arranged across the field with Clydesdale and Percheron horses assembling for the Heavy Horse division. Along the far side, cows were being unloaded from stock trailers for the Holstein show. The midway rides were just starting up, and the place was bustling with activity. Boo was pawing in the trailer as they parked, and Kella knew the best strategy was to unload the horses as soon as possible and let Megan and Sage lead them around for a while to get them accustomed to the new surroundings. Kella sent the mothers to the entry booth to enter the girls in the classes that she had selected, and Corby stayed close by, hanging up hay bags, fetching pails of water, and unfolding lawn chairs.

A lumberjack show was underway, and the buzz of the chainsaws drowned out all other sounds—the chink, chink, chink of the harness on the heavy horses as they trotted by with a large wagon, the mooing of cows and calves, the roar of the midway rides, and the shouts of the carnival barkers offering games of chance and skill. Kella and Corby had skipped breakfast at home, so they made their way to the Rotary Club food tent. Back bacon and egg on a bun and a coffee for Kella. An apple fritter and an orange juice for Corby.

"Kella Major, how are you?" came a voice from behind the table. Jane Whetstone was the wife of one of the Rotarians and was taking a shift at the food booth.

"Oh, hi, Jane," Kella replied.

"Can you believe this place? What a zoo! You wouldn't catch me showing my horses here if my life depended on it. That's for sure."

Jane was a prominent hunter class exhibitor on the A circuit. She and Kella competed against each other growing up, and Jane continued a successful show career as an adult amateur. She qualified annually for the Royal Agricultural Winter Fair held in Toronto in

November, and then she would spend a large part of each winter competing on the show circuit in Wellington, Florida. "So what brings you here today, Kella? Checking out the lumberjacks?"

"Actually, I've just got two novice students competing in a couple classes here today. No big deal," said Kella.

"Oh, so you're coaching here? That's so sweet," said Jane, faking a look of shock. Jane thought that working at the food booth would be embarrassing, but Kella's position seemed much lower, and this suited Jane just fine.

"Yes, just a little warm-up really. These are new horse and rider combinations and not quite ready for prime time, if you know what I mean."

"I'll try to come watch some of the little show when I'm done here," said Jane in her most condescending manner.

"Great," said Kella. "We've got to go get the horses ready."

Back at the trailer, Banjo and Boo were tied up with hay bags to nibble on while they waited. Kella offered them water from a bucket, but neither of them drank any. Boo was fidgeting and pawing, but Banjo was standing patiently and resting a hind foot.

Megan and Sage took turns getting dressed in their show clothes in the tiny tack compartment at the front of the trailer. Megan's mom helped with their hair and tied exhibitor numbers onto their backs as Kella put saddles on the horses.

"Can I go see if my project got a prize?" asked Corby.

"Okay, but I want you to check back with me in a half hour or so."

Corby took off at a run.

"Don't run around the horses!" Kella shouted, but Corby was quickly out of sight.

Corby made her way to the homecrafts building. Inside there were displays of quilts and flowers, 4H Club projects, commercial displays for water softeners, a bathtub refinisher, and a paving company. She found the centerpieces next to the amateur photography wall. Her creation featured six hockey pucks standing on edge and glued together to form a circle. Red letters painted on each puck spelled out DEVILS. They supported a platform made of sawed-off hockey sticks, and on top of that was a large candle in a jar that was wrapped in red paper. Painted in white on the side of the candle jar was #1. A second-place ribbon was stapled to her name card next to the item.

Corby continued through the building and into the agricultural exhibit building. Inside there were flakes of alfalfa hay that had been judged, as well as giant pumpkins with their colossal weights painted on the side of them. Vegetables of all descriptions were shriveling on platters, with colored ribbons for each placing. She watched a woman sitting at a spinning wheel turning wool from a sheep into yarn. Another man sat next to a display of bees in a glass-sided hive, and she looked closely at the insects until his description of the honey-making process started to sound too much like school, and she politely wandered away. Eighth grade would be starting in a few days, and she didn't think her brain was ready for any new information too soon.

Kella had both Megan and Sage up on their horses and trotting them around the warm-up area, which was just another part of the grass that was surrounded with a temporary snow fence. Another ring had jumps set up, and the jumper classes featuring higher jumps taken at speed were underway.

Banjo was being his reliable self. Boo was still whinnying occasionally and was already in a sweat. There was one small jump set up in the warm-up area, and the girls took their turns going over it without incident.

"I got a second place," said Corby as she came up behind her mother.

"That's awesome," said Kella. "Were there a lot of entries?"

"I'm not sure. I only saw mine and the first-place winner."

Over on the jumper course, a horse had refused a fence and dumped its rider. The horse was trotting around the ring as a few people attended to the fallen teen. Others were waving their arms and shouting, "Whoa," to try to stop the horse. He finally put his head down and started grazing, and it was actually the judge who got hold of the horse and held him until someone led him out of the show ring behind the teary-eyed girl.

"Okay, girls, let's take the horses back to the trailer for a while before your classes come up."

Megan and Sage dismounted and led the horses to the trailer. They put halters on the horses and left them tied up. Boo was still not settled, and he pawed at the ground and at the side of the trailer. Next, he pawed at the trailer so aggressively that his front shoe caught on the running board and bent back. It was now twisted and hanging on by just three of the six nails. Megan started yelling for her mother. Boo couldn't completely put the foot down, and he hopped in place on the other foot.

"Go to the entry booth and ask them if there is a farrier on the grounds," Kella said to Corby. This time when Corby ran, it wasn't a problem.

Very soon, the group heard the show announcer call for the fair blacksmith to report to the entry booth as soon as possible.

"Is she going to miss her class? Will there be a refund?" Megan's mother was questioning Kella as Kella supported Boo's leg and tried to pull the bent shoe off with her bare hands.

Damien Rhodes poked his head into the entry booth. "Somebody need me?" he said.

"Yes. Follow this girl to her trailer. A horse has pulled his shoe."

"Oh, hi, Corby. Is it your mother's horse?"

Corby recognized Damien but couldn't remember his name. "Not her own horse but another one we brought. I'll take you to our trailer." Damien was carrying a set of basic tools rolled up in a leather pouch for emergency use.

"Oh, it's you," said Kella, smiling as he arrived. "I didn't know you'd be working here."

"Neither did I until my father told me this morning that I was now the official farrier of the Duckville Fall Fair. Just what I always wanted." He laughed.

Damien took over holding Boo's leg, then took the shoe puller tool out of his kit and pried the twisted shoe off. Boo was relieved to be able to place his hoof flat on the ground.

"What now?" asked Kella.

"We've got two options. Either I pull off the other front shoe so at least he can travel evenly, or I can bring my truck over with the forge and hammer this one back into shape. How much time have you got?"

"Not very much."

"I'll go get my truck and pull it over here. If I run out of time, I can always pull off the other shoe, but I'd like to get this one back on him since you're gonna be showing on the grass."

"This is a disaster," said Megan's mother "I'm going to text my husband and tell him not to bother coming now."

"It will be fine," Kella assured her. "We've got this under control. She's not going to miss anything."

"Can I get back on Banjo now?" asked Sage. "I think they're setting up the hunter fences."

"Sure," said Kella. " You might as well just take him over to the ring and hang out until your class. We will be over soon to go over the course with you."

Damien backed the truck up near Kella's trailer, then quickly opened up the back and lit the propane forge. He tapped the remaining nails out of the shoe and took a wire brush to it for a vigorous cleaning. Then he used the tongs to place it in the red-hot forge.

He set up his anvil and then took a rasp and smoothed off the bottom of Boo's foot. Everyone was watching and hoping he would be done in time.

"Working hunter for junior riders will start in five minutes. Have your horses ready please," the show announcer's voice boomed across the fairgrounds, adding to the panic.

"I haven't even looked at the course," said Megan.

"It will be fine," assured Kella. "He's almost done."

Damien pounded the shoe flat again against the anvil and placed it back against Boo's bare hoof. He held six nails in his mouth and quickly tapped each one into place. He finished the hoof off with a few swipes from the rasp and threw his hands in the air. "Done," he said as if he was being timed with a stopwatch.

"Amazing," said Kella.

"What do we owe you?" asked Megan's mother, reaching in her purse.

"I can just add it to your bill the next time I'm at the farm if you want," said Damien.

"We've got to get to the show ring," said Kella as she gave Megan a boost into the saddle.

"Wanna see my Devil's centerpiece?" Corby asked Damien.

"Where is it?" said Damien.

"In the homecraft building."

"Sure. I'll just leave my truck here for now, I guess."

"Damien Rhodes, please report to the Heavy Horse Show Ring," came the announcement over the loud speakers.

"Looks like I'm needed somewhere. I'll catch you later," he said as he gathered up his tool kit and headed off.

Jane Whetstone was giving Sage some last-minute, unsolicited guidance as she entered the ring for her first class, just as Kella arrived with Megan on Boo.

"Poor thing didn't have a clue what she was supposed to do," said Jane. "Looks like she's here all on her own. Who does that to a kid?"

"Actually, she's with me, Jane. We got delayed at the trailer. She'll be fine. Thank you."

They all watched as Banjo picked up an even pace at the canter and took the first three fences flawlessly. Then Sage guided him diagonally across the arena and did a small circle before heading for the closest jump. The judge blew her whistle. "Off course!" shouted the ring steward, and Sage calmly brought Banjo to a halt and then walked out of the ring.

"What a shame. She was doing so well. Just needed some more time to be properly prepared," said Jane.

"She's got a couple more classes to make up for it," said Kella.

"But she won't be eligible for the championship ribbon now," said Jane. "Too bad." And she walked back toward the Rotary food tent.

Megan was a quick study, and Kella went over the course with her. She watched as the rider ahead of her completed the course accurately but with a knockdown.

"Next on course is Megan Riley showing Tickety Boo" came over the speakers as she trotted in and then picked up the canter. Eight perfect jumps later, she rode out of the ring at the walk, bending down to hug Boo.

Kella gave a "Woot, Woot!" and a slow, loud clap. She looked around to see if Jane was still watching, but she was out of sight.

8

It was late on a Saturday afternoon two weeks after the Duckville Fair, and Kella was feeling restless. Corby was spending the weekend with her dad, and Danby had gone to a horse auction two hours away in Listowel and wasn't expected home anytime soon. She finished up the barn chores on her own and went into the house to enjoy a long, hot shower and a glass of wine.

Kella had not been in a serious relationship for a few years. She had dated the single father of one of her riding students for a while, but like many men, he made himself scarce when he found out how time-consuming the horse business was. When their dating tapered off, so did the riding lessons for his daughter. Lesson learned. She had looked through the online options. Picture after picture of guys standing next to their jacked-up four-by-four trucks, others in backward ball caps holding their latest fish or sitting on a snowmobile. None of those scenes appealed to her. Where could she find that unicorn of a man she was looking for? Single and sophisticated with a connection to the horse industry. She would happily settle for two out of three.

Kella stepped out the sliding door in her bathrobe and sat down in a Muskoka chair on her back porch to enjoy one of the last warm evenings of September. Cider flopped down next to her. The weather would be cooler soon with the beautiful changing colors of the leaves. The outdoor horse show season was winding down. Winter would bring another set of challenges around the farm. She had a glass of Chardonnay in one hand and her iPhone in the other. Opening the Facebook app, she typed Damien Rhodes into the blue space at the top of the screen.

Creeping into his profile page, she found it to be not surprisingly sparse. The profile picture of him grinning for the camera with a beer in his hand looked like it was cropped from a group shot at a party. It was slightly blurry and dated 2014. Four years ago. His page said that he lived in Fredericksburg, Virginia. His list of friends was not available for public viewing; neither were any other photos except for his cover photo, which was a stock photo of Canadian and American flags superimposed against a sunset background. Kella wondered if he was genuinely into horses or if it was just a job.

She thought about how confident and skilled he had looked when she first met him and watched him at work. She thought about his strong, leathery hands with the bulging veins and dirt ground into the calluses. She thought about how he saved the day at the fair by fixing Boo's shoe. She also knew he had a troubled past. He had demons that would haunt him forever. *How does he deal with what happened in that hockey game?* she wondered. *Does he even think about it, or can he keep it in a locked compartment in his brain?*

Kella was always attracted to the horses with a questionable history, the ones that other trainers had given up on. She looked for the best in every living thing. She loved to prove the people wrong who had written off a horse as being dangerous and unmanageable. She knew that horses, like people, can change and soften and become the best version of themselves, depending on how they are treated.

She scrolled through her contact list and started to compose a text to Damien.

"Hey, what are you up to?" she began. Then she deleted that and started again.

"Hi Damien, this is Kella. I'm going to need more Venice Turpentine for Banjo's feet. Can I buy a jar from you?" She pressed send and waited. Staring at her phone, she took another sip of wine and saw the text bubble moving to indicate that he was texting back.

"I can drop off some next time I'm driving by. Prob Mon."

"I don't mind swinging by to pick it up," she typed.

"I'm home now if you want to come over," he responded.

Kella stood up and rapidly typed, *20 min :)*

She sprang into action to get ready. She hoped that he realized as much as she did that the Venice Turpentine for Banjo was a lame excuse. They had discussed on day one that he was staying in a house trailer at a Thoroughbred racing stable about fifteen minutes away. He was doing the morning feeding and turnout of the horses in exchange for the little trailer, and the farm owners were happy to have another experienced horseman on site in case of any emergency.

She scrunched her damp hair into a messy bun and pulled on some tight jeans that she could never ride in, then slipped into some sandals. *Bra? No bra. Bra? No bra.* Kella threw on a sweat-shirt without a bra and a quick spritz of perfume, and she was out the door.

The nine-year-old Lexus SUV she was driving was her last splurge from the settlement she got when she divorced. She had never been too careful with money, preferring to live for the moment and keep up appearances rather than doing any long-term financial planning.

She drove across the rolling countryside on the other side of

Duckville. The fields of corn were high and interspersed with dairy farms, estate homes, horse stables, and a few remaining mixed farming operations, with the Century Farm designation sign marking their long laneways. Large, round bales sat in hay fields that had been gleaned of their second cut for the season, ready to be gathered and stockpiled for the winter.

She rolled up to the long, paved driveway of Bear Claw Racing Stable. The last time she was here was in the spring, when she picked up Millennium Blue Jay for her new owners. It was a well-kept facility that had been purchased and extensively renovated four years ago by a property developer from Toronto. It was a weekend home for the owner, and the farm manager lived in a house on an acre of land that had been severed from the front corner of the farm. Black steel buildings with white trim and black board fencing contrasted against the bright green pastures. The stable kept a few broodmares and foals, some yearlings that were being prepped for the fall sales, and assorted other race horses on layup. Their primary racing stock spent the season stabled at Woodbine Racetrack in Toronto, and most spent winters racing at Gulfstream Park in Florida.

Kella parked in front of the stable and walked around to the house trailer parked permanently against the side. Alfonso's truck, which was now Damien's work truck, was parked there, as was an old Honda Civic hatchback with Virginia license plates. The smell of a barbecue greeted her—and then Damien, holding a new jar of Venice Turpentine in his hand. He was standing on the small deck attached to the house trailer. His hair looked wet, like he had just gotten out of the shower. He was in clean jeans and bare feet and was wearing an untucked floral Hawaiian shirt. Kella could hardly make out what he said over the sound of "Wake Me Up When September Ends" by Green Day coming from inside.

"Here you go," he said. "I could have brought it over."

"Not a problem," said Kella. "I didn't have anything to do tonight."

"Want a beer?" offered Damien.

"Why not?" she said.

Damien opened the screen door and disappeared inside to retrieve a beer for Kella. She heard him turn down the volume of the music. "Have you eaten?" he asked as he handed her the cold can of Molson Canadian. "I'm just doing burgers. If you want one, I can throw one on for you."

"That would be great actually. It would be nice to not have to do the cooking for a change." Kella took a seat in one of the two folding lawn chairs.

"Whose car is that? Is someone else here?" she asked.

"No, that's just my old beater," he said. "I'd waste a lot of gas driving the work truck around. I've had that beast forever. I still need to get Ontario plates for it."

Kella sipped on her beer and watched him at the barbecue. Here he was again, wielding tools amid smoke and fire. He looked as sure of himself in front of the grill as he did at the blacksmith forge.

"So, how are you enjoying life back in Duckville?" she asked.

"It's like a time warp. Not much changes around this town, but most of my buds are married or moved away. I can't believe how close the city is coming up this way."

"How's work going for you?" Kella asked. "Are you keeping most of your dad's clients?"

"That's no problem. There's lots of work around here. I honestly don't know how my old man lasted at it so long."

Damien stepped back inside, while Kella looked at the sunset. There were a half a dozen broodmares in a large pasture with a loafing shed. She watched them grazing and swishing their tails as the flies and mosquitos started to feast on them in the early evening. One dropped down and rolled vigorously in the lush grass and then rose quickly and cantered to a new spot.

Damien came out using an empty pizza box as a tray, carrying buns and containers of ketchup and mustard. "I hope this isn't too fancy for you," he said sarcastically.

"Are you kidding? Having a handsome man cook for me? This is total luxury," she said.

"Here you go," he said, handing her a burger on a bun. "I'll let you doctor it up the way you want it. How's that beer doing?"

"I'm good, thanks."

Damien turned off the grill and took a seat with his burger in his hand and his beer can on the deck beside him.

"How is it?" he said.

"This is perfect. So good," Kella gushed.

Damien was finishing his first burger and got up to put a second one together.

"Come over here," said Kella.

"What?" said Damien.

"You've got mustard on your cheek."

"Where?" he said. Kella got up and wiped it off of him with her finger. She looked around for somewhere to clean it off and then slowly licked her finger, looking Damien in the eyes.

"Thanks," he said.

They finished eating, and Damien took some things back inside. He returned with a cigarette lighter and a little box that usually carried horseshoe nails. He opened the box and took out two joints. "Weed?" he said to Kella, offering her one.

"Oh, no thanks. You go ahead though."

Damien pinched the joint into his lips and lit it. She watched as he inhaled. Then she turned away, smiled, and shook her head. *What am I doing here?* she asked herself.

The mosquitos were starting to become a problem, and Kella's bare ankles seemed to be a favorite target.

"Ready for another beer now?" he asked.

"I could go for that, but these bugs are eating me alive," she said.

"Let's go inside then," he said, and they both got up to step into the trailer.

As Kella took a step forward, her sandal slipped off, and she skidded the sole of her foot across the deck. "Shit, shit, shit!" she yelled.

"What happened?" asked Damien.

"I think I got a sliver in my foot!" Kella said, hopping on her other foot.

"Hang on, let me help you," said Damien. He put one arm around her waist and guided her through the door before depositing her onto the sofa. "Put your foot up. I think I've got some tweezers."

Kella lay back on the sofa with her arm across her forehead as Damien went down the narrow hall to the bathroom. He returned with tweezers, ointment, and a Band-Aid. He switched on the lamp on the little table next to the sofa.

"Thanks," said Kella, reaching for the supplies.

"Let me do it for you," said Damien. He sat down and gently put her foot on his lap.

"Are you going to be still, or am I going to have to hobble you?" he joked.

"You really don't need to—" Kella started.

Damien cut her off. "Of course I'm doing this," he insisted.

Kella lay still with one hand tightly over her mouth as he pried into her foot. "You're right, that's a big one," he said. "You might want to take it home and use it in your fireplace."

"Very funny," she said.

"There. I've got it," he said, setting down the tweezers on the table. He squirted some ointment onto the wound and then carefully applied the bandage.

"Thank you, Doctor Rhodes," she said.

"Now I'll just kiss it better, and you'll be jogging soundly in no time." He bent over and kissed the top of her foot. Then he sat back and admired his work, still holding her foot in one hand, with the other hand on her ankle.

Kella pulled herself up, holding onto his arm, and kissed him on the cheek. "My hero. You're the best," she said.

"You're not so bad yourself."

Then they both sat still and looked awkwardly at each other. They were both trying to read the other's mind. *Is this business or are we friends? Are we friends or are we flirting? Are we flirting or are we taking this further?*

Damien stood up. "Can you stand on it?" he asked, and he put out both hands to help her up. She took his hands, and he pulled her to her feet. Once they were both standing and face-to-face, he put his arms around her and pulled her into a hug. Kella held on tight and ran her hands up and down his back, reaching under his loose Hawaiian shirt. He held her by the back of her head and kissed her slowly.

"Follow me," he said. Taking her by the hand, he led her down the narrow hallway to the tiny bedroom at the back of the trailer. He didn't turn on a light, but there was a glow to the room provided by the setting sun coming through the Canadian flag that was used as a curtain over the one small window. "This is more comfortable," he said as he took off his shirt and lay on the double bed. On the bed was one of those tacky blankets that were sold at gas stations and truck stops, with a picture of a wolf on it.

Kella immediately climbed on top of him and kissed him as he ran his hands under her sweatshirt and reached for her breasts.

"I hope you're not sleeping with all of your clients," she said.

"Not yet," he replied, and Kella gave him a playful slap on the cheek.

"Well, I don't kiss and tell, and neither should you," said Kella as she sat up and pulled her sweatshirt off over her head.

She reached for the buckle of his belt, and he fumbled for the button fly on her jeans. "Oh God, it's been too long," she said.

They both shimmied out of their clothes and grabbed for each other, kissing and stroking and licking and thrusting. After twenty minutes of nonstop, mindless sex, out of breath, they both collapsed and rolled aside. Kella lay on her back and stared at the room. The lack of decor was striking. Three bare, oatmeal-colored walls and one covered in a floral wallpaper that must have come with the trailer when it was manufactured. A tall dresser stood with assorted caps, cologne, coins, a pocketknife, and a flashlight on top. The room carried the smell of Damien's work clothes, which were tossed into a pile in the corner. The aroma of man and horse sweat, manure and scorched hooves.

Damien was lying flat on his stomach, and she ran her fingers over his strong back. Then she rolled on top of him and straddled him. She began to rub his back and then stopped suddenly. Now, for the first time, she noticed the small tattoo of single name at the base of his neck between his shoulder blades. She looked closely at it in the fading light.

"Who's Camden?"

# 9

When Damien's hockey playing days came to an end and the investigation into the death of Justin Semper was over, his family decided it would be best for him to get out of town for a while. His father enrolled him in the same horseshoeing school in Oklahoma that he himself had attended in the seventies, and Damien hit the road. Alfonso paid the tuition for the full twelve-week program that included accommodation and would provide the young man with all the skills needed to become a professional farrier. When Damien was a child, he often went on calls with his dad during school holidays or weekends, but as a teenager, he was more focused on sports than horses. He knew that working at Morden's Modern Printing Inc. was only temporary, and he wasn't going to miss it one bit. Mr. Morden had terminated his position anyway, without notice, following the hockey incident.

Damien quickly made friends at the shoeing school and found the work easier than most. While his classmates' hands, forearms, and backs were sore every morning, Damien's hockey conditioning was coming in handy, and so was all of Alfonso's tips that he had absorbed over the years. Damien kept quiet about his hockey life and soaked in the football culture that defined Oklahoma.

Talk around the school quickly turned to the subject of career plans following graduation, and his closest classmate, Scott Hames from Denton, Texas, told him that he was already apprenticing with a guy named Bugsy, and he could put in a good word for Damien too.

Once they both finished in Oklahoma, they made a plan to catch up with Bugsy in West Palm Beach, Florida. Scott enticed Damien with the promise, "If you are interested in wealthy, athletic, good-looking women, then you should do well at the horse shows in Florida." The two headed for West Palm Beach in Damien's Civic with their certification in hand and big dreams in their heads.

Bugsy was a legendary farrier in his fifties who followed the horse show circuit. Charismatic and knowledgeable, Bugsy was in high demand in the show-jumping world. It was not unusual for clients to pay for a plane ticket for him to fly to wherever their horse was just to reset his shoes. When Damien first met him, he was holding court in the farrier tent at a horse show. There was line of grooms holding horses, waiting for his services. He was never in a hurry, and nobody cared. "This is the dude I told you about," said Scott to Bugsy, introducing Damien.

"Damien Rhodes, sir. Nice to meet you."

"Sir? It's just Bugs, if you don't mind. So you're a Canuck, are you, eh?" He laughed. "You two can go and pick up my order at the Farrier Supplies truck next to the feed and shavings office. Take my golf cart; you'll need it." Damien had trouble understanding Bugsy's thick southern accent, made even less intelligible by the wad of chewing tobacco inside his lower lip. Bugsy had a great setup, with an aluminum cargo trailer that held his gear and supplies and carried his beat-up old golf cart with toolboxes mounted on the back fenders.

In the days and weeks that followed, Damien and Scott worked next to Bugsy doing trims and prepping shoes, while Bugsy did the specialized forge jobs and worked his magic to make sore horses sound. They made trips on the off days to shoe at barns within a three-hour radius and filled their pockets with cash while they learned the business. Bugsy stayed in a camper mounted in his truck bed, and the boys shared the cheapest motel rooms they could find.

For two young, single men, the horse show world was paradise. As advertised, there was no shortage of women to get their attention. They danced with them at the exhibitors' parties, they met up with them at the local bars, and they followed them back to the living quarters in their horse trailers or to their hotel rooms. Bugsy and the crew followed the circuit to Georgia, back to Oklahoma, and up to Columbus, Ohio. By now, Duckville, the Devils, and Justin Semper could not have been further from Damien's mind.

For the winter, they were back in Florida again, and Damien got reacquainted with an exhibitor from Virginia he had met the previous season.

Shonna Weber brought her horse down to Florida in her own two-horse gooseneck trailer, with small living quarters in the front. Her gelding was stabled with her trainer, but Shonna was one of the few riders who was showing on a tight budget. She had two weeks off of work that she stretched from Christmas until the second week of January. Shonna was twenty-four years old and had been showing horses since she was twelve. She lived alone in Fredericksburg in a small house that she inherited when her grandmother passed away last year. Shonna worked at a local garden center, which made it easier to get time off in the winter. Her parents lived in Washington, DC, and her father was still begrudgingly funding her horse habit. If only he knew how much it actually cost, she thought. She was competing in the Amateur Owner Hunter division, and although her eleven-year-old gelding wasn't fancy by national standards, he was steady, and even in stiff competition, she could pick up the odd ribbon.

Shonna helped cover her expenses at the shows by braiding

manes and tails of horses for other exhibitors. Damien would hang around the showgrounds in the evenings and keep her company while she was braiding, helping to hold the horses that were being difficult. Conversation came easily for both of them, even though in many ways they were from different worlds. Shonna grew up as a rather privileged only child in the Woodley Park suburb of Washington, DC. Her father was generous with her, but she was expected to pull her own weight, and gradually he was tightening the purse strings and letting her manage more and more of her expenses on her own. She loved the outdoors and was never suited for an office job, so she had found the garden center job to be a perfect fit for her lifestyle. It was also close to her grandmother's house, where she was now living. Shonna and Damien talked about how things were different in Canada from the United States. She had never been there, but she pictured it being wild and uncivilized, much like how she thought of Damien.

Damien knew he was way out of his league, but he was very attracted to Shonna and figured they could have a little fun together and then get back to their lives. His list of horse show girlfriends was growing, and he was starting to struggle with juggling them all. The women came from all over the east half of the country, and he met up with them at different locations. So far, none of the overlapping had caused him a problem, but he knew it was only a matter of time.

During the two weeks that Shonna and Damien spent in Florida that winter, they spent almost all of their free time together. Her coach and the other ladies from her barn saw him around the stalls more and more, and Bugsy and Scott were starting to give him a hard time about it. "That's four nights in a row that you haven't been back to the motel," said Scott. "That's got to be a new record. You're still paying for half, you know, even if you're not sleeping there."

"Trust me. It's worth it," said Damien.

Saying goodbye in mid-January was hard. Shonna delayed and delayed her departure until her job pressured her to return. They promised to keep in touch and planned to see each other at the Virginia Horse Center in Lexington for a show circuit in a couple months.

The texting and phone calls tapered off until early March when Shonna called Damien and started the conversation with "I'm pregnant."

"Whoa, what?" Damien replied. "From me?"

Damien could hear Shonna crying and didn't need any more explanation.

"Look, it's fine. I can manage this on my own. I just thought you should know. I already told my mom. She's going to tell my dad. He's going to freak out, but it will be fine."

"So, you're going to have it?" asked Damien.

Shonna paused. "You know what? Never mind. You go ahead and do your thing, Damien. I'm not asking you for anything. You take care, okay?"

Damien called her right back, but it went straight to voicemail, and he couldn't think of anything to say.

Damien's head was spinning. When he got the call, he was working with Bugsy at a Quarter Horse ranch in Pilot Point, Texas. They were trimming some weanling halter horses that were still on their mothers and were barely broke to handle. The two of them were getting tossed around by these little powerhouses. Damien put the phone in the holster on his belt. "I need to get some air," he said, and he stepped out of the barn and took a seat on a bench outside.

He was rubbing his head and neck when Bugsy checked on him. "You okay there, cowboy?"

"Yeah, sure, I just need some water or something," said Damien.

"Anything I need to know about?" asked Bugsy.

"It's all good," said Damien.

Damien lay in bed that night staring at the ceiling and considering his options. He could ignore the situation, put Shonna out of his mind, and let her deal with it. Or he could make an effort to do the right thing and take responsibility for his actions for a change. He had enough secrets to keep track of in his head, and he didn't want this to be one more thing that would haunt him for the rest of his life. What could Shonna want from him? Did she want him to be involved? What would her parents think of him? Once again, it looked as though life as he knew it was never going to be the same.

The next day, he told Bugsy that he had something he needed to take care of, and he was going to have to hit the road for a while. He decided not to let him in on the details just yet. Depending on how things played out, he might never need to tell him anything.

He loaded up his car with everything he had and started the drive to Fredericksburg, Virginia. Shonna had never given him her home address. However, she had told him the name of the garden center where she worked, and he would try to find her there. The second option would be to look her up at the barn through her coach, but that would open a can of worms if he ran into people he knew.

With more than nineteen hours of driving ahead, he could arrive tomorrow afternoon if he drove most of the night and slept in his car at rest areas along the highway. He headed northwest to Little Rock, Arkansas, through Nashville, and up to Staunton, Virginia. Past Charlottesville, he was heading through the heart of Civil War battlegrounds, and every rest stop and roadside monument or lookout area was a history lesson.

The drive gave him plenty of time to think. What would Shonna's reaction be to him? He was prepared for everything from rejection to elation. He expected something in between.

When he was officially within the Fredericksburg city limits, he stopped at a gas station that had a rare payphone with a phonebook. He looked up the address for the garden center. The gas station staff gave him directions, and he was finally hoping to see Shonna face-to-face.

Damien could feel his heart pounding as he pulled up in front of the garden center. It was five thirty in the evening, and the hours posted on the door said they closed at six.

Damien went inside and asked the man at the counter if Shonna Weber was there.

"You should find her in garden decor. Head down this way past the bird feeders and turn right."

As he made the turn, he bumped into some wind chimes, and Shonna turned around at the sound. "Oh no you didn't," she said and hugged him and started to sob against his chest.

"We need to talk," he said.

Shonna composed herself and wiped her face with her shirt. "I finish in about twenty minutes, if you can stick around."

"Well, yeah, I'm not going anywhere," he said, and she laughed. "You do what you need to do, and I'll just look around until you're done."

Damien wandered around the shop as Shonna was arranging bird baths and gazing balls. It was early spring, and the peak season was just around the corner. Inventory was arriving every day to be unloaded. He checked out the wine-making supplies, the horse and livestock feed selection, and took a seat on a chaise lounge in the furniture department until the man from the front counter gave him a look.

When she was done, they went outside, sat in Shonna's pickup truck, and talked for two hours. Damien said all the right things. He was going to be supportive in any way he could. He would find work in the area and settle down with her if she would have him. He wanted to be a father, and he already loved this baby. Shonna hadn't had time to process everything. She had thought parenting was going to be a solo act.

In the end, she said, "Let's go back to my place and continue this conversation." He stayed one night and then another. He found household jobs to do when she went to work. She was getting used to the idea of having a man around the home. She worried about what her parents would think of the arrangement, but to her surprise, they were agreeable. This was only the second most shocking news that they had heard in the past two weeks.

Damien found blacksmith work slowly but steadily, starting at the barn where Shonna kept her horse. On the weekends, he would travel to horse shows of every kind to drum up some extra cash.

On September 28, 2010, Shonna gave birth to a healthy baby boy, and they named him Camden.

# 10

"So you're telling me that you've got a son in Virginia who is what? Eight years old?" asked Kella.

"He'll have his eighth birthday next Friday actually. I'm going down to see him," said Damien.

"Holy shit, man. You've got more secrets than North Korea," said Kella as she started to get dressed. "So why aren't you living there with Shonna and Camden anymore?"

Once Camden was born, Shonna and Damien settled into a functional routine. He found just enough work to make ends meet, and with babysitting help from Shonna's mom, she was able to get back to her job at the garden center. Damien scheduled his appointments around Shonna's flexible work hours and did his part to take care of Camden. Damien spent extended long weekends working at horse shows, some that Shonna was competing at and some farther away. Shonna's pickup became his work truck, and she used his Civic to commute to work.

The in-laws tolerated Damien and loved Camden. Damien got Camden started in ice hockey as soon as he could find skates small enough to fit him. Damien even started coaching kids hockey programs at the Prince William Ice Center. He had a dream of making Camden the best young hockey player in the area. Damien's mom and dad came down twice a year to visit and spoil their grandson for a week at a time.

By all appearances, life was good, but then Damien started to spend more time away, shoeing at horse shows. He'd catch up with Bugsy and Scott, and they would be the three Musketeers again, pillaging and plundering and leaving a trail of broken hearts. Damien considered his faithfulness to Shonna somewhat optional since they weren't officially married. Five years into the relationship, he knew he was leading a double life. Dutiful father and husband at home and badass playboy on the road. He owed a lot to Shonna. She gave him a stable life and home that he never could have created on his own, but in doing so, he still never had to grow up. He continued to operate his shoeing business out of his pocket. He never officially had status to be working in the United States, and he avoided all the adulting stuff, letting Shonna deal with it. He figured as long as he was paying his own way and contributing to raising Camden, it was all good. Until he met Tracy Renault.

Tracy worked for a major tack shop that set up a semitrailer at horse show circuits up and down the East Coast. She could easily be described as the female version of Damien—a bit dangerous and mysterious, feeding off of the horse show world while never totally being part of it. They had some fun together after hours occasionally and enjoyed an unspoken "don't ask, don't tell" arrangement. Damien knew little about her and didn't want to. He had an itch that he needed scratched, and that was all she was to him. They might go a couple months without seeing each other, and there was very little in the way of texting back and forth. If Tracy wanted more from him, she kept it to herself, and his personal life was definitely not on the table for discussion. He was becoming skilled at keeping the various compartments in his head locked and separate.

In June 2018, Damien was back to his regular clients after a lengthy stint at the horse show in Devon, Pennsylvania. He was finishing up a long, hot day at a boarding stable that had several lesson horses and assorted boarders that needed trims and resets. He packed his gear into the back of the truck and headed home. Camden would be home, and he was hoping that Shonna would have some dinner underway. All he wanted was a shower, a beer, a bite to eat, and to sit with Camden and watch the Washington Nationals baseball game on TV in air-conditioned comfort.

When he got home, he saw a Volkswagen Beetle parked out front and figured it must be one of Shonna's friends.

He walked in the side door, and Camden ran to greet him. Entering the kitchen, however, the greeting was not as pleasant. Sitting at the table drinking tea were Shonna, with reddened eyes, and Tracy.

"Is there something you want to tell me?" Shonna asked.

Damien knew for the third time in his life that from this moment forward, nothing was going to be the same. He got a room at a motel for a few days while he got his meager affairs in order. He took his shoeing equipment to a farrier supply shop, and they gave him twenty-five cents on the dollar for everything. He called his father, packed up his Honda Civic, and headed back to Duckville.

"You are a bad, bad boy, Mr. Rhodes," said Kella as she slipped into her sandals.

"Am I still your farrier?" he asked.

"Yes, but you're still on trial." She poked her index finger into his bare chest. She gave him a quick kiss. "Thanks for dinner … and dessert," she said and then left.

**11**

In 1974, Kella's father, Danby Major, was a young horse trainer trying to make a name for himself in the Quarter Horse industry. He was competing at open horse shows and shows for registered American Quarter Horses and was steadily moving up the ranks. Danby had a reputation for taking on the rougher stock. Sometimes he would get a horse that was four or five years old and had never been ridden. Sometimes he would get a stallion with a bad disposition or a spirited, young horse with an inclination to spook or buck. No matter to Danby. He was determined to make a living horseback, and he couldn't afford to be choosy at this stage of his young career. While he was competent enough with the horses, the business side of his endeavor was usually lacking. When it came to the bookkeeping, banking, invoicing, and bill paying, Danby was borderline irresponsible, but he survived.

Danby Major, like a lot of western trainers at the time, competed in almost any event that was offered—halter classes, trail, western pleasure, reining, and even barrel racing, often with the same horse in every event. Horses in those days were not as specialized, and the reputation of Quarter Horses as the most versatile breed was widely promoted.

The 1974 show season had gone better than ever for Danby as he hauled his own favorite mare, Miss Honey Pine, all around

Ontario and across the border into Michigan and New York. The five-year-old, solid bay mare had all of the attributes of the breed at the time. She stood 14.3 hands tall on a stocky build, including a large hip and wide chest, with the prettiest head and tiniest ears you ever saw. Danby campaigned her for high point awards in multiple events, but her specialty was the western pleasure class. Exhibitors in the class entered as a group and were judged on the rail at the walk, jog, and lope while they showed off their smooth gaits, seamless transitions, and impeccable manners. More often than not, Danby and Miss Honey Pine took home the first-place red ribbons.

Word spread throughout the year that the American Quarter Horse Association had decided at their annual convention to create the first ever World Championship Quarter Horse Show, and it would be held in Louisville, Kentucky, in November. Danby decided that the time was right for him to take his career to the next level, and he mailed the one-hundred-dollar entry fee to the association office in Amarillo, Texas.

He planned to enter just one class, the Junior Western Pleasure for horses aged five and under. Other top exhibitors from Ontario were also making plans to attend, and when all the contestants were tallied, there were going to be 692 entries from forty states and five Canadian provinces competing.

Keeping a horse slick and shiny in Ontario in November was going to be a challenge, and Danby combined a vigorous grooming routine, diligent blanketing, and a lightbulb placed in Honey's stall with a timer that kept it on for sixteen hours per day. This would combat the effects of shorter daylight hours at that time of year, which trigger the growth of a long winter coat on the horses. Left to Mother Nature, the mare would start growing her winter coat in August and would no doubt resemble a furry Shetland pony by November. Danby's efforts paid off, and by the time he led her into her stall at the Kentucky Fair and Exposition Center, she was slick as a seal.

The stall that Danby was assigned was a temporary wooden crate type of stall located under the stadium seating of the arena. If there was a hierarchy system of who would be eligible for the more permanent stalls in the other covered barns, Danby clearly didn't qualify.

Miss Honey Pine settled in nicely, and after Danby had checked in at the show office to get his exhibitor's pass and his number to wear in the class, he took a quick look around the grounds. Commercial exhibitors with the latest tack and clothing, farm and ranch supplies, feed and supplements, and gifts were set up on the upper level behind the seating around the arena. The show arena itself was covered in wood shavings that had been dyed bright green in a gaudy attempt to simulate an outdoor, grassy setting. Ponderosa Steakhouse restaurants were the signature sponsors for the event, and their signs and banners were prominently displayed. Danby was shocked at the high prices of the fancy show halters and saddles on sale. Some silver adorned halters were as much as $200, and he took some time to admire a saddle under a spotlight on a revolving saddle rack with a $2,000 price tag.

While Honey was enjoying an extra flake of hay, Danby wandered through the aisles of the other stabling. He saw names of breeders and trainers that he had only read about in magazines. Bob Anthony, Tommy Manion, Gaylon Delfer, John Hoyt, and Jerry Wells were all legendary in the industry, and Danby walked slowly past their stalls, studying how they had things set up so elegantly, with stall curtains on their tack room and color-coordinated signs on every stall.

An outdoor ring was available for warmup, and although the weather was turning colder and damp, Danby took Honey for a ride outside, where floodlights lit up the arena as dusk approached.

Honey was as steady as could be, unflustered by the strange environment and the noise and activity. Danby felt that if she rode as well in the class tomorrow as she did in the warmup, he should be a serious contender.

Danby had a cap on the back of his pickup truck and had set up a bedroll on a cot inside. That night, as he lay in the back of his truck, eating potato chips and a drinking a Coke, he dreamed of having his name announced at the World Championship Quarter Horse Show. This could be just the shot in the arm that his horse-training business needed. His excitement kept him from sleeping, and when his wind-up alarm clock went off at six thirty, he felt as though he hadn't slept at all. Frost covered the inside of the truck cap windows, and he scrambled into his clothes before taking his shaving kit and a towel to the public washrooms.

His Junior Western Pleasure class would be in the late afternoon. There were enough entries to warrant two splits of the class, and the top ten from each group would be returning for the finals. Earlier in the day, the halter classes were scheduled, with the first AQHA World Championships being awarded. Danby caught a glimpse of some of the halter horses entering the show arena. He had never seen horses with so much muscle and such detailed grooming.

Before his class, he warmed up Miss Honey Pine the same way he always did, and she felt like she was as ready as she had ever been. He left her tied in her stall while he ran out to his truck to put on a clean white shirt and then waited for announcements regarding the timing of his class.

He was in the first section, and as he made his way into the show arena, Miss Honey Pine sensed his excitement and perked up a bit more than usual.

Most of the next five minutes were a blur as Danby struggled to keep Honey at the slow pace of his competitors. Even at the jog, he felt like he was trotting too fast, and when the lope was called for in the second direction, Danby squeezed her a little too hard and took a few strides on the wrong lead before slowing her back to a jog and correcting her.

Contestants then lined up across the middle of the arena and backed up individually for the judges. He waited for the announcement of the exhibitors who would be invited back to compete in the finals. His number was never called.

Back at his stall, he untacked Honey while he listened over the public address system to the rest of the class. The second split of the group was already underway and then the finals. He managed to squeeze into a spot in an alleyway with a view of the arena while they announced the final placings. Danby was shocked to see that the same filly that won the two-year-old mares halter class had also won the Junior Western Pleasure. He felt defeated and woefully underqualified to be competing at this level. He chalked this one up to experience and returned to his stall to give Honey a good grooming.

"Is this your horse, son?" a voice came through the wooden slats of the stall.

"Yes, sir, she is," said Danby as he stepped out into the aisle.

Peering in to see Honey was none other than Gaylon Delfer. Delfer was a renowned breeder of Quarter Horses, and his Gee Bar Dee ranch in Centennial, Nebraska, was legendary. Danby had never seen the man before in person but recognized him from his ads in *Western Horseman* magazine and the *Quarter Horse Journal*. For Gaylon Delfer even to acknowledge that Danby and his horse existed was a victory.

"Well, she sure is a pretty one," said Gaylon.

"Thank you, sir. I really appreciate that," said Danby.

"How's she bred?" Delfer asked. "I could swear she was a daughter of my stud Dee Bar Beaumont."

"No, sir. She's sired by a horse in Ontario. I doubt you've heard of him."

"Look at the little ears on her," Delfer said. "Could sure pass for a Beaumont, and not a single white hair on her. Are you showing her in any other classes?"

"Just the Junior Western Pleasure. I'm afraid it wasn't our best," said Danby.

"Well, she looked good to me," said Gaylon. "I like the way you had her moving out and natural. Too many of these horses are starting to look phony. I like a good *using* horse. Do you know what I mean?"

Danby could hardly argue with Gaylon Delfer. The man was everything that Danby hoped to become. He was polished and elegant with a plaid polyester western suit and a turquoise bolo tie with silver tips. He had a brown felt cowboy hat and a horseshoe-shaped ring that sparkled as he gestured with his hand.

"Usually I do pretty well with her in the shows at home," said Danby.

"Where's home?" asked Gaylon.

"Near Toronto, Canada," Danby replied.

"I'm sure you do well up there, son," said Gaylon. "Most of these judges don't know shit from Shinola."

Gaylon took out a cigarette and lit it right next to a No Smoking sign.

"She wouldn't be for sale, would she?" he asked.

"Everything is for sale," said Danby, trying to measure up to Gaylon with his casual horse-trading ways.

"What sort of price do you have on her?" asked Gaylon.

"I was thinking five thousand," said Danby.

"I was thinking more like three," said Gaylon.

"Can you do four thousand?" asked Danby, eager to make a sale of any kind to the great Gaylon Delfer. This would be a negotiation that would live in infamy. Danby could potentially stretch this into a biblical tale of victory as a horse sale version of David slaying Goliath.

"Let's split the difference and say thirty-five hundred," said Gaylon.

Danby stuck out his hand for Gaylon to shake.

"Tell you what. You bring her registration papers around to my stalls in a half an hour, and we can get settled up. Okay?" said Delfer.

"I'll be there," said Danby.

Danby was walking on air as he went back to his truck to get the mare's original registration papers out of his folder. He wasn't thrilled with the price, but he was willing to take a discounted amount from Gaylon. He couldn't wait to get home and place a full-page ad in the *Ontario Quarter Horse Newsletter* congratulating Gaylon Delfer of Centennial, Nebraska, on his purchase of Miss Honey Pine. The sale price, he thought, would be a figure of great speculation by his peers, and he would never disclose the private treaty amount, but selling a horse from Duckville to someone in Nebraska would be quite a coup.

At the Gee Bar Dee stalls, Gaylon ushered Danby behind the curtains and into his tack room. The converted stall had saddle and bridle racks covered in the fanciest tack. There was a card table in the corner with bottles of whiskey and gin, and there was an ice chest under the table.

"Can I get you a drink?" asked Gaylon, taking a beer bottle out of the chest.

"No, I'm fine," said Danby.

Delfer opened his carved leather briefcase and took out a transfer report that they would need to send to AQHA to verify the transaction. Danby filled out the information, identifying the plain bay mare and signing it as the seller.

"Now let me find you a check," said Gaylon.

Danby waited patiently as the man shuffled papers around in his briefcase.

"Damn it," he said. "It looks like I'm all out of checks right now. Tell you what, I'll give you five hundred in cash today, and I'll send the rest to your address up in Canada as soon as I get home. How does that sound?"

However it sounded to Danby at that moment really didn't matter. Whenever he presented the check in American Funds at his bank was going to be a moment of great pride, whether it was in a few days or a few weeks.

"I guess so," agreed Danby as Gaylon opened his thick wallet and peeled out five one-hundred-dollar bills.

As they shook hands, the two men agreed that Danby would leave her at her stall with a halter on her, and Delfer's staff would care for her for the rest of the weekend before they trailered her back to Nebraska.

Danby went back to take one last look at Miss Honey Pine. In the arena, a demonstration of traditional roping by cowboys from the Mexico Quarter Horse Association was underway, and the crowd was cheering with excitement. Honey, unaffected by the noise, was quietly munching on some hay.

"Goodbye, ol' girl. It's been quite a ride," he said as he scratched her behind her tiny ears.

# 12

Damien continued to take over the farrier duties at Major Meadows, and his work was top-notch. Introductions between Damien and Danby had been brief and tense from Kella's perspective, and she continued to try to book Damien's visits when Danby was most likely to be off the property. She knew how he felt about Damien, and nothing Damien could do with his blacksmith tools was going to change that. Danby thought he at least owed it to his old friend Alfonso to give his son a chance. He remembered that they had all been young and made mistakes before, but he wanted to keep him on a short leash. One hint of trouble, and he didn't want him around.

The days were getting shorter, and the leaves were off the trees. Kella's business was slowing down for the approaching winter. A couple of new boarders moved in to take advantage of the indoor arena until spring, but the training and showing part of her business was winding down.

The last big event of the season would be the ninety-sixth Royal Agricultural Winter Fair held each November in Toronto. It was a great spectacle that brought the country to the city with all forms of agricultural competition. There were crops and vegetables, sheep, goats, pigs, and cattle. You could see rabbits and chickens, ducks and geese, and demonstrations of all kinds. It featured dog agility events, a rodeo, lectures and clinics, commercial vendors, art and artists, cooking and food displays, lots of shopping, and of course the horse show.

The Royal, as it was known, would bring out the who's who of the North American equestrian community. Kella had been invited by a couple of friends to join them and split their VIP skybox seats for one night of the event. The couples would meet ahead of time at the Tanbark Club for dinner and drinks and then take in the show from the posh venue. It had long been a tradition at the Royal that box seat holders dressed in formal black-tie attire, and although the Coliseum had been reconfigured to accommodate the American Hockey League affiliate of the Toronto Maple Leafs hockey team, attendees still adhered to the formal dress code.

Kella had taken along a girlfriend before or occasionally gone on her own, but she was tired of being the third wheel, so when she replied to the invitation, she said that she would pay for two tickets and expected to bring a "plus one."

"Someone we know?" replied Jessica Stewart, who, with her husband, Oliver, was putting the group together for the night.

"Just a friend, no biggie," said Kella, downplaying the fact that she and Damien had been seeing each other on the down low for almost two months.

Kella texted Damien: "Do you own a suit?"

"WTF kind of question is that?" he replied.

"I guess that's a no," she messaged.

"I don't need one," texted Damien.

"Every man should have a suit. You should always be ready for a wedding or a funeral."

"Who died?" asked Damien.

"LOL, nobody died," replied Kella. "I'll explain when I see you tonight."

Corby's dad, Reese, was picking her up and taking her to her hockey game tonight, so it was a perfect opportunity for Kella to slip out and visit Damien at his trailer.

Kella was excited to talk to Damien about going to the Royal together. Their hookups had become predictable, and she knew that beyond the sex, they didn't have a whole lot in common. This would be a big step to go out in public as a couple, and she secretly was just dying to see him all dressed up. She predicted a transformation that would rival the makeovers on the daytime TV talk shows.

Kella arrived at the trailer, kicked off her boots just inside the door, and then flopped down on the sofa. With the doors and windows closed during the cooler weather, the sweet scent of marijuana permeated everything in the place. Kella hoped she wasn't taking the smell home with her on her clothes.

"Ever been to the Royal?" she asked.

"Sure, tons of times. I used to help the Watsons with their Holstein cows down there when I was a kid," said Damien.

"I mean the horse show, the evening performances that you need a ticket for," said Kella.

"The fancy part? Not officially, I don't think. Why? What's up? Has this got something to do with me needing a suit?" said Damien.

"My friends Jessica and Oliver invited us to join them in their skybox seats on Friday night."

"Us?" said Damien.

"I said I'd be bringing someone. The dress code is formal, black tie, so you'll at least need a dark suit. You should have one anyway."

"I don't know. I'm not exactly a suit and tie kind of guy, if you know what I mean."

"Please," said Kella. "Tell you what. I'll pay for the horse show tickets and for dinner and drinks, and you go get yourself a black suit with a white shirt and a black tie. That's all you need."

"What are you going to wear?" he asked.

"Don't worry about me. It will be a surprise. Do you have black dress shoes?" she asked.

"I've got black cowboy boots," he said.

"Uh, no. Add black shoes to the list."

"You sure you want to do this?" he asked.

"I wouldn't ask you if I wasn't, would I?"

Kella planned to wear a dress that she had worn last winter to a cousin's wedding. She was sure that nobody who saw her in it before was going to see her at the Royal, so it would do double duty seamlessly.

On the day of the event, she said goodbye to Corby and Danby, all dressed up for her night at the Royal Horse Show, and she conveniently left out the part about who was going with her. Danby tolerated Damien's role as the farrier for Major Meadows, but if he knew they were seeing each other socially, he would throw a fit.

It was a cool November night with the threat of snow flurries in the air. Kella wore a dark red velvet gown with a black wool cape. She arrived at four o'clock at Damien's trailer. He was ready and standing inside the door. They both stood and stared at each other, speechless. Neither had seen the other in anything but the most casual attire, and they were both overwhelmed by the transformation. Damien looked polished and elegant, and his crisp white shirt contrasted perfectly with his groomed but stubbly beard. He studied Kella up and down and admired everything about her, from her hairstyle to her jewelry to her shoes. "I might be the luckiest guy in the world right now," he said.

"You clean up pretty good there, cowboy," Kella replied. Damien reached for his coat. It was a black and gray nylon snowmobile jacket with bright yellow logos embroidered on the chest, back, and sleeves. "You're not planning on wearing that, are you?" she asked.

"It's supposed to snow tonight. What else am I going to wear?"

"Well, you can leave it in my car. We will get valet parking any-way. so you won't need to walk far outside. We'll take my Lexus," she said and tossed him the keys.

It was a one-hour drive into Toronto going in the opposite direction of the rush hour commuter traffic. Damien drove the SUV up to the valet parking, and attendants opened their doors and handed him a claim check. Kella had their e-tickets ready in her phone, and they breezed through the turnstiles and entered the shopping area of the fair.

They had an hour to kill before meeting the others for a pre-show dinner, and there was plenty to see. They had a slight awk-wardness between them now that they were out in public and exposed as a couple. They both were likely to see lots of people they knew in the horse industry, and they each silently did an inventory of who they wanted to see and who they didn't.

Damien tried to take Kella's hand as they walked around the booths, but he sensed a chilly response, so after he conveniently let it go, he didn't try again. They looked at the displays of the finest in saddles and bridles, trucks and horse trailers, equestrian themed decor and artwork. Kella insisted that they needed a slab of the best fudge in the world. They agreed on a flavor, and Damien was assigned to carry the fudge in a bag after they both had a sweet sample.

They wandered into the cattle area and saw dairy cows being groomed and vacuumed and clipped for the show. Sheep wearing coats to keep them clean and gigantic pigs ready for competition. They strolled through the horticultural displays along the inter-locking brick pathways next to manicured shrubbery and artificial waterfalls. Damien felt conspicuous in his suit and tie when most of the visitors at the fair were dressed more casually. Kella was in her glory. She watched women checking out her dress and checking out Damien, and she loved the attention. They went into the Horse Palace, where all the horses competing in the show were stabled in the two-story, historic structure. Aisles of neatly adorned stalls were filled with draft horses, tiny ponies, and everything in between. The exercise arena in the middle was crowded with horses warming up for the evening show, and there was a buzz in the air with whinnying horses and clip clopping hooves mixed with the smells of horse manure, wood shavings, leather, and horse grooming sprays. The vintage stables were famous for being used in scenes of movies filmed in Toronto, including *The Black Stallion*, and the stalls were once used to house soldiers during World War II.

"Kella, how are you? I haven't seen you since that little show at the fair," said Jane Whetstone as she gave Kella a weak hug and an air kiss on the cheek.

"Jane, this is my friend Damien Rhodes," said Kella.

"You know my husband, Donald," said Jane, presenting Donald Whetstone to Kella and Damien. Jane was dressed in a long black gown covered with sequins, and she wore a black mink shawl over her shoulders. Donald looked like royalty with his full head of silver hair, and he was dressed in the scarlet-red, formal attire of their hunt club. "Here for the show?" Jane asked, then continued without waiting for an answer. "My new horse was amazing in the Derby on Wednesday night, and I showed my old, faithful gelding yesterday and again tomorrow. Tonight is my night off to watch."

"Well, good luck, Jane," said Kella.

"Nice to meet you," said Damien, and the two couples continued in different directions.

"Look at Mr. Fancypants over here," said a man in overalls and a greasy ball cap as he slapped Damien on the back.

"Hey, Doug," said Damien. "Kella, this is Doug Prentice. I shoe his Standardbreds."

"I guess I'll see you on Monday, Damien. Enjoy the horse show.

Don't get any mustard on that pretty tie," said Doug, laughing and spitting bits of chewing tobacco out of his lips as he spoke.

The couple made their way to the Tanbark Club, which was a temporary upscale restaurant set up in a curtained-off area next to the warmup ring. They gave the name Stewart at the front desk for the reserved table and were escorted in. Damien finally realized that there were a whole lot more people here that were dressed formally, and he decided that since this part wasn't costing him a dime, he might as well enjoy it.

They met up with Jessica and Oliver Stewart, plus Connie and Bryan Winters and enjoyed a light dinner and drinks. Kella sipped white wine, while Damien downed two beers. The other couples were even more dressed up, with the men both in black tuxedos and the women in full-length gowns.

During dinner, Kella slipped Damien two hundred dollars in cash so that he could at least appear to be paying for them. The six of them then took the elevator up to the skybox level to watch the horse show. The room included six seats across the front with a glass panel railing overlooking the show ring. In the back was a small lounge with a counter and stools. The women poured themselves glasses of wine and settled into the front seats. The men stayed in the lounge area.

"So, Damien, what do you do?" asked Bryan.

"I operate my own farrier services business," said Damien in an attempt to give it as much importance as possible.

"Oh, so you must love horses as much as these girls do," said Bryan.

"I just shoe them. I don't ride them," he replied. "What about you?" asked Damien.

"I'm a stockbroker. I stay as far from the horses as possible. I just pay for them," said Bryan.

The evening program featured a wide variety of horse show

classes, including the perennial favorites. Men in brightly colored silk jackets showing their speedy roadsters with the crowd roaring each time the "Road Gait" was called by the announcer. Two-wheeled sulkies fishtailed on the corners as the trotters flew around the arena. Next was the Green Meadows Four In Hand class, where antique carriages were pulled by four horses carrying formally attired guests, while their well-appointed footman played a tune on a hunting horn. Then a Hackney pony class with the high-stepping and spirited ponies pulled their well turned out four-wheeled carts. Next, they watched the heavy horse class where teams of six Clydesdales tugged big, shiny wagons. The feature act of the night was a "natural horseman" trainer presenting his five horses at liberty in the arena in a moving demonstration set to music. The night concluded with the exciting International Jumper Challenge that featured the best of the best equestrians from the up-and-coming professionals to the seasoned Olympic medal winners.

During the performance, everyone enjoyed a chunk of the fudge that Damien had been carrying all evening.

With the show over, the couples made their way to the crowded elevators, and Kella and Damien stood in the back. Damien put his hand around Kella's waist for the ride down to the main floor. They retrieved Kella's car from the valet parking service and were back on the highway to make their way to Duckville.

"Well, that was fun," she said.

"That was amazing," said Damien. "I still can't believe you invited me."

"Did you get along okay with Oliver and Bryan?" she asked.

"Oh yeah, we're best buds now. I'm going curling with them next week."

"Seriously?" she asked.

"What do you think?" he said, and they both laughed.

Pulling into the driveway at Bear Claw Racing Stable, Damien said, "That dress looks great on you, but do you know where I'd really like to see it?"

"Where?" asked Kella.

"On the floor in my bedroom," said Damien.

"Very funny," said Kella. "I'm going to take a rain check on that offer. I better get home before Dad starts wondering where I am."

They both got out of her car, and he held the driver door open for her to get in.

"Thanks for a great evening," she said.

"I should be the one doing the thanking. I had a great time." They kissed quickly, and she drove off.

Once home, she made her way quietly into her house. Corby was in bed, and the lights were off in Danby's apartment, but she knew he would have seen her headlights come in and noted the time.

She took her phone out of her purse and found a text from Damien.

"My jacket is still in the back of your car. I'll need it tomorrow."

Kella typed back, "Okay, we can figure it out in the morning. Goodnight and thanks again. XO"

# 13

Two weeks after the Royal Winter Fair, Damien was at Major Meadows finishing up the last horse on his list for the day. Kella was busy putting hay in horses' stalls before she brought them in for the night.

"Hey, do you and Corby want to come to the Devils game with me tonight?" he shouted down the barn aisle as he packed up his tools.

"Sorry, I can't. I promised Jessica and Connie that I'd go with them to a painting party thing tonight. I don't know why. I can't even draw a stick man," said Kella.

"Do you think Corby would want to come with me? I haven't been back to the arena for years, and I'd rather not go in there alone, if you know what I mean," said Damien.

"I'm sure she would absolutely love to. Dad hasn't taken her to a Devils game yet this season, but he's speaking at a 4H Club meeting tonight. She's been so busy with her own games that she hasn't mentioned the Devils. I'll check with her and text you later," said Kella.

Back at his trailer, Damien got showered and dressed and found a text on his phone from Kella: "Corby wants to go. She will be ready at 6:20. I'll give her money. I'll be gone when you get here."

Damien replied: "Awesome. Have a nice night."

As an only child of single parents, Corby was used to being passed around among family members and acquaintances. She had seen Damien around the barn numerous times, and they could always find common ground in a conversation about hockey. Kella gave her money for admission and a snack, and she was waiting at the front door, watching for Damien to arrive. She didn't recognize the Honda Civic he was driving, but she met him on the front porch before he could get to the front door.

"All set for the big game?" he asked.

"I sure am. Who are they playing tonight?" she asked.

"Miskatung Hawks," said Damien. "Should be a good one."

Miskatung was a First Nations community two hours north of Duckville in the lakes region. Most of the players were First Nation boys, and what the team lacked in coaching and facilities, they made up for in effort. A lot of them saw hockey as a pathway to get off the reservation and make a better life for themselves and their families. While the Hawks were perennial last-place finishers in the standings, they were feared by the other teams in the league. Damien fondly remembered many battles with Miskatung, and he had a scar that divided one eyebrow as a reminder.

It was lightly snowing with big, wet flakes as they arrived at the Preston Giles Memorial Arena. Damien had practically grown up there. He played hockey in the winter and indoor lacrosse and floor hockey in the summer. He knew every hall, every door, every seat in the place. As usual, the parking lot was nearly full, with spectators arriving for the game and figure skaters leaving the building at the end of their practice.

Corby saw her friend Angel coming out of the arena carrying her white figure skates. "Hi, Corb," she said.

"Hi, Angel. You staying for the game?" said Corby.

"I can't. I have to babysit. Watch for my brother. He's number thirty-four," said Angel.

Inside, the arena was buzzing with Devils supporters, and the distinctive clan from Miskatung were keeping to themselves near the side entrance. The place had the familiar smell of fresh popcorn, and through the glass of the lobby they could see the Zamboni ice machine prepping the surface for the game.

There was a line at the snack bar for hotdogs, nachos, soft drinks, and candy bars. At a side table, an elderly couple was selling fifty-fifty draw tickets. "Five bucks apiece, three for ten!" the man called to Damien as he walked by. At another table was the registration for the Chuck-A-Puck game. People paid two dollars to get a puck with a number painted on it. Between the first and second periods, they could toss their puck on the ice, and the person who had the puck closest to center ice would win half of the money collected.

"Wanna chuck a puck?" Damien asked Corby as he took a couple two-dollar coins out of his pocket.

"Only if you do it too," she said. Corby grabbed puck number ten and wrote her name next to number ten on the page. Damien took number forty-five and signed the page as he placed the two coins on the table.

"Come here. I want to show you something that should be down here," he said as he led Corby toward the trophy case that took up most of the hallway to the dressing rooms. "See anyone you know in that picture?" he asked, pointing to the Mid Ontario Junior B Champions team photo. "That's me in the back row on the left," said Damien.

"Nice mullet," said Corby. "Just kidding."

Damien scanned the names listed under the photo and noticed that his own name had been whited out. He said nothing more to Corby, then moved toward the snack bar, where he saw something he had not seen in the arena before. It stopped him cold. A hockey sweater was mounted in a frame under glass. It was a green

Beaverwood Loggers sweater with the name Semper on the back. Attached to the framed was a corroding brass plaque that read "Justin Ryan Semper, January 10, 1991–April 6, 2008.

It was a chilling reminder of a night more than ten years ago that Damien and the citizens of Beaverwood and Duckville would never forget.

"Want anything to eat or drink?" Damien asked Corby.

"I'd like a large popcorn and a small Coke. My mom gave me money."

"That's okay. I'll get it for you," said Damien.

"Thanks. I've got to go to the bathroom." Corby headed down the hall while Damien got in line.

Damien felt a tap on the shoulder. "Long time no see there, handsome." Damien recognized the voice before he turned around. It was Nicole Esposito. Damien and Nicole had dated during most of grade ten and eleven, but they weren't ready for monogamy and finally broke it off for good in the summer before grade twelve. "Who's the kid? Not yours, I hope," she said.

"No, that's Kella Major's daughter. Just a friend."

"Well, look at you! Moving up in the world, are we? Kella Major, eh? Right on. Good for you, buddy."

"We're just friends," he said. "The kid's dad isn't around much, so I thought I'd bring her."

"Friends with benefits if I know you," said Nicole with a wink, and she walked away before Corby returned.

The muffled sound of the Canadian national anthem was filtering into the lobby and snack bar area, and everyone stood quietly until it ended.

"Let's get some seats," said Damien as he handed Corby her snacks. Damien wanted to maintain as low a profile as possible. He was still shaken from seeing Justin's sweater hanging in the lobby, and he didn't want to be recognized. There was a whole new generation of Devils fans in the seats, and he was ten years older. He didn't expect many people to know who he was—or care.

The first period opened with a quick goal by the Miskatung Hawks just thirty seconds into the game. The early goal silenced the Devils fans until Duckville tied the game on a power play goal while one of the Hawks served a penalty for tripping. The announcer had just finished saying, "Last minute to play in the first period," when the Devils scored again to take a 2–1 lead into the first intermission.

The Zamboni made its way around the ice to scrape it and flood it, creating a new smooth surface for the second period.

"Ladies and gentlemen. Boys and girls. It's time to chuck your puck!" said the announcer with great fanfare, and immediately pucks began flying onto the ice from all directions. Some fell short and bounced off the glass and back into the front row where kids were waiting to toss the extra pucks over the boards and onto the ice. Corby's puck grazed the top of the glass and dropped just onto the ice next to the wall. Damien cocked his arm like a quarterback and launched his puck toward center ice. It ricocheted off of a few others before resting near center. As others flew in and bounced around the face-off circle, they lost track of which puck was his.

Once all the puck chucking stopped, a young woman in an oversized Devils sweater approached center ice with a microphone, a clipboard, and a tape measure. After some measuring and deliberation, she announced. "Winning tonight's Chuck-A-Puck Jackpot of ninety-six dollars is number forty-five, Corby McLaren."

"Hey, that was yours, not mine!" she shouted to Damien over the applause.

"Don't worry about it. Just go get your money," he said to her, smiling.

The second period resumed, and the Hawks were ready to push back. Again they opened the scoring, tying the game with a slap shot from a defenseman on the blue line that was tipped in by their center parked in front of the goalie. The Miskatung fans erupted with cheers and applause, and even some Devils fans were nodding in agreement that it was a nice goal. The game stayed tied at 3–3 to the end of the second period as the players retreated to their dressing rooms and the Zamboni took to the ice again. After the fifty-fifty draw winner was announced, winning $245, the second intermission entertainment came out on the ice.

Against one goal, a plywood sign was placed that filled the gap except for a small rectangular hole in the bottom at the center. Morden's Modern Printing Inc. *For All Your Printing Needs* was printed in red on the white panel. Across the bottom were the black scuffs from wayward pucks that had missed the target at previous games.

Three audience members were given a chance to shoot a puck through the target from the closest blue line. The first two were teenaged boys who both shot straight through the hole. The third shooter was a middle-aged woman who missed the goal entirely, to the amusement of the audience, and then slipped and fell on her way off the ice, which ignited more laughter.

The two boys then moved to center ice to take their next shots. The first boy took a slow and steady approach, but the audience groaned when the puck came to a stop a few feet short of the target. The next boy took a firm wrist shot that arced off the ice then settled back down on a straight path through the opening. The audience roared with appreciation, and the boy raised both hands and the stick in the air and nodded his head up and down as he slowly rotated to acknowledge the applause like a prize fighter. The girl with the clipboard and the microphone handed him the Devils replica sweater that she had draped over her arm, and he put it on to more cheers from the crowd.

The third period was shaping up to be a classic clash between the Devils and the Hawks. With the score tied, there was little room for error, and both teams opened the period with a cautious and defensive approach. During a struggle for the puck in the corner, a Miskatung player unleashed an elbow into the head of Angel's brother, number thirty-four. Everyone in the arena saw it except the referees, and no penalty was called on it as play continued. Two more shifts, and the Miskatung player with the wayward elbow was back on the ice. Duckville's coach gave a tap on the shoulder to Brendan Deschamps. Brendan stood and waited for one of the Devils to get off the ice and then launched over the boards and straight toward the unsuspecting Miskatung skater. Deschamps plowed him into the boards right in front of where Damien and Corby were sitting and then dropped his gloves to uncork a flurry of blows before his opponent had a chance to get reset. The Hawks player recovered quickly and met Brendan punch for punch as the audience erupted with approval. Damien clenched his jaw and tilted his head to one side as he made a tight fist with his right hand. Instinctively, he was mimicking the movements of the Devils player and was feeling every jab and uppercut that he threw or received. Both players began to slow their assault, and the referees moved in to separate the pair, sparing their honor and protecting them from further damage. Before they pulled apart, Brendan gave the Miskatung player a rub on the head to signal his approval of a fight well fought. They were both ejected from the game, and play resumed.

"What did you think of that?" Damien asked Corby.

"That was awesome. We aren't allowed to fight in our league," she replied.

"Well, they aren't really allowed to fight in any league," said Damien. "Trust me, it's not worth it."

With three minutes left in the third period, the Hawks took the lead with what would be called a "garbage goal." There had been a scramble around the net, and the puck deflected into the corner of the net off the back of the leg of one of the Devils' own players.

The Devils made one last bid to tie the game up again by pulling their goalie from the net with a minute and a half to go in the game and putting an extra forward player on the ice for an all-out, go-for-broke attack on the Hawk's net. Miskatung cleared the puck up the boards and into the Devils' zone. and then with just twelve seconds remaining, they sealed the game in their favor with an empty-net goal.

"That's okay. It was still really fun," said Corby as they made their way to the lobby. "Can I get a hot chocolate to take home?" she asked.

"Sure, you're the one with the big bucks now," said Damien, and he waited next to the skate-sharpening booth while Corby went to the snack bar.

"Coulda used you out there tonight, Rhodes," said team owner Richard Morden, spotting Damien by himself.

"That's all behind me now, sir," said Damien.

Morden extended his hand to shake Damien's. "Good to see you, son. You're looking well."

"Thanks, Mr. Morden. It's nice to be back."

Corby arrived with her hot chocolate, and they headed out to the parking lot. It had been snowing heavily since they arrived, and Damien got in and started his car, then got out and used his bare hands and jacket sleeve to clear the snow off of the windshield and back window. Corby sat shivering in the passenger seat, warming her hands with her Styrofoam cup of hot chocolate. He had the wipers on to clear the accumulating snow, but they barely gave him any view other than straight ahead. It was a traffic jam getting positioned to leave the parking lot. The entrance sloped up to the road, and a snowplow had left a pile of snow across the lane, making it difficult for any vehicles that didn't have four-wheel drive to exit.

Damien approached the road with his tires spinning and came to a stop in the drift of snow. "Hang on," he said. "I'm going to have to rock it a bit." He gunned it forward and then slammed into reverse, backed up a bit, and took another run at it. The second jolt caused Corby to spill her piping-hot chocolate onto her lap.

"Ouch, ouch, hot, hot, hot!" she screamed. Damien looked toward her and was briefly distracted as his car gained traction and launched across the road and into the path of a vehicle emerging from the snowy darkness to the right.

Damien's Civic was no match for the crew cab pickup truck, and the last thing he remembered was the deafening sound of breaking glass and crunching metal as it slammed into the passenger door.

# 14

Connie and Jessica convinced Kella to join the event page on Facebook and attend a painting party. Connie had been to this place before, and she told the others it was going to be a lot of fun. They would all be following the instructor's demonstration to make a painting on canvas. To help get the creative juices flowing, they were allowed to bring their own "refreshments of any kind," so the girls were all set with wine and some plastic wine glasses.

Kella was secretly terrified of doing anything art related. She was certain that she was going to embarrass herself with her painting. She had already visited the artist's website and seen how great everyone's paintings looked, and this made her feel worse.

The artist's space was in a converted old mill that had been renovated and restored to be used as art studios and galleries. It was located in the tiny old village of Hawthorne, one of many quaint hamlets in the region that was a popular day trip for tourists from the city. Visitors enjoyed the small-town charm and shopped in the one-of-a-kind stores for everything from local foods to pottery, repurposed textiles, and jewelry. In addition to the agricultural influences in the area, it was becoming a favorite spot for the arts, with a flourishing local theatre scene as well as attracting writers, musicians, and painters. The local landscape provided inspiration with its rivers and lakes, fields and forests, trails and wildlife.

Kella arrived at the studio in the old mill to find an eclectic space with a comfortable vibe. Classic rock music was playing, and about twenty women were taking their spots at the tables to do their paintings. At the front of the room, Malcolm Lancaster, the artist in residence, was calmly guiding the giggling women into position. Malcolm was a fifty-something artist who had long since discovered that the key to marketing his own paintings was to develop a following among the women in the area who needed a night out with the girls, without the bar scene. His strategy was obviously working, because his Girls Night Out Painting Parties were often sold out, and as a result his commission orders and sales of his own paintings were flourishing.

Connie and Jessica were already seated and had saved Kella a spot, printing her name onto a name card and starting some introductions around their paint-stained table. Mercifully, the first thing that Kella discovered when she stared at the intimidating canvas was that Malcolm Lancaster had taken the time to predraw the image in pencil on each of the canvases to match the sample painting that he was about to do. "That will be our little secret," he said as he welcomed Kella to her seat. "You didn't want to draw the horse yourself, did you?" he joked.

"Oh my god, I'm so relieved," she said. "You have no idea. I'm going to be the worst student you've ever had."

"You don't scare me," said Malcolm as he went to his easel and brought the group to attention.

He gave them all the information they needed about the process and the paints and then spoke more specifically about the painting that they were going to replicate.

"This image is from a photograph that I took last year. The

picture is of a gray horse, but as you can see, I decided to paint the horse blue."

Kella studied the paints on her palette and her little reference picture and tried to guess where he was going to begin to paint.

She watched as he used each brush as an extension of his hand. Like a musician with an instrument or a carpenter with his tools, under his control the brushes started to bring the image to life. All the women tried to keep up as he swapped from one brush to another, changing the angle of the bristles to create a different effect. He showed them how to blend two or three colors together, and they marveled as the new mixture became the perfect hue to match the reference picture.

Halfway through the evening, the group took a break from the painting, and the girls topped up their wine glasses. Others had brought cheese and fruit trays, squares and cupcakes, and there was plenty to go around. A few stepped out to smoke, and when they came back in, they were covered in snow. "It's really coming down out there," one said as she stomped her feet and shook the big flakes off of her clothes.

"What's Corby up to tonight?" Jessica asked.

"She's at the Devils game with Damien actually. She's crazy about hockey. She's probably having the time of her life."

"Damien, yes. Let's talk about Damien, shall we?" said Connie.

"What exactly is going on with your latest boy toy?"

Kella continued to downplay their relationship. She explained that he was doing their farrier work at the farm, but Danby wasn't too comfortable with him yet.

"What's he think about Damien taking Corby out for the evening?" they asked.

"Dad doesn't know, and he probably never will if the timing works out tonight. Corby and I will be home before he gets back from his meeting."

Kella instinctively looked at her phone to check the time and see if she had any new texts. Nothing. No news was good news.

Back to the painting, and Kella wondered if it was the wine, Malcolm's encouragement, or her own latent artistic talent that was making her blue horse painting look so good. As they finished, Malcolm said, "Sign it however you normally sign your paintings," and Kella laughed, saying that she had never done a single painting since she was twelve.

Malcolm then asked them to line up as a group with their creations. He was going to take a photo to post on his social media pages. "This one is for my website, so pretend you had fun," he said, and all the women chuckled on cue as he took the photo with his phone.

"That was awesome. Thanks so much," Kella said to Malcolm as he was cleaning up the paints and brushes.

"I'm glad you enjoyed it. Hope to see you again," he said. " Like my page on Facebook if you want to see my upcoming events."

Kella checked her phone again. Four percent battery was left, but she was going to be back to the farm in twenty minutes. She knew the hockey game should be over and that Corby and Damien would be on their way home. *Perfect timing*, she thought as she hugged her friends and bundled up for the snow outside.

Kella got a snow scraper out of the back of her vehicle and cleared the snow off of the windows as she let it idle to warm up. The flakes were still coming down heavily when she drove through the sleepy little town and back onto the road that would take her east toward Major Meadows. She had finished three small glasses of wine in the past three hours, so she felt fine to drive, but she didn't want to encounter any police check stops. These backroads were a favorite spot for the local law enforcement to check for drinking drivers who had been out at the pre-Christmas office parties this time of year and were avoiding the main roads back to their country homes.

Kella arrived home at Major Meadows without incident but was surprised that there were no tire tracks in the driveway and no lights on at home. *Maybe the game went into overtime or something*, she thought as she carried her painting into the house, trying to keep the snow from falling on it.

She got inside and took off her coat and boots, hearing the tapping of Cider's toenails trotting across the tile kitchen floor to greet her. Kella let Cider out the door, but the dog took one look at the snow from the porch and turned around to give two scratches on the front door to signal that she wanted back inside. Kella set her painting proudly on the mantel over the fireplace so that she could show Corby as soon as she got home. She checked her phone again. No battery. It was shut down, so she plugged it into the charger cord on the kitchen counter and filled up the kettle to make a cup of herbal tea. Picking up her tea, she settled in a chair that gave her a good view of the driveway so she could see headlights arriving. She just hoped that Damien and Corby would arrive before Danby.

Her phone vibrated and beeped and came to life on the kitchen counter. She set down her tea and picked up her phone to check for messages. There were four in a row from Damien.

"We've had an accident. Meet us at the hospital."

"Bring Corby's Ontario health card if you can."

"Are you getting these messages?"

"Hello?"

Kella stared at the screen. She was foggy from the wine and tired from a long day, and it took a moment to process the information she was reading. She tried to call Damien's phone, but it went straight to voicemail.

She read it over several times before texting a reply: "I'm coming. Is she okay? Are you okay? What happened?"

Kella unplugged her phone with just 5 percent battery life and headed out the door. There was already snow covering her car, but she just got in and turned on her windshield wipers and started driving. She lowered all four windows and then raised them again to clear the snow off of them and give her enough visibility for the half-hour drive to the hospital.

In her rush, she had forgotten to bring a charger cord with her to plug her phone into her car. Her mind was racing. *I never should have sent her alone with Damien. How bad was the accident? Is she injured or worse? How am I going to tell Dad? How could I have been painting while this was happening?*

She pulled into the parking lot at the hospital. Snow covered the automated, gated entrance, and she fumbled with the ticket machine. *Do I put money in this? Do I insert my credit card? Just open the gate and let me in.* "Push Button for Ticket," she read, poking frantically at the green button. Finally the gate went up. She parked haphazardly in two spots and ran to the emergency entrance of the hospital.

Kella's eyes had to adjust to the bright lighting in the emergency department. She hadn't been here for a few years, since she had to bring her dad in to get stitches in his forehead when a piece of wood he was chopping flew up and hit him in the face.

The waiting area was crowded with all the usual suspects you'd find on a typical Friday night. Mothers holding crying babies, men who had a minor injury at work and waited until evening to get it taken care of. A man with chest pains who had been shoveling snow was being given top priority as Kella approached the triage desk.

"I'm here for my daughter. Corby McLaren. She came in from a car accident with a man named Damien Rhodes."

The nurse typed for a moment on her computer. "McLaren, Corby. Yes, here she is. Are you the mother?" she asked.

"Yes, Kella Major."

"Do you have your health card with you?" the nurse asked, and Kella rifled through her purse and handed it to her. "Take a seat, and a doctor will be out to speak with you."

"Well, is she okay? What happened? Can I see her?" Kella was becoming frantic.

"Ma'am, a doctor will be right out to speak with you," said the nurse in such a calm and well-trained manner that it irritated Kella.

She turned to look for a seat and heard a man's voice call from within the patient area. "McLaren, Corby?" he said, holding a clipboard. He appeared to be a doctor. He was about forty years old and dressed in green scrubs and running shoes.

"I'm Corby's mother. Is she okay? Can I see her?" she asked as she approached the man. Looking at his clipboard, he said, "Kella Major? Follow me please."

"Will somebody please tell me if she is okay?" she shouted at the man.

Kella took great pride in being cool under pressure. This had given her an advantage showing horses from a young age. She had immeasurable patience, which helped her when she was training the difficult horses. She had been around animals all her life, and her father didn't shield her from the trauma of the blood and gore from birth to death in the raising of livestock. She had assisted with minor surgeries from suturing hernias to castrations, and she had delivered foals dead and alive. She had held horses as they took their last breath when they had to be euthanized due to severe injury or old age. She was tough when she needed to be, but tonight she felt weakened and vulnerable and lonely, and she was terrified that Corby could be severely injured or dead.

"Oh sure, she'll be fine," he said. "I'm Dr. Larose. I thought you knew that already."

He pulled back a curtain and let Kella into a small treatment room where Corby was lying on the bed, and Damien was sitting in a chair beside her.

"I am so, so sorry, Kella," Damien said when she walked in. Kella didn't answer but immediately went to hug Corby.

"Easy, easy," said the doctor. "She's pretty tender on the right side."

Corby's right arm was in a cast in a sling. She had two bandages on the right side of her face—one on her forehead and one on the side of her chin.

"She's a lucky young lady," the doctor reported. "The x-rays showed a fracture at the bottom of the humerus, which we have set. Technically that's an olecranon process fracture. Not uncommon in collisions when a vehicle doesn't have side airbags. She will be in a cast for about six weeks. She has two lacerations on her face. The one on her forehead had some glass fragments, which have been debrided, and she received nine stitches there and six more on her chin. Luckily our plastic surgeon was on site, so he did a beautiful job, and it shouldn't affect her modelling career."

"I broke my funny bone, but it wasn't funny," said Corby.

"She does have a mild concussion, attempts at comedy notwithstanding. She can go home tonight, but she should not sleep for more than two hours at a time for now. The nurse will give you some literature to read about managing the symptoms, and please don't hesitate to call us if there are any changes in her condition. She also has some very minor burning on the skin in the pelvic area, but we established the cause of that, and it's nothing to worry about. The nurse will give you a few tablets for managing pain, and I will write you a prescription for some more, but the more we can keep her off of the pills, the better. Just wait here, and someone will be with you to discharge."

"Thank you, Doctor," said Kella as he excused himself. Kella then turned her attention to Damien. "So, do you mind telling me what the hell happened?"

For the first time, she noticed that Damien also had a bandage across his forehead. He looked exhausted as he explained what he remembered about the accident. It was snowing, the car couldn't make it out the driveway because of the snow, Corby spilled her drink, he didn't see the truck coming.

"Can you give me a ride home?" he asked. "My car is a write-off. I'll go to the wrecker yard tomorrow and get my stuff out of it."

Not much was said in the car from the hospital to Bear Claw Racing Stable. The long driveway wasn't cleared of snow, but Kella put her SUV into four-wheel drive and plowed through.

She dropped Damien off without much of a goodbye, and he wondered how this was going to change things between them.

"It's almost one in the morning. Your grandfather is going to wonder where the heck we are. Let's just get to bed, and we can give him the full report in the morning, okay?" Kella said to Corby.

"Okay, Mom. Devils lost, by the way, but I won ninety-seven dollars."

# 15

In the weeks that followed the accident, Kella felt as though she needed to create some space between herself and Damien. Danby was livid when he found out that Damien was out alone with Corby, and it gave him even more ammunition to try to convince Kella that he shouldn't be doing their farrier work either.

Kella was torn. On one hand, Damien was an excellent farrier. He had skills and techniques that she had never seen Alfonso do. He was prompt, he was good with the horses and her boarders, and he had reasonable prices. On the other hand, she couldn't afford to have Danby upset, and she was tiring of the struggle to keep them separated.

Damien knew things had definitely changed. For the past two appointments, Kella had texted him a list of horses to do and left a check for him in an envelope on the bulletin board in the barn. She had conveniently been absent whenever he had been to the farm.

Christmas holidays arrived, and Corby was growing weary of the cast on her arm. She was scheduled to get it removed in the week between Christmas and New Year's, and it couldn't come off soon enough.

"Can I at least go to public skating?" she had asked. "I'm not going to fall or anything."

Doctor's orders said to stay off the skates. She had gone to watch a couple of her hockey team games to cheer on her friends, but it wasn't the same as getting on the ice.

Corby was also keeping an eye on the ice on the pond. Freezing temperatures were forecast for the next two weeks, and with any luck, the homemade ice rink would be ready at the same time that she got her cast removed. She was spending this Christmas with her father. Reese and Kella alternated years, splitting up the family holidays. This year, Kella had Corby at home for Thanksgiving and not for Christmas, and next year it would be the other way around.

In the morning of Christmas Eve, Corby's father picked her up, and they drove two hours north to the McLaren family cottage on Sugar Maple Bay. Corby's grandfather Corwyn had spent his summers at the family's rustic retreat as a boy, and after he inherited it, it was renovated and winterized for year-round use. Corby loved Christmas at the cottage and was really looking forward to it, even if she wouldn't be skating on the lake this year.

"Looks like it's just the two of us again this year, honey," Danby said to Kella as they finished up the barn chores.

"That's okay, Dad. There is nowhere I'd rather be," said Kella.

Kella kept some Christmas decorations in an old trunk and decided how much of an effort to make each year based on whether or not Corby was going to be around. Danby planted a stand of spruce trees years ago on the property and made a tradition with Corby of cutting down a tree each year and putting it up in the living room. In the early days, the trees were all too small to really qualify as Christmas trees, so he would cut a little tree and put it on a small table. Then for a few years, the trees were the perfect size. These days, they were so tall that they couldn't come in the house, so he would just take a chainsaw and cut the top of the tree off to make it the perfect size, using just the top. Once the tree was in place, Danby's decorating efforts came to a halt. He would let the girls take over, placing the ornaments, while he sat in his favorite spot and supervised.

His Christmas trees were always a great opportunity for him to get in the spirit, as he always invited a few old friends to come over and pick out a tree. The annual visits to the farm became a tradition for several families. There were prettier, more manicured trees available from the serious sellers, but taking home a Major Meadows tree made them more special.

Christmas Day was not a holiday on the farm. The horses got fed at seven thirty in the morning, just like every other day of the year. Stalls would need to be cleaned, horses would get turned out, the barn would be swept. Boarders frequently visited their horse's on Christmas Day to bring them a special treat or a new halter or blanket. Kella and Danby always agreed to save the gift opening until after Corby got home from up north. She would be home on the twenty-seventh, and that would be their Christmas.

Early in the afternoon on Christmas Day, Kella was in the house alone. She was playing some Michael Buble Christmas music and feeling lonely. She sent at text to Damien.

"Merry Christmas!" she typed.

"Ho ho ho. Same to you," he replied.

"What are you doing today?" she texted.

"Doing the family thing," he replied.

"Get any good gifts?" she asked.

"Dad got me new snow tires for the truck," he replied.

"Maybe we could have lunch this week and get caught up. I'd love to see those tires," Kella messaged.

"That would be awesome," he replied.

Kella was still undecided over what she was going to do with Damien. They were probably never going to have a conventional relationship. They both knew what they wanted this to be, and for the time being, she was fine with that. She hadn't seen him in almost six weeks, partly because of how Danby felt about him and partly to punish him. She also knew that if she gave him any more slack, he would find someone else. Maybe he already had. That gave her a feeling in her stomach that she didn't like.

"Let's meet for lunch at the Dirty Duck the day after tomorrow," she texted.

"I'll be there at noon," he replied.

On the day that they were meeting for lunch, Kella did some work around the barn in the morning and rode Milly in the indoor arena. Milly had progressed to jumping two-foot jumps, and she could change leads at the canter when Kella rode her in a figure eight pattern.

She came in to the house and got showered and dressed to go meet Damien at the Dirty Duck Café. She found herself fussing more than usual over what to wear, and she put on a bit of makeup for a change. It was the coldest day so far this year, so she had to pile on layers of clothes.

Danby saw her leaving.

"Where are you heading?" he asked.

"I thought I'd pick up another gift for Corby before she gets home tonight. Everything is on sale now. I might find a bargain."

"Sounds good. I'm going to try to fix that heater on the water bowl in the run-in shed," he said. "It's not too reliable, and I don't want that water line freezing up right now or I'll never get it thawed."

Kella was glad that Danby had a project to keep him busy for the afternoon. He wouldn't be keeping track of how long she was gone, and this gave her some leeway just in case she decided to go back to Damien's for a little visit after lunch.

Kella parked out front and then entered the café and found a table where she could look out the window to watch for Damien. The little restaurant was filling up with the regular lunch crowd.

Farmers in their barn coats sat at the stools at the counter. It was a quiet time of year, and they enjoyed a chance to stay in out of the cold awhile longer and take advantage of the bottomless cups of coffee. Families with children that were tired of leftover turkey were now feasting on chicken fingers and grilled cheese sandwiches. The Dirty Duck Café had been the hub of Duckville for two generations. When a franchised Sub Shop moved in at one end of town and then a Tim Horton's Coffee shop at the other, people thought the café was a sitting duck, but business didn't change at all. People still appreciated the home-cooked meals and the comfortable surroundings. Photos of hockey teams, soccer teams, and baseball teams, all sponsored by the Dirty Duck, covered the walls. Next to the sports photos and numerous certificates of appreciation for support of every cause and charity in town was a framed photo of a local racehorse that won the Queen's Plate, Canada's oldest and richest horse race. Tacky Christmas decorations were taped to the windows, and "Rocking Around the Christmas Tree" was playing on the antiquated sound system.

"Cold enough for you?" the waitress asked as she set a mug in front of Kella and started pouring a coffee.

"Sure is," Kella said. "There will be two of us."

"Need menus?" asked the waitress.

"Yes, please," said Kella as she looked out the window for Damien's truck.

Two Ontario Provincial police officers came in and sat at the last two seats at the counter. Their walkie-talkies squawked with something indiscernible, and they quickly turned down the volume as everyone turned around to see where the noise was coming from.

Finally, Kella saw Damien's truck pull into a spot across the street. Damien hopped out with his snowmobile jacket unzipped and held it closed against the cold wind as he walked into the café.

Damien's eyes went immediately to the two uniforms sitting

at the counter. Then he spotted Kella and came over to sit down. They weren't yet comfortable with any public displays of affection, and she wasn't going to make this the first time she greeted him with a hug, even though she wanted to.

"Nice tires," she said.

"Thanks. Those are still the old ones. I'll get the new ones put on tomorrow afternoon."

The waitress came over and set down a mug and poured another coffee.

"Merry Christmas, Damien," she said.

"Hi, Vicky. This is Kella," he replied.

The women exchanged polite smiles and nods, and then Vicky left them alone.

"Friend of yours?" Kella asked.

"We were in high school together. I've seen her in here a few times," he said.

Kella looked at her menu. How many girls was he seeing? she wondered.

"What are you going to have?" he asked her.

"I'm just going to have the beef stew."

"Mac and cheese for me," Damien said.

They were about to place their orders with the waitress when Kella looked out the window and saw Danby's truck drive by.

"Oh shit," she said.

"What?"

"My dad is in town. I thought he was working on a water heater or something. If he sees my car, he will probably come in."

Moments later, Kella's father walked right past the window where she was sitting and saw her through the frosty glass.

When Danby Major entered the Dirty Duck café, he didn't notice the two police officers sitting at the counter. He knew exactly where Kella was sitting, and he was focused on her.

"I thought you were going shopping," he said, and then he noticed Damien. "What the hell is he doing here?" he asked.

"Dad, we're just having a quick lunch."

Danby squared his shoulders and spoke directly to Damien in a raised voice. "Look, young man, I'm going to tell you to stay away from my granddaughter, stay away from my daughter, and unless you've got specific business to do, stay the hell away from my farm. Do you understand me?"

Damien stood up as the café got quiet and everyone looked at them. "Sir, we are just friends having lunch right now, if you don't mind," Damien said.

"Well, I sure as hell do mind. Damien Rhodes, you've been nothing but trouble your whole life, and it doesn't look as though that's going to change anytime soon. You take my granddaughter to a hockey game and almost get her half-killed. If I ever catch you around my family again, there's gonna be trouble. You hear?"

One of the police officers stood up and took a few steps toward the commotion. When Danby noticed him, he said, "Everything's fine here. I was just leaving," and stormed out the door.

"I'm so sorry," said Kella as they watched Danby march past the window, looking straight ahead.

"You know what? This probably isn't such a good idea. I'm going to go," said Damien.

"You don't have to," Kella said, but Damien was heading for the door. Both officers took a long look at him as he left.

Vicky came back to the table with a fake smile on her face as she asked Kella, "So just the two coffees then, or will there be anything else?"

# 16

The next morning when Corby woke up at home, the first thing on her mind was getting the cast off her arm and getting back to playing hockey.

"The doctor's office is closing at three o'clock today, but they can fit you in around two thirty to get your cast off," said Kella. She had already been out to the barn and fed the horses and was now making breakfast.

"We can also go to the mall and try to exchange the sweater that Poppa got you for something you will actually wear," said Kella.

"I think I should tell him first," said Corby.

"Okay, I think you'll find him putting a new heater cable on the water pipe in the run-in shed," said Kella.

After breakfast, Corby went out to see Danby. She found him kneeling next to a pipe coming through the wall. His toolbox was laid out beside him, and Cider was guarding it. "Thanks again for the sweater, Poppa," she said.

"I'm glad you like it, darling," Danby replied.

"Mom and I were wondering if you mind if we see if there are any others in the store that I could exchange it for. I don't wear purple very much," she said.

"Of course, sweetheart. You get whatever you want."

"Poppa, if the doctor says that I can skate after I get my cast off today, do you think you can clear the snow off of the pond and make me a rink again?"

"I'm not sure if it's fully frozen yet," he said. "We've only had a few days of freezing temperatures. I'll check how thick the ice is later on and see if it's safe."

"Okay," said Corby. "Do you need any help with anything?"

"You can hand me those pliers," he said.

"Do you want me to fill up the water buckets in the barn?" she asked.

"I would, but I've got the water shut off right now while I'm working on this, so that will have to wait."

Kella and Corby left Danby with his project, and they got to the doctor's office in time to get the cast off.

"How does it feel?" Kella asked.

"It feels strange," Corby said. "It feels like my arm is floating now. My elbow hurts a bit when I straighten it out."

"The doctor said that's normal," said Kella.

"He also said that I can start skating," said Corby.

"If you're careful," said Kella. "No hockey for a couple more weeks."

Kella and Corby made their way into the mall. It was packed with shoppers looking for Boxing Day bargains. "Let's get your sweater taken care of first, and then we can look around," said Kella.

The line at the checkout had about twenty people in it. Transactions were taking longer with lots of returns and gift cards to deal with. "First, let's find you something you like," said Kella. Corby found a red hoodie with a canoe on the front and also a pair of jeans. They joined the line to exchange the gift and then decided to look around the mall for a while longer.

When they got home, Corby went straight to Danby's apartment to show him what they got. "That looks perfect for you, Corb. I probably should have just got you one of those gift certificates, but I wanted you to have something to open last night."

"Did you get a chance to check the ice?" Corby asked.

"I didn't actually. I was busy getting that water line fixed up, and then I came in to warm up and take a little nap. I'll go out and check it in a little while."

To check the ice, Danby would take an old manual ice auger that he used to use for ice fishing, drill a hole into the ice, and measure the thickness. By the time he found the auger tucked away in his workshop, it was starting to snow, and he considered waiting until the next morning, but he had already promised Corby he would check it. Tomorrow would be Saturday, and it would be the perfect day to clear the snow off and get the rink ready.

Cider followed him out to the pond. Snow was piling up on her back as she followed his footprints in the snow.

The edge of the pond was hard to distinguish from the ground around it except for a few dried-up bullrushes defining the perimeter. Danby scraped one boot against the ice surface, clearing away a layer of snow to reveal the smooth glasslike ice underneath. He bounced up and down a few times, hearing some crackling, but that was not unusual. The ice only needed to be four inches thick to walk on, and he would assure people that if it was six inches thick, it could hold a tractor.

The edge of the pond was always the first to freeze, but it was the middle that needed to be tested to be sure. Cider followed Danby out to the center, and he jabbed the pointed end of the sharp spiral auger into the ice. He placed one hand over the rounded handle on the top and leaned into the tool as he gave it a turn with his other hand. The first few turns were slow, with the friction of the ice slowing the blade, and then he leaned a bit harder into it to get the bit to drive deeper into the crust. Suddenly the auger broke through the ice unexpectedly, and Danby dropped to his knees. The ice was not nearly as thick as he had anticipated, and the weight of his body hitting the surface with such force cracked the ice in all directions around him. As he scrambled, he dropped the auger through the hole, and when he tried to make a quick grab for it, the ice broke away from under him, sending him plunging into the frigid water. Cider jumped back and barked frantically, watching Danby struggle to get back onto the surface. He had fallen completely under water, and even his head was now freezing from the wet and cold. He struggled to get a grip on the broken edges of the ice and kicked his legs under the water to propel him onto the ice surface, but the ice kept breaking away in front of him under his weight. Danby was losing strength as he felt his legs seizing up from the cold. Inch by inch, he broke through the ice, trying to make it to the edge of the pond. With a few feet to go and with Cider barking at him, he felt a stabbing pain in his chest as his arms went numb. He had no more fight left in him, and he collapsed at the water's edge with his lower legs still in the water. Cider lay beside him, licking his face as the snow blanketed both of them.

Damien Rhodes was making his way home from getting his new snow tires installed, and his route took him right past Major Meadows. As usual, he looked toward the farm as he drove by. He could see lights on in the barn and knew it was feeding time. Then he noticed Cider sitting at the edge of the pond. "That's weird," he said to himself, slowing down to take a longer look. It appeared that she was sitting next to an animal in the snow. Maybe it was a deer or something, he thought. Damien turned into the driveway to investigate. He left his truck running as he got out and walked over to Cider. The sun was almost completely set, and just the light of the snow was reflecting to create some visibility. As he approached Cider, she began wagging her tail. "Whatcha got there, girl?" he said to her, and then he stopped suddenly. "Oh shit! It's Danby!" he said. He grabbed him by the jacket and pulled him onto the shore. There was no doubt he was dead.

Damien looked around for a few moments before deciding what to do. *Kella must be in the barn*, he thought. He grabbed Cider by the collar and loaded her into the passenger seat of his truck. He left Danby where he was lying and drove quickly to the barn. Cider followed him out of the driver door and into the stable. He slammed the big barn door against the blowing snow and looked around for Kella. He could hear her singing along with Bing Crosby on the radio.

"Dad, can you throw down two more bales from the loft?" she said, and then she saw Damien. "Oh, it's you. What are you doing here?"

Damien paused and cleared his throat as he walked toward her to hug her. "Kella, something terrible has happened."

# 17

In August 1976, young Danby Major needed to raise some cash and sell a horse, so he decided to take his chances on a horse auction in Ada, Oklahoma. The Ada Horse Sale had a reputation for marketing some of the top Quarter Horses in the industry from broodmares to prospects and from show horses to world champion breeding stallions. He found out about the sale from the advertisements in the *American Quarter Horse Journal* and in *Western Horseman* magazine. Danby studied the sales results page in the journal and tracked the averages. Buyers and sellers were flocking to the sales from across the United States, Canada, and Mexico, and Danby wanted a piece of the action.

He contacted the sale company by phone in advance and was instructed to mail them a Xerox copy of his horse's registration papers as well as a full description for the catalog. He went to the library to get the copy made and sent it along with the consignment fee in the form of a bank draft check payable in US funds.

Danby was planning to sell a two-year-old gelding that he had owned for just five months. The horse had been brought to him for training the previous November, but the owners had been slow to pay their bills with him. Then two checks bounced, and then he couldn't get hold of them at all. In order to settle the bill, he was entitled to sell the horse himself by public auction under an antiquated law called the Innkeepers Act of Ontario. This allowed stable owners to sell the horses or tack of owners who were delinquent on their bill. The American Quarter Horse Association would issue new registration papers to the new owner, provided that all of the procedures were followed. The first step was to hire a licensed auctioneer to facilitate the transaction. Next he had to place a classified ad in the *Duckville Dispatch* stating the name of the owners, a description of the horse, and how much was owing as well as the time, date, and location of the proposed auction. Harlan Wilson was a local auctioneer who specialized in livestock sales, estate sales, antiques, and collectibles, and he was happy to collect a forty-dollar fee to take care of the official auction at Major Meadows. The day of the auction came without any word from the horse's owners. One local farmer showed up out of curiosity but without any intention of bidding. The amount owing on the horse was $1,300, and that would be the starting bid. At the posted time, Harlon made all of the official proclamations as if there were a sale barn filled with buyers, but only Danby and the farmer stood there as witnesses. With no bidders, it was Danby's right to claim the horse for his own without any further notification or charges to the owner. Harlon Wilson collected his fee, the farmer left, and Danby Major was the not so proud owner of a two-year-old Quarter Horse gelding that he didn't particularly like.

Just like a shoemaker's kids go barefoot, a horse trainer's horse is usually the last one to get trained. Danby, however, put in the time to make the best of the situation, and by the time he entered the horse in the sale in Oklahoma, he was starting to dream about cashing in on some big American dollars. In those days, the Canadian and American currencies were nearly at par, but Danby was going to get to present his horse to hundreds of potential buyers that he had no hope of attracting in Ontario.

He also had a second purpose for his trip to Oklahoma. He was going to try to track down Gaylon Delfer. For almost two years, Danby had waited for a check to arrive for the $3,000 that was still owing from the sale of his mare in Louisville in November 1974. Danby had tried calling the number listed in the ads for the G Bar D Ranch, until he got a message that the number was no longer in service. He wrote letters requesting payment but got no response. He considered contacting the American Quarter Horse Association for assistance, but he was embarrassed by his stupidity for letting this happen, and he assumed that AQHA would take the side of a well-known member like Gaylon Delfer if it came down to Danby's word against his.

He rehearsed in his mind how he was going to ambush Delfer at the horse sale. Hopefully he would find him standing among a group of horsemen, and Danby would confront him with the replay of their transaction and demand payment immediately.

Danby set out early in the morning in his '72 GMC pickup truck with a two-horse trailer in tow. He had his horse's blood test results and export papers prepared by his own veterinarian and had them stamped by the federal veterinarian at an office in Brampton, so he didn't anticipate any trouble getting the horse over the border.

He crossed the Blue Water Bridge at Sarnia, Ontario, into Port Huron, Michigan, by nine in the morning. The border official looked briefly at the paperwork and, unsure of what to do with a horse, told Danby to park and take the papers inside. From there, he was instructed to check in with the federal veterinarian's office about a half hour west on Highway 69 in Wadhams, Michigan. When Danby arrived there, a semitrailer filled with Angus steers was being loaded after the routine health inspection of the animals and recording of ear tags.

"I'll be with you in a minute!" shouted the vet over the noise. "Let me hose the cow shit off my boots first."

Danby checked on the gelding and opened up the escape doors to let a breeze blow through the trailer. The horse had finished a net filled with hay, so Danby refilled it from one of the bales in the back of the truck. He took a water bucket and found a tap on the side of the small brick building next to the holding pens. He offered water to his horse, but he just flapped his lips on the surface and didn't drink any. This wasn't unusual. Some horses didn't like the taste and smell of strange water. Danby hoped he would drink when he got thirsty enough.

"So, what do we have here?" the vet asked, taking the paperwork from Danby.

"I'm bringing this horse to a sale in Oklahoma, so I have permanent export papers here."

The vet poked his head in the trailer to check out the horse and make sure that he matched the description on the export papers and the blood test results. "Okay, looks good. Follow me inside, and I'll stamp these for you, and you can get on your way."

Danby planned to get as far as Rolla, Missouri, on his first night, and he had called a Quarter Horse breeder there ahead of time to arrange a stall for the night. By the time he drove into the farm, it was dark, but there was a light on in the barn, so he pulled up to the long, galvanized steel stable. As soon as he was getting out of the truck, a teenaged girl was standing there to greet him.

"Dad said you can have a broodmare stall," she said. "The mares are all outside right now, and the stalls are big, so your horse will be happy."

Danby unloaded his gelding and followed the girl down a long aisle of stalls with steel gate fronts on them. Every stall appeared to be about fifteen by twenty feet—probably the biggest horse stalls he had ever seen. The girl swung open a stall gate, and Danby put his horse in. The stall was bedded deeply with fresh straw, the water bucket was filled, and there was a pile of beautiful alfalfa hay in the corner. "This is great. I really appreciate it," said Danby. "What do I owe you for the stall for the night?" he asked.

The girl looked like she didn't understand the question, then replied, "No, Dad said you don't have to pay anything."

"Thanks," said Danby. "That really helps me out. Can you tell me where the closest motel would be around here?"

The girl gave Danby detailed directions to the Cloud Nine Motel just fifteen minutes away. He waited to watch the gelding settle for a few minutes. The horse rolled in the straw, took a few bites of hay, and then drank half of the bucket of water. "He'll be fine," said the girl. "I'll come out and check him again before I go to bed."

"Thanks again," said Danby.

Danby unhooked his horse trailer and promised he would have the horse out of the barn by seven the next morning.

The next day, Danby continued west on Highway 44 through Tulsa and then south on Route 377 to Ada, Oklahoma. It was three o'clock in the afternoon when he arrived at the sale facility. It was Thursday afternoon. The auction didn't start until the next day, but the grounds were already packed with trucks and trailers of every size. Danby noticed license plates from Texas, New Mexico, Florida, and Louisiana. A man with a binder in his hand stepped up to the truck window to greet Danby. "Buyer or consigner?" he said.

"Consigner," said Danby.

"Your name?" asked the man.

"Danby Major."

The man flipped through the binder to find Danby's name and stall assignment.

"Major. Here you are. Wow, you're a long way from home. You're in barn seven, stall 341. Just keep driving down this alley, and barn seven is on the left. After you unload, you'll need to park your trailer way at the back. Check in at the sale office as soon as you can and get your hip numbers. No horses are allowed in the warm-up pens without hip numbers. There will be two bales of straw in the stall. If you need anything else, you can go to the feed and bedding barn between barns two and three. Any purchases there will be added to your account and deducted from your payout."

"Got it. Thanks," said Danby.

The Ada Horse Sale had grown to an impressive 525-stall facility since it began fourteen years ago. Danby parked beside barn seven and grabbed a bale of hay and the water bucket out of the back of his truck before he went in to find the stall. Inside the barn, other sellers had farm signs and color-coordinated curtains on the stall fronts, and some had lawn chairs sitting in front of their stalls on green indoor/outdoor carpeting. Danby felt insignificant as he opened the stall door and found an empty concrete floor and no bedding. A Mexican man was sweeping in front of the stall across the aisle.

"Aren't we supposed to each get two bales of straw?" he asked the man. The man just shrugged his shoulders and kept sweeping. *I guess it pays to get here early,* Danby thought. Danby filled the water bucket from the hydrant at the end of the aisle and tied it inside the stall with one of the strings off of his hay bale. He tossed a few flakes of hay in the stall and headed for the feed and bedding barn. He could hear his horse pawing in the trailer outside. The sooner he could get bedding in the stall and get him unloaded, the better.

After carrying two bales of straw back from the feed and bedding barn, Danby shook them out in the stall and got his horse unloaded and settled into the stall before parking his trailer. He unhooked the hitch from the ball on the bumper on his truck and threw a grooming box and his tack into the back of the truck. He found a spot to park a bit closer to barn seven, then checked the horse once again before heading to the sale office with his original registration papers.

The line of people at the sale office extended out of the room and down the crowded hallway. Consigners were checking in with their paperwork, and buyers were providing identification and getting their buyers number cards. Ranch cowboys in Levi Strauss jeans mixed with oil tycoons in their fancy western suits. As Danby got closer to the front of the line, he could see there were two women working at the counter and a few men behind them making notes in their sale catalogs, discussing each horse. Danby recognized one of them as the legendary auctioneer Lionel Van Klink. He had seen pictures of him in magazines, advertising his own sales barn and his auctioneering services. A sign on the wall said Ada Horse Sales. The Sale Built on Fact, Not Fiction!

One of the women said, "Next," and Danby stepped up to the counter and handed over the registration papers for his horse. She had a beehive hairstyle and looked at Danby over her cat's-eye glasses that were secured with a chain around her neck. "Any reserve?" she said.

"Pardon?" said Danby.

"Do you have a reserve bid amount on your horse? We still charge the commission on the reserve if it doesn't sell, but you can take your horse home."

"No thanks, ma'am," Danby said. "I'm here to sell him no matter what."

The man behind him in line overheard and said, "You should always have a reserve, son. The market is funny this time of year."

"I'll take my chances," said Danby. The last thing he wanted to do was try to prove that he knew more about the price of horses than five hundred educated buyers in Oklahoma and haul his gelding all the way back to Ontario to try to sell him there.

"Can you tell me if Gaylon Delfer is here?" Danby asked the woman. This inquiry got the attention of the men behind the counter.

"I can tell you that he doesn't have any horses consigned in this sale," the woman said.

"Is he registered yet as a buyer?" asked Danby, hoping he would be able to corner him to get his money before he spent any on more horses.

"The buyers' list is confidential, I'm afraid," said the secretary.

"Delfer's not here," Came the loud voice from the man behind him. "Someone brought the last six head he had at the sale in March," said the man.

"It's terrible what's become of him since what happened to his son," said the woman.

"What happened to his son?" asked Danby.

The secretary looked to the left and right and then leaned forward and whispered, "He was killed in Vietnam."

"Seems ol' Gaylon pretty much has given up since then," said the man. "That son of a bitch was a bit of a snake, but nobody deserves what's happened to him. Goddamn war. No horses left at the Gee Bar Dee Ranch as far as I know. I don't think he has been sober a single day in eighteen months."

Danby's head was spinning. How could this be? The Gee Bar Dee Ranch was a flourishing breeding and training center with the respected Gaylon Delfer at the helm. This wasn't at all the reception that he was planning. Where was his mare now? he wondered.

"Say, did there happen to be a little bay mare with no white markings in that group of horses that were sold in March?" asked Danby. "Her registered name is Miss Honey Pine."

At this point, another man in a tie behind the counter stepped forward and said, "We sell a lot of horses here, young man. You don't expect us to remember every single one, do you?"

"She would be seven years old, pretty headed with tiny ears. Mr. Delfer bought a mare from me and never completely paid for her. I was hoping to track him down and get it settled."

"There was a bay mare, but she was sired by his own stud, Gee Bar Beaumont," said the man from behind. "Had his own G Bar D brand on her and everything."

"My mare doesn't have any brands," said Danby.

The man behind the counter stepped forward again. "It wasn't your horse, son. Now if you're all checked in, you should take that card there and head to barn one to get your hip number stuck on your horse. Good luck with your sale."

Now the wheels started to turn in Danby's head. This was starting to make sense. Gaylon Delfer had swapped the AQHA registration papers on Danby's horse for some other bay mare that he had in his herd, or maybe one that was already dead, and nobody would be the wiser. If she was believed to be a daughter of Gee Bar Beaumont, she would be worth five times as much at an auction sale.

Danby turned to leave, and the man behind him spoke in a low voice into his ear before he stepped up to the counter. "The brand on that bay mare looked awfully fresh, if you know what I mean. That's all I'm saying. I don't want to get involved."

"Next," called the woman behind the counter, with the other man looking over her shoulder.

On a hunch, Danby looked at his watch. It was 4:45 p.m. He looked for a pay phone and gathered all the coins in his pockets to make a call to the American Quarter Horse Association in Amarillo, Texas. He wanted to catch someone there before they closed for the day.

"American Quarter Horse. How may I direct your call?" came the sweet voice with the Texas drawl.

"Records Department please," said Danby.

After a brief pause, a woman said, "Records. How can I help you?"

"Yes, I hope you can help me. I'm trying to find out who is the current registered owner of a particular horse. Can you do that?"

"Certainly, sir. Do you have the horse's registered name?"

"Miss Honey Pine," said Danby.

"Okay, just give me a minute here, and I'll look that up for you."

Danby waited as he heard file cabinets opening and closing and a shuffling of papers.

"Well, that horse is way up in Canada, sir. It says here she is owned by a Danby Majors in Duckville, Ontario. Will there be anything else?"

"No thanks. You've been very helpful," said Danby as he hung up the phone.

# 18

Danby woke up early Friday morning with mixed emotions. He was looking forward to selling his horse and the possibility of getting a big paycheck. He was also wondering how he was going to ever connect with Gaylon Delfer and if he had any hope of collecting his money from him. From what he had heard yesterday, it sounded like things were pretty desperate at the Gee Bar Dee Ranch. Depending on how it went at the sale, he was considering driving up to the ranch in the Nebraska Sand Hills to pay him a visit him in person.

In Danby's motel room, there was a tiny kitchen counter with a hot plate and a tea kettle. He mixed a packet of instant coffee with some boiling water and drank it to help kickstart his day. He filled the kettle with more water and let it boil again. From the bathroom, he took a hand towel and gave his gray felt cowboy hat a vigorous wiping. Then he held the edges of the hat over the steam from the kettle and let it saturate the brim. He pulled the hat out of the blast of steam, and before it cooled down, he gently reshaped the edges of the brim to form a new crease. He noticed that the cowboy hats he had seen the day before were more curved from front to back. He placed his hat against his chest and bent the brim down lower in the front and again at the back to get the desired effect. As the steam cooled from the felt fibers, the hat regained its stiffness and held the new shape. He put it on his head and looked in the mirror. With a slight adjustment to raise the left side a bit to make it balanced, he stood back and admired his cowboy hat shaping ability. *Looks just like Mickey Gilley,* he thought as he gulped the last sip of bad coffee and headed out the door to his truck.

Back at the sale grounds, he could barely find a place to park. He had taken all his tack back to the motel with him, and he had a long way to carry it from his pickup truck to barn seven.

He fed and watered his horse and borrowed a pitchfork to fluff up his bedding. While the horse ate, he took a sponge and dampened it in the water bucket to wipe off the manure stains that the gelding managed to acquire overnight. Buyers were walking up and down every aisle. They carried the sale catalog with them while they peered into every stall, checking the hip number on each horse and referring to the details in the write-up.

"Is he broke?" a voice asked through the door of the stall.

"Yes, sir, I've got nearly six months in the saddle. Walks, jogs, lopes. Got a decent stop and turn on him. I'll be warming him up outside in about a half an hour if you want to see," Danby said.

The buyer studied the gelding's unremarkable pedigree. "You from Canada?" he asked.

"That's right," said Danby. "Near Toronto." The man gave no response but was already looking in the next stall. Clearly, being from Ontario was not going to increase the interest in his horse.

Danby's horse was hip number 162. It was eight o'clock in the morning, and the first day of sale was about to begin. Danby knew that the average horse auction sold twenty horses per hour, and at that pace, his horse should sell just after four o'clock that afternoon. He had plenty of time to ride him around to show him off to potential buyers and get him all cleaned up in time to go into the sale ring.

There were several areas where Danby could take the horse for a ride so people could see him. He saddled the horse and led him to one of the more popular areas where there were plenty of horses already working. The staccato chant of the auctioneer boomed through the speakers all over the grounds and added to the excitement for the young horse. As he was getting into the saddle, he realized that he probably should have picked a more private area to warm up. His horse was higher headed and more alert than he should be. The gelding started to whinny loudly, possibly having bonded with the other horses nearby in barn seven. The gelding's attitude attracted the attention of several spectators. They were all scoping out the 162 printed on the white cards glued onto each hip and then flipping pages in their catalogs to read up on the horse. Danby swung smoothly onto the saddle, and as soon as he got a foot into the stirrup on the right side, the horse started to pitch and buck across the arena. Shouts of "Let 'er buck!" and "Ride 'em, cowboy!" came from the good-natured audience who appreciated the unscheduled show. The commotion he caused attracted some dirty looks from other riders who were jogging around slowly on their dead broke show horses. Before Danby could gather up his horse under control, he nearly got clotheslined by someone lunging their horse in a corner. *Not the best way to make a first impression,* he thought as he gathered his mount into a controlled jog. After fifteen minutes of jogging, his horse was settled, and a new crop of spectators had taken positions along the rail, none of whom were aware of the antics from earlier.

The sun was getting higher in the sky, and it was going to be a scorching hot day. The gelding had a good sweat all over him quite quickly, and Danby decided to quit while he was ahead and take the horse back to the barn to cool off.

A man with a teenaged daughter followed Danby and caught up to him. "Ya think he'd make a good 4H horse?" the father asked. Finally Danby felt like he had a fish nibbling at the bait; he just needed to set the hook.

"Sir, this is the quietest horse I've ever trained. He loves people, he wants to please, and is the smoothest mover you're going to find. All he needs is someone to love him and give him the chance he deserves to be a great show horse." Danby was laying it on thick.

"Do you think you could let my daughter take him for a little ride?" the father asked.

Danby thought quickly. A test ride could go one of two ways, and both were risky. "I wish I could, but with the heat and all, I'm going to save him for the sale. He's just a two-year-old, and as quiet as he is, he doesn't need a whole lot of riding." This seemed to satisfy the pair, and the girl followed Danby into the stall and held the horse while he unsaddled him. She was petting his neck, and Danby told her that she could take off the bridle and put the halter on him if she wanted. A clear bond was forming, and Danby was pretty sure that they were going to be bidders.

Danby spent the rest of the day leading the horse around, hosing him off, grooming him, and discussing him with anyone who showed even the slightest interest.

Before sale time, Danby went back to his truck and put on a clean floral western shirt that hung behind the bench seat. He tacked up the horse for the final time and sprayed on some fly spray and some Grand Champion gloss spray to enhance the shine. When he heard hip number 155 selling, he made his way into the row of horses in front of the building that housed the sale ring. An assortment of buyers were crowded along both sides of the alleyway leading to the sale ring. Hushed conversations were going on between the horse handlers and potential buyers right to the last minute. The auctioneer's voice was keeping a steady pace, interrupted briefly by another man who was reading the pedigree and catalog description of each horse. Their excitement as each horse entered the ring was only outdone by their enthusiasm for the very next horse. Danby had heard some prices in the ten to twenty thousand range being shouted, and his hopes were high for a record sale of his own.

"What do you need for him?" a man with a horseshoe moustache asked from behind mirrored sunglasses.

"Well, I'm just going to see whatever he brings," said Danby.

"What do you want for him right now?" the man asked. Danby was puzzled. He wasn't anticipating such an inquiry. Danby wasn't familiar with the business of "pinhooking" at an auction. Buyers would make a firm deal on a horse before it ever entered the auction ring, taking a chance that the horse could sell for more than they paid and make a quick profit. It was perfectly legal, and the sale company would be notified before the horse entered the ring that it had already changed hands. Commissions would still be collected on the sale.

"I'm hoping to get about $7,500," Danby shot back with as much confidence as he could muster.

"Not gonna happen, kid. I'll give you $2,000 for him right now."

Danby was crushed. "Thanks for the offer, but I'm going to take my chances in the auction. I'm pretty sure I'll do better than that."

"If you say so," the man said before turning his attention to hip number 163 in line behind Danby.

The pedigree man was introducing Danby's horse as he rode up the dirt ramp and into the tiny sale ring. Bleachers on three sides were packed with buyers, and bright lights shone down on Danby's horse, giving him a glow like he had never seen. A yellow rope supported by white posts defined the edges of the ring, and Danby had just enough room to jog a few strides in each direction before turning sharply and returning. Danby recognized the man on the podium reading the catalog as the one who assured him that the mare sold in the March sale by Gaylon Delfer was not his horse. Next to him, the auctioneer was none other than Lionel Van Klink himself, and as soon as the first man finished his announcement, Lionel snapped his microphone to his mouth and started his melodic call. "What am I bid, can I getta five thousand?" he shouted between the stutters and clicks that formed his hypnotizing tune. "Four thousand, who's got three thousand?" he called to the quiet and educated audience. Danby spotted the man with the young girl who had displayed such a fondness for the horse just a couple hours earlier. "Two thousand, now who's got a thousand-dollar bill to start us off?" Lionel coaxed the crowd some more. Finally the father's hand went up. "Thousand bid and now fifteen, who'll give me fifteen hundred dollars now?" Danby was starting to sweat. His hopes for a big payday were fading. "Fifteen bid and now two!" Mr. Van Klink shouted as he acknowledged the man who had tried to make a deal for $2,000 earlier.

The father shouted, "Sixteen!" and Lionel pointed back at the man in the mirrored sunglasses.

"Sixteen bid and now seventeen to you, sir," and the man flicked an index finger to signal his bid. "Seventeen bid and eighteen, eighteen hundred dollars?" Lionel called out directly to the father. There was a pause. The pedigree man saw the opportunity to jump in and try to stir it up again. "Look, folks, I think we are still way off on this nice two-year-old gelding. This horse has come all the way from Canada, and it looks like this young man has done a real fine job getting him broke. Lets' see if we can send him home with a few more greenbacks."

Lionel jumped in on cue with "Eighteen anywhere?" A nod from the dad broke the tension. "Can I get nineteen now?" Lionel looked to the other man who chopped the air sideways with a flat hand in front of his chest to indicate half of a bid. "Eighteen hundred and fifty now going once." Everyone looked at the teenaged girl who was sitting on her hands, staring at the shiny young horse, rocking forward and back, hoping her dad could bid again. "Going twice. Open the gate," Lionel said, directing Danby out the other side of the ring before the hammer dropped. Danby swung around and made eye contact with the girl just before Lionel Van Klink tapped his gavel on the counter and said, "Sold for eighteen-five to the man in the sunglasses. Eighteen hundred and fifty on lot 162." The man smiled as he took a pen out of his pocket and made a note in his catalog.

"Now pay attention, everyone. Next horse is lot number 163," said the pedigree reading man whose voice was getting fainter on the echoing speakers as Danby slowly led his horse back to the stall. "Now this is the kind of horse that a lot of you have been waiting for. Who'll gimme thirty thousand?" shouted Van Klink to start the bidding.

# 19

Danby wasn't going to waste any time getting out of Ada. He put his horse back in the stall and left him with a new halter and lead rope and the water bucket that was tied inside. He abandoned the remaining bale of hay in front and said, "Adios, amigo," to the gelding as he carried his tack back to his truck.

He was angry and humiliated, and he didn't even want to add up what his income and expenses had been on that horse, but he did it anyway. He figured that including the halter and the bucket, he was down about four hundred bucks, and with gas at fifty-nine cents a gallon, this trip was costing a lot more than expected.

He was now certain that the only way to make this odyssey more profitable was to drive north to Nebraska and ambush that sneaky son of a bitch Gaylon Delfer and demand payment from him.

Once he had his empty trailer hitched to his truck, he briefly considered checking in at the sale office to see if he could get paid to trailer any horses that needed to go north or east, but he quickly talked himself out of that idea. He would get a check in the mail in a few weeks for the horse, and he had no interest in running into the man with the mirrored sunglasses and allowing him to gloat over his shrewd horse purchase. *I hope that horse kicks him right in that big, goofy moustache,* he thought as he drove through the exit gate.

Looking at the mileage legend on the map in his well-worn atlas and doing some rough measurements, he figured he had about an eleven-hour drive to get to Centennial, Nebraska, and the Gee Bar Dee Ranch. He would drive as far as he could tonight, and then he hoped he would be able to surprise Gaylon in the middle of the day tomorrow.

The sun was starting to set to his left, and he rolled down the window of his truck and rested his arm on the opening. He turned up the radio and listened to Waylon Jennings sing about a good-hearted woman. According to the map, he could get around Oklahoma City just after the Friday-night traffic, and he would try to make it as far as Salina, Kansas, before he stopped for the night. He kept replaying the day's events, and each time he questioned himself more. Maybe he should have let that girl ride the horse. No doubt he should have negotiated with the man in the sunglasses before the sale. Maybe he should have put a reserve bid on the horse, but then he would have been hauling him home right then without a penny to show for it. Danby consoled himself with the notion that if the horse business was easy, then everyone would be doing it.

At ten thirty, Danby spotted a Vacancy sign on the Wagon Wheel Motel just a few miles north of Salina, Kansas. He entered the small room with the fake wood paneling, cranked up the air conditioner in the window, and turned on the TV before he got into the shower to rinse away every speck of horse sale dirt that he'd brought with him. He set his cowboy hat upside down on the dresser rather than on the bed, honoring the cowboy superstition that it's bad luck to place your hat on a bed. He wondered how much worse his luck could get anyway.

He watched the eleven o'clock news as he lay in his underwear on top of the cool sheets. The presidential election was a hot topic, with Jimmy Carter and his vice presidential running mate, Walter Mondale, gaining ground on the incumbent Republican president, Gerald Ford, with Bob Dole. In sports, California Angels pitcher Nolan Ryan added another win to his impressive career, but the reporter forecasted that at twenty-nine years of age, his arm probably wouldn't last much longer, considering how hard he threw the ball. In other news, doctors were still searching for clues in the strange deaths of twenty-nine people at an American Legion convention in Philadelphia.

Danby flipped through the four TV channels and settled on an episode of *Charlie's Angels*. He fell asleep with the TV on and woke up at two with nothing but static on the screen, as the station had shut off for the night.

The next morning, he was on the road at seven thirty. An hour later, he stopped at a café in Concordia and got a coffee in a Styrofoam cup.

Just north of Interstate 80, Danby was looking for a spot where he could park his horse trailer and pick it up on his way back to Ontario. This would make the drive a bit easier and more fuel efficient. In York, Nebraska, he located the York County Fairgrounds and drove in to look for a place he could abandon the trailer until tonight. He noticed a man cutting grass, and he got out of his truck and approached him. "Good morning, sir. Is there any chance I could park my horse trailer here for the day? I'm coming back this way tonight, and it would be easier if I didn't have to tow it all day."

"It ain't stolen, is it?" the man replied.

"Oh no, it's mine. Ontario plates, just like my truck."

"I suppose you can leave it next to the mercantile building over there."

"Thank you, sir. I really appreciate it."

By noon, he was into the renowned Nebraska Sand Hills. This

was a region very different from the Platte River Valley of southern Nebraska. He passed herds of red Hereford cattle as well as Black Angus. Next to a lake, Danby spotted some mule deer grazing on what was known as some of the best grasses on the planet. He drove by a ranch that had an old cowboy boot nailed upside down over every fence post along the highway frontage and down the lane. This region was also known for its migratory bird population with sandhill cranes, geese, pheasants, and quail that feasted on the wild choke cherry and wild plum thickets.

Engrossed by the landscape, Danby hadn't noticed until now that his gas tank was nearly empty. The last town he drove through that was noted on his map was nothing more than a crossroads with a boarded-up general store and a few grain silos.

As he feared getting stranded without any gas in the middle of nowhere, he began looking for farms that might have fuel tanks on the property for their trucks and machinery. It wasn't long before Danby could see two galvanized steel five-hundred-gallon tanks propped up on a rusty scaffold next to some buildings by the road. He drove in and pulled up next to the tanks, then got out of the truck and started to look around to find someone to buy some gas from. The property included nothing more than a few weathered implement sheds and a feedlot containing about twenty assorted commercial beef steers hovering around a concrete water trough next to a windmill. There was a stand of overgrown trees surrounding the crumbling foundation that used to support a farmhouse. The windmill gave a screech, tick, tick sound that repeated with each revolution of the blades. The cows started bawling when he approached, but there was no sign of human life anywhere.

He decided the only thing to do was to put enough fuel in the truck to get to the next town and leave some money in the spout handle. The fuel tanks were painted in dripping red letters. One had the word *GAS*, and the other had the letters *DEISEL*. Danby tapped his knuckles on the tanks to determine if they had anything in them. He had no sooner removed the truck's gas cap and inserted the nozzle into the tank when a cloud of dust announced the arrival of a black Chevy four-by-four pickup coming down the driveway toward him. Attached behind the truck was a low trailer loaded with aluminum irrigation pipe.

The truck came to an abrupt stop just in front of Danby's truck, as if to block his escape, and the driver quickly stepped out and called to Danby, "What the hell is going on here?"

The thickly built man looked to be about twenty-four years old. He was wearing a dirty Nebraska Cornhuskers cap and a plaid western shirt with the sleeves cut off. Danby couldn't help noticing the fact that he was missing half of his left arm just below the elbow.

"I was hoping I could buy enough gas to get to the next town. Seems I didn't plan too well," said Danby, smiling and trying his best to deflect the tension of the situation.

From the passenger side of the truck, a boy about thirteen years old got out. He was shirtless and dirty and looked like he had spent his summer doing a man's work. He walked up to Danby, stood with his hands on his hips, and looked him up and down.

The man relaxed his stance and said, "No problem at all. We can fix you up." Then he spoke to the boy. "Bo, put some gas in the man's truck."

"Just five dollars' worth would be great," said Danby. " I don't want to trouble you."

There was no gauge on the tank and no way to know exactly how much fuel was being dispensed.

"You're a long way from home," the man said, looking at the license plate on Danby's truck.

"Is Ontario a state?" the boy said.

"It's not a state, you idiot. It's a providence. It's up north in Canada," said the one-armed man.

"Actually, I live straight east from here," said Danby to blank stares.

"Are you really from Canada? Do you live in an igloo? Do you play ice hockey? Do you drink maple syrup?" the boy asked in rapid succession.

"Shut up and just pump the gas, will ya," the man scolded.

"What brings you round here?" he asked.

"I'm going up to visit someone in Centennial," Danby said.

"Centennial!" the man said, laughing with disbelief. "There's nothing in Centennial. Who the hell are you gonna find up there?"

"I'm looking for a man named Gaylon Delfer actually. Ever heard of him?"

"Sure I've heard of him. I played high school football with his son, Jimmy. Helluva ball player. We were even in Nam together. I got off lucky, I guess." The man looked down at his stump of an arm. "Poor bastard," he said quietly as he looked off across the horizon. The three stood in silence for a moment.

"That should be enough," Danby said to the boy, handing a five-dollar bill to the man. "Thanks again. You saved me from getting stranded."

Danby turned the key in his truck and watched the red needle on the fuel gauge go all the way up to the F as he drove out the laneway.

For the next twenty minutes, he passed only one other vehicle. There was a pickup truck heading south, pulling a stock trailer with no roof over it. In the trailer were two horses with saddles on them.

The next town he came to was Redman, Nebraska, which consisted of four corners and a stop sign. There was a gas station with a mechanic's garage on the side, and the Crazy Crane café, which was a welcome sight. He parked in front of the café and went inside.

Inside the door was a bulletin board with announcements and posters and handwritten advertisements of all kinds. A farm and livestock auction, a county fair and rodeo, hay for sale, ranch help wanted, Australian shepherd puppies available.

The place was empty other than a waitress wiping off the long counter in front of a row of red swivel stools with chrome bases.

Her name tag said Myrna, and she was quietly humming along to Olivia Newton John singing "Have You Ever Been Mellow."

There was a framed photo of President Gerald Ford on the wall, an autographed picture of Miss Rodeo Nebraska '75, and even an eight-by-ten photo of the stallion Dee Bar Beaumont himself.

"Coffee, honey?" said Myrna as Danby took a seat at the counter.

"Yes, please, and a menu. Not exactly a full house for lunch on a Saturday, eh?"

"Hoose? Did you say hoose? Where y'all from, darlin'?"

"I live just about an hour out of Toronto, Ontario," said Danby.

"Well I could tell from that accent that you ain't from 'round here. What on earth brings you to Redman, handsome?"

Myrna looked to be in her early sixties. She was wearing blue eyeshadow and deep red lipstick. Her sizeable bosom was packed into a red gingham blouse, and she was wearing tight white jeans tucked into red cowboy boots.

"I'm out here to visit someone. Gaylon Delfer. Have you heard of him?"

"Heard of him?" said Myrna. "I've known him all my life." Then she called to the cook, who was scraping the grill at the other end of the open kitchen.

"Earl, this fella's from Canada, and he's come to see Gaylon."

"Gaylon Delfer?" said Earl without looking up.

"No. Gaylon Eisenhower. Who the hell do you think? Meathead!"

Earl came over and stood in front of Danby. He lowered his chin to his chest and stared seriously at Danby with his eyes up under his bushy eyebrows.

"What sort of business do you have with Gaylon Delfer?" he said in a deep voice.

"Actually, we've done some horse trading in the past, and I just needed to settle a few things with him," said Danby.

"Well, there ain't much left of him to settle," said Earl.

Myra stepped in and broke the tension with "Anything on the menu that suits your fancy?"

"Can I still get breakfast even though it's afternoon?" he asked.

"Just a sec, sugar. Let me check. Earl, are you still serving breakfast?" she shouted to Earl, who had gone back to the stove.

They both chuckled as she said, "Of course, baby doll. You're the only one here. You can have whatever you like."

"Okay, I'm pretty hungry. What are teddy bear pancakes?" he asked, pointing at the menu.

"Oh, those are something Earl does for the little kids. He makes a teddy bear face out of the batter and uses chocolate chips to make the eyes and nose," said Myrna, smiling.

"Okay, I'll just have two regular pancakes, three eggs over medium, and sausages please."

"Comin' right up," she said as she topped up Danby's coffee, spoiling the ratio of cream and sugar to coffee.

Danby spun around in his stool to take a look around the Crazy Crane. He wondered if there was ever a time when all the tables and chairs were filled. There was a jukebox against one wall and an assortment of taxidermy mounts hung above—a whitetail buck with impressive antlers, a largemouth bass, and a comical jacka-lope, which was a taxidermist's classic prank to create a mythical cross between a jackrabbit and an antelope with horns mounted on a rabbit's head.

In the parking area, a brown Dodge Monaco with *SHERIFF* painted on the side in yellow letters pulled up and parked next to Danby's truck.

Danby watched the driver door open, and the sheriff stepped out as he put on a crisp straw cowboy hat. He took a long look at Danby's license plate before he came into the café.

"What took you so long, Cordell?" Myrna said as she set a tall glass on the counter and poured some brewed iced tea from the side of the pitcher, letting a few ice cubes splash into the glass.

Cordell Wyman didn't miss much in this region. When he saw a strange vehicle with out-of-state plates at the café, he made it his business to check it out. Sheriff Wyman looked as though retirement couldn't be too far off. His potbelly spilled over his belt that carried a holstered pistol and a walkie-talkie.

"You're a ways from home," he said to Danby as he sat next to him and took a sip of tea.

"He's here to see Gaylon," said Myrna before Danby could answer.

"Delfer?" said the sheriff.

"Seriously?" said Myrna. "Are there other Gaylons around here that I don't know about?"

"I don't know if you're aware, son," said Cordell, "Gaylon Delfer hasn't been doing too good since his boy Jimmy passed."

"Fucking war," said Earl without looking up from the stove. "Boy coulda been playing pro football by now instead of getting shot in the jungle by some Chinamen."

"Simmer down, Earl," said Myrna.

"I guess the Gee Bar Dee is in jeopardy," Earl said in a singsong voice that he had used for that line before.

The sheriff turned to Danby.

"Truthfully, there ain't much left of Gaylon Delfer. I don't know what you're gonna find when you get up there. Last time I saw him was about six weeks ago when I had to go out with the utilities rep to shut of his electricity. I'd been out there months ago when they unplugged his phone lines. When we saw him, I convinced the electrician to leave him alone. I doubt he will need it too long. Seems he's planning to drink himself to death."

Myrna leaned over the counter between the men and set down Danby's meal. Three eggs and sausages with white toast on one plate, and next to that, a plate with two teddy bear pancakes with chocolate chip smiles looking up at Danby.

The sheriff stared at the plate and then raised an eyebrow to Danby. Earl was watching the reaction from behind the counter, and they all had a good laugh at the Canadian's expense.

Danby attacked the meal, while Cordell sipped his tea, and Myrna and Earl busied themselves behind the counter. As he was finishing, Earl came over with a paper bag and set it in front of Danby.

"That's for Gaylon," he said.

"A club house sandwich. It's his favorite. That's what he always orders when he comes in," said Myrna. "He'll be back. He's just got a touch of melancholy; that's all. Everyone grieves in their own way. I know Gaylon. He's gonna be fine."

Earl and the sheriff looked at each other and rolled their eyes with the unanimous belief that the next time Gaylon Delfer left his house, it would be in a pine box.

"What do I owe you for the breakfast?" asked Danby.

"That's on the house, good lookin'," Myrna said.

"You deliver that sandwich and check in on Gaylon, and we'll be all square."

Cordell Wyman followed Danby out the door and to his truck.

He reached into his police cruiser and got a fresh pack of Marlboro cigarettes from the glove box. He tossed them to Danby. "Give these to Gaylon, will ya? Tell him Cordell sent them. And another thing." The officer paused and squinted his eyes as he looked far off across the hills. "Like I said, I don't know what you're going to find up there, but if there is anything we need to know about, then you check back in and let us know, okay?"

"Yes, sir, I sure will," said Danby as he closed his door and started the truck.

# 20

Danby left the Crazy Crane with some apprehension. He didn't want to kick a man when he was down, but he'd come this far, and he wasn't going home empty-handed.

He drove another twenty minutes toward Centennial, and then before coming to any sort of town, he saw a weathered sign with G BAR D and an arrow pointing down a narrow gravel road. A wall of dust kicked up behind the truck as he left the blacktop and headed down the final leg of his journey. Up ahead, a collection of farm buildings came into focus on the horizon. Rusted steel pipe fencing surrounded knee-high grasses in each pasture and corral. At the farm entrance, Danby drove over a cattle guard gate filled with weeds. This consisted of a ditch across the entrance between the fences that had a steel pipe grid overtop that allowed vehicles to pass through but would stop livestock from escaping.

A rusting metal sign hung from a post at the road: Gee Bar Dee Ranch. Home of Gee Bar Beaumont.

As Danby slowly approached the farmstead, he saw what was left of a once-renowned Quarter Horse breeding and training operation. The main stable had a large sliding door at the end that had fallen off its tracks and lay cockeyed against the barn. An open-ended hay barn had a few faded and molding round bales that were now just a home for snakes and mice. A two-horse inline trailer that had once been painted proudly in the brown and tan farm colors had grass growing on the running boards, and the back door was missing. A gold 1972 Cadillac Eldorado was parked next to the house but slumped to one side with a flat tire.

Danby stepped out of his truck and took the sandwich bag and Marlboro pack with him as he went to inspect the barn first. He called, "Hello? Anyone here?" Every stall door was open. Old, dry manure was piled up in the corner of each enclosure. Danby walked down the aisle with just the sunlight filtering through the cobweb-covered windows. He heard some scratching and scuffling. "Hello?" he called again as a chicken came scrambling out of a stall half-running and half-flying, nearly running right into his legs. In the next stall, a half dozen more hens were clucking and cooing and stepping around their randomly laid eggs on piles of hay.

The largest stall at the end of the aisle had an engraved brass plaque on the door: Gee Bar Beaumont. This was the stall of a once famous stallion, but where was he now? Traded? Castrated and sold as a pet? Dead and buried on the ranch somewhere?

Danby retraced his steps out of the abandoned stable and approached the farmhouse.

In the trees around the house, the chirping sound of male cicadas created an almost deafening drone. Danby expected to encounter a barking dog, but none appeared as he stepped up onto the front porch. The front door was swung wide open, but an aluminum screen door with a torn screen covered the opening. Danby tapped on the frame of the door. "Hello?" he called.

"Jimmy?" called a crusty man's voice from inside. "Jimmy, is that you?"

Danby took the opportunity to let himself in and explain that he was not Jimmy.

"No, sir, I'm Danby Majors. From Canada. Do you remember

we met in Louisville at the AQHA World Championships a couple years ago? You bought a bay mare from me?"

Danby hadn't actually seen Gaylon yet as he made his introductory announcement and closed the screen door behind him. To the right was a kitchen with a counter covered in dirty dishes, empty soup cans, and raw eggs. To the left was a small, dark room that appeared to be the ranch office. Piles of unopened mail covered the desk.

Danby explored further and found Gaylon Delfer lying on a brown leather sofa in the living room next to the kitchen. He was dressed in a sleeveless undershirt and blue jeans with no belt. Dirty white socks covered his feet, which were propped up on the arm of the sofa. He looked like he had lost fifty pounds since the last time Danby saw him. On the coffee table beside him were some empty beer cans, an overflowing ashtray, and a half-empty bottle of Jack Daniel's Whiskey.

"Who the hell did you say you are?" said Gaylon as he swung around to a seated position, elbows on his knees and rubbing his mop of uncombed gray hair. He was growing an uncharacteristic beard and smelled of body odor, whiskey, and cigarettes.

"Do you remember buying a mare from me at the show in Louisville two years ago?" asked Danby.

"Sure, I remember that mare. Pretty as hell. Coulda swore she was a Beaumont," he said, slurring his words.

"You were supposed to send me the other $3,000. But you never did."

"I don't remember anything about that, son. I'm sure I paid you in full for her."

"No, sir, just a deposit. I gave you the papers and the signed transfer report, and you promised to send me the balance."

Gaylon paused and gave Danby a menacing stare. "That's your word against mine, boy. What are you going to do about it?"

"If you don't pay me, I'm going to report you to the AQHA," said Danby.

Gaylon reached for his pack of cigarettes, but it was empty.

"Here," said Danby, handing him the unopened pack of Marlboros. "Sargent Wyman told me to give you these."

Gaylon maintained eye contact with Danby as his hands frantically and methodically opened the package, tapped out a cigarette, stuck it in his mouth, then struck a match and lit it in a long-rehearsed and choreographed routine.

"To be honest, I don't give a shit if you report me to the AQHA, the CIA, and the FBI. What's in the bag?" he asked.

Danby handed over the sandwich bag. "This is from the cook at the Crazy Crane Café down in Redman."

Gaylon opened the bag and pulled out the sandwich with the cigarette dangling from his lips.

"Earl made this for me?" he asked.

"They said it was your favorite."

"Well, ol' Earl probably woulda wiped his ass with the bread if he knew how many times I've fucked his wife, Myrna," said Gaylon as he laughed at his own coarse brand of humor with a cackle that turned into a smoky cough.

"I don't have anything for you," said Gaylon, devouring the sandwich between drags on the cigarette.

When he was finished, he butted out the cigarette and took a long swallow from the whiskey bottle to wash it down. Then he lay back down on the sofa and closed his eyes.

Danby stood there staring at him. He didn't know what to do next. Arguing was going to be pointless. He walked back through the kitchen and poked his head into the little office room. Behind the desk on the wall was an original oil painting of Dee Bar Beaumont signed by the artist Orren Mixer. The shelves were covered in trophies and ribbons, and there was an engraved trophy saddle on a stand that had never been on a horse. NQHA High Point Horse was stamped into the fenders of the saddle.

On a side wall was a collection of football trophies. There was a small photo cutout of a high school football player mounted on a stand. On the wall was a framed military photograph of a young marine in dress uniform. His eyes stared straight ahead, his neck as wide as his square jaw. Below the portrait, sitting on a shelf, was an American flag folded into a triangle, and on top of the flag were several medals.

Danby took a moment to think about James Delfer. He was just a few years younger than Danby himself. *What a waste of a fine man,* he thought. *More than one Delfer was killed that fateful day in Vietnam.* "Thank you for your service," Danby whispered as he felt a lump forming in his throat and his eyes welling up.

He walked out of the room and returned to check on Gaylon. He was passed out and snoring.

Danby steeled himself for what he was about to do. He was angry and tired of being taken advantage of. One way or another, Danby Major was going to get paid for that mare.

He returned to the office. Rummaging around the edge of the room, he saw a few paintings leaning against the wall.

Danby also noticed a beautiful headstall with silver accents and an elaborate spade bit with rawhide braided romal reins attached on silver chains. He wanted to grab the bridle, but he figured its absence would be too noticeable. Going back to the stash of paintings with dust on the tops of the frames, Danby found one framed painting with two cowboys riding with some cattle in a snowstorm. Since it was tucked between a couple others, he figured that nobody would even notice it missing. He was not an art connoisseur of any sort, but he knew what he liked, and this was the kind of thing that he would never find in Ontario.

Danby checked again to make sure that Gaylon was sound

asleep. Then he plucked the painting from it' position and quietly slipped out the screen door with it under his arm. He took long, smooth steps straight to his truck and tucked the painting safely behind the bench seat.

Danby never looked back as he drove over the cattle guard and left the Gee Bar Dee Ranch in his dust as he headed for the main road.

Half an hour later, Danby was cruising through Redman again and passed Sheriff Cordell Wyman parked next to the road in the café parking lot. Danby never even turned his head as he drove by.

Within seconds, the sheriff wheeled out of the parking lot and onto the road behind Danby.

Danby felt a chill through his body as he looked at the cruiser getting closer in his rearview mirror.

He reached over the back of the seat, instinctively feeling for the painting and confirming its hiding spot.

Checking behind him again, he saw the blue and red lights on the roof of the police car come on and start their flashing rotation. A "whoop, whoop" from the siren confirmed their intent.

Danby smoothly pulled his truck over and rolled down his window. He watched as the sheriff paused to speak into his car radio for a moment and then step out of the car.

Could he know already that the painting was stolen? Did Gaylon already report the robbery? Was his only phone really disconnected?

The officer strolled up and stood at Danby's window with one arm resting on the roof of the truck.

"Well? Do you mind telling me what's going on?" said Wyman.

Danby had collected his Ontario driver's license out of his wallet before the sheriff approached his truck. He fumbled for a response to the officer's question and stalled for time by repeating the inquiry. "What's going on?" said Danby.

"You were going to let us know what's going on with Gaylon, remember?" said Wyman.

"Oh right. Well, he's okay. I guess, I mean, he's alive anyway," said Danby.

"Did you give him the smokes and the sandwich?" asked the sheriff.

"Yes, sir. He was very appreciative. I really need to get down the road though. Say goodbye to Myrna and Earl for me and tell them I said thanks for the meal. I hope their friend gets better."

"All righty then, drive safely. Remember, fifty-five saves lives," said the sheriff as he began walking back to his car.

Danby eased the pickup back onto the road and again reached his right hand behind the bench seat to touch the frame of the painting. Safe and sound, he exhaled and set his eyes on the southern horizon. Next stop, York County Fairgrounds.

It was nine at night when Danby pulled up to the mercantile building at the fairgrounds to hook up his horse trailer. At the same time, a 4H Club meeting was just getting out, and people of all ages were swarming the foreign trailer to help guide Danby as he backed his truck bumper under the trailer hitch.

"Buying or selling?" asked a man as Danby cranked the handle to lower the trailer onto the ball.

"I was selling a horse down in Ada. Heading home now," replied Danby.

"Are you interested in buying anything?" the man asked. " I've got a half a dozen yearlings at my place about ten minutes from here. They're out at pasture, but we could take a look at them with the headlights from my truck if you're interested. There's a couple Zippos, a few Beaumonts, two Thoroughbred cross fillies if you like some size and speed."

"Thanks anyway, but I'm not in a buying mood on this trip," said Danby as he hustled back behind the wheel in his truck and drove toward the highway.

Danby now headed east on Interstate 80. Across the heartland of America, he drove through Lincoln and around Omaha, then crossed the state line into Iowa, which gave him some sense of relief since he was technically carrying stolen goods.

By midnight, he pulled off the highway to find a room for the night in West Des Moines, Iowa.

Not far from the interstate was a strip of motels and bars, and the promise of air-conditioning and color TV lured Danby toward the ironically named Tropics Motel. He found a larger parking area at the back at the motel to park his truck and trailer, and he checked into room number six. Next door, he noticed a nondescript square brick building with several motorcycles parked in front. A doorway with a sign stating No Shirt, No Service welcomed patrons to the Hammer Down Bar & Grill.

Danby unloaded his gear into his motel room, stowed the painting behind the dresser, and took a quick shower. Getting dressed again in his cleanest dirty clothes, he decided that, considering the events of the past couple days, he deserved a drink or two. As he entered the Hammer Down, he took in the typical Saturday-night crowd in a Midwestern biker bar. Women appeared to be in short supply in this town. A smoky haze filled the dark space, and six or seven men sat around the bar. One couple was shuffling in each other's arms on the small dance floor to Tammy Wynette singing "Till I Can Make It on My Own."

Danby found a stool at the end of the bar away from the regulars. Behind the bar was a pretty woman, a bit younger than Danby. "Welcome to the Hammer," she said. "Whatcha drinking?"

"I'll have a scotch and soda," he said. "Is the kitchen still serving food?"

The waitress checked her watch. "I think I can get you a plate of fries, but that's about it," she said, sliding him a half-empty bowl of peanuts.

"Fries would be great," said Danby.

The waitress set his drink in front of him and then walked back to the kitchen. Danby's eyes followed her as he sipped his drink.

Danby Major was a handsome young man with a lean build and a boyish charm that was a magnet for women. Something stirred inside him as he admired the waitress. She returned a moment later with a large plate of french fries and set them on the bar with a knife and fork wrapped in a paper napkin. She then slid the salt and pepper shakers to him and a red squeeze bottle of ketchup. "Do you have any vinegar?" he asked.

"Vinegar? What do you need vinegar for?"

"For the fries," he said.

"You put vinegar on french fries?" she said.

"Didn't know that was strange," he said.

"Who the hell puts vinegar on a french fry?"

"Everyone."

"Not around here. Where are you from?"

"I live near Toronto, Ontario."

"You're from Canada? Right on! I've never met anyone from Canada before."

"I'll be fine with just salt and ketchup tonight, but you really should try them with vinegar," he said.

The waitress laughed. "I'm Rose," she said, reaching to shake Danby's hand.

"I'm Danby," he said. "Nice to meet you."

The other patrons were thinning out of the place as the waitress continued wiping tables and rinsing glasses in the sink.

"What are you doing so far from home?" she asked, trying to keep up a conversation as she worked.

"Just passing through," he said. "I sold a horse in Oklahoma, then I had some business in Nebraska, and now I'm heading home."

"Where does a Canadian cowboy stay when he's passing through West Des Moines?" she asked.

"I'm next door at the Tropics."

Rose leaned forward and lowered her voice. "I get off at one thirty if you'd like a little company tonight."

Danby was somewhat surprised by the proposal, but given the fact that they were in a seedy little bar after midnight, he could hardly be too shocked.

"I'm in room number six," Danby said as he pulled the plastic, diamond-shaped key tag out of his pocket and checked it to make sure.

"Another scotch?" said Rose.

"Make it a double," said Danby.

"This one's on me," she said as she set the glass in his hand.

Danby finished the fries and his drink and left a twenty-dollar bill on the bar as he left. Rose was settling the bill with another patron, and she gave Danby a wink as he went out the door.

Back in his motel room, Danby made preparations for a visitor.

He tidied up the bathroom, tucked all his dirty clothes back into his duffel bag, and turned on the TV. On television was an episode of *Wild Kingdom,* and Marlin Perkins was narrating a scene with large snakes laying eggs. Danby decided that might be inappropriate background ambiance, so he turned off the TV set.

He lay on the bed staring at the ceiling and waiting for a knock on the door, with just the light from the bathroom on. At 1:35, there was a gentle tap on the door. "Danny, are you in there?" said Rose in a loud whisper.

Danby opened the door. "It's Danby, with a *b,*" he said as he let her in and slid the deadbolt to lock the door behind her.

"Mind if I use your bathroom to freshen up?" she said.

"It's all yours."

Rose went into the bathroom with her purse. Danby lay back on the bed listening to water running, the toilet flushing, and more water running. He adjusted himself on the bed in an attempt to look sexy and not awkward.

After what seemed like an eternity, Rose came out of the bathroom wearing just her bra and panties. She turned off the bathroom light and then turned on the bedside lamp with a matter of factness that gave Danby the slightly uneasy feeling that this was pretty much a regular routine for her.

She pulled back the sheets on the bed and said, "Okay, partner, get those jeans off for me."

Danby complied. Rose was already taking off her bra and panties and said, "You got any quarters? This thing only takes quarters." She pointed to the coin box and start button for the vibrating bed.

"I'm not sure. Let me check my pockets," he said.

"Just hand me my purse," she said.

Rose fired three quarters into the slot and turned the dial.

"That will give us fifteen minutes." Then she climbed onto Danby like she was getting on a bicycle.

The bed shook like a jackhammer under them, adding to the raw excitement.

They dispensed with the preliminary foreplay and got right down to business as quickly as possible. Danby considered the fact that he didn't have any protection with him. He should have checked for a condom vending machine in the Hammer Down men's room, but he hadn't thought that far ahead.

"Is this, you know, safe?" he asked Rose as she was riding him like a bucking bronco.

"Sure it's safe, baby. I'm on the pill. I just started a brand-new prescription today. You can give me all you got, cowboy."

As he expected, Danby finished before the bed stopped vibrating, and they lay there silently on the shaking bed, waiting for it to finish. When it did, Rose reached up to turn off the bedside lamp, and they held each other and drifted off to sleep.

Danby was exhausted mentally and physically, and to be cuddled up next to a pretty woman's soft body was just what he needed.

After some deep sleep, he was awoken by the sound of Rose stirring and then the sliver of light under the bathroom door. He looked at the bedside clock. It was quarter after five in the morning. He turned over and pretended to be asleep as Rose came out of the bathroom and made her way out of the motel room door, closing it quietly behind her.

Danby lay in the darkness, replaying the wild, vibrating sex that he had just enjoyed with a stranger. He sat up and turned on the bedside lamp. Before going to the bathroom, he checked again to make sure the painting was still behind the dresser. Of course, it was. He entered the bathroom and turned on the light, squinting as he looked at the mirror. Between him and his reflection was a red maple leaf and a heart drawn in lipstick.

# 22

It had been nearly a month since Danby's death, and Kella was getting used to her new normal barn routines. Fortunately, in late January, the workload was lighter than in the summer, and she was managing both the barn and the household chores for now.

Corby had a rare Friday off of school while the local school board provided its teachers with a day of professional activity without the students. She had her friend Angel stay overnight, and Kella knew they would be hungry for breakfast when she came in after feeding the horses.

They were in their pajamas, playing her NHL video game, with Cider lying between them when Kella interrupted.

"Who's ready for breakfast?" she called to them as she put away the dishes from the night before.

"We are!" they shouted in unison without looking away from the screen.

"What do you feel like? Cereal, porridge, eggs?" she asked.

"Mom, can you make us teddy bear pancakes like Poppa always made?" said Corby.

"I guess I can try. As long as I have some chocolate chips."

Kella had never actually taken on the duty of making the famous teddy bear pancakes, although she had eaten them all her life. Her dad always told the story of how he was tricked into eating them in a restaurant on one of his many trips out west. The story was always made funnier when a big, tough sheriff sat down beside him before they arrived.

Kella assembled the ingredients while the girls played.

She mixed the batter and heated up the skillet, then poured one big circle for the face and two smaller portions at the top to form the ears. She poured some chocolate chips into her hand from the bag and carefully arranged two small groups to form the eyes and then a couple in the middle to make a little nose. She made a curved row at the bottom with more chips to make a smile on the bear face. Kella stared at the bear smiling back at her and thought of her father. She thought about all of the joy he had brought her over the years, all the sacrifices he had made. He was a selfless man who would do anything to provide a comfortable life for her and Corby. Tears welled up in her eyes, and she wiped them away with a dish towel as she flipped the pancake. Content with her first attempt, she made several more before calling the girls to the table.

"What do you girls have planned today?" she asked. "You're not going to be sitting inside playing video games all day; that's for sure."

"Can we skate on the pond?" Corby asked. "Angel brought her figure skates."

Kella hadn't thought about the pond since Danby's death at the end of December. She knew that by now the pond would be frozen solid. Several other outdoor pond rinks in the area had been in use for weeks. She knew that she was eventually going to move past the tragedy and let Corby enjoy the pond ice like her dad would have wanted.

"As long as you two are ready to help shovel it," she said. "I've got a meeting with Poppa's lawyer later this afternoon, but you can skate before I go. I don't want anyone on the ice when I'm not here."

After breakfast was finished, the three of them bundled up and collected an assortment of shovels to take to the pond. They put the shovels, two old hockey sticks, a few pucks, their skates, and a hay bale in the back of the truck and drove down the lane to the pond. They dragged the hay bale through the snow to the edge of the pond so that they could use it as a bench to put on their skates.

"How did Poppa do this?" Kella asked Corby as she surveyed the vast ice surface covered in four inches of snow.

"He always pushed it out from the middle," said Corby. "We will put our skates on first. It makes it easier to push."

The girls sat down on the bale and took off their boots, then carefully slid their feet into their skates without touching down in the wet snow. Kella took a shovel out to the middle of the pond. She was wearing sunglasses and had a scarf around her neck, which she pulled up over her mouth and nose as she set the shovel into the fresh snow and pushed the first path toward the shoreline. Tears and weeping turned to sobs, and she felt her wet cheeks freezing while she struggled against the snow in her boots, slipping on the ice surface as the load increased. She didn't want Corby to see her crying, so she took a deep breath and assigned them their zones to clear away from hers.

The three of them worked for half an hour to push the snow to the edges and create a beautiful, smooth skating surface for the girls to play on. All the while, Cider was trotting back and forth around the edge of the ice, looking agitated.

Corby skated up to Kella with a hockey stick in her hands. "It's my fault that Poppa died, isn't it," she said.

"Oh, honey, of course not. It was just an accident. Poppa was doing what he loved to do. He wouldn't have it any other way."

She hugged Corby, while Angel awkwardly stickhandled a puck around them.

"I'm going to warm up in the truck while you two play for a while. Try not to lose any pucks in the snowbanks."

Later after lunch, Kella got ready to go to a meeting with Danby's lawyer. At his request, she had dropped off as many "important papers" as she could assemble from his office. The purpose of this meeting was to assess his financial position and the disposition of his assets, insurance policies, and so on.

"Will you two be okay to just stay in while I'm gone for a couple hours?" she asked Corby.

"Of course, Mom," said Corby, rolling her eyes, embarrassed to be treated as though she was any younger than she was.

Kella arrived at Gibson & Crawford, Barristers and Solicitors in the town of Bonne River, twenty minutes north of Duckville. The offices were located in a converted Victorian house on a beautiful tree-lined avenue, one block away from the main street. She entered and was met by the legal secretary/receptionist, who offered her a cup of coffee while she waited for the lawyer Glenn Gibson. "Mr. Gibson will be with you in a few minutes," said the secretary. Kella checked out the magazine selection in the tiny waiting area—*Ontario Out of Doors, Ski Canada, Canadian House and Home.* She picked up the home-decorating magazine and started to flip the pages as Glenn Gibson stepped out of his office to greet her. Gibson was in his late sixties and was about as dull a man as Kella knew. He had as much personality as the legal journals that lined his office walls and had spent the past forty odd years going through the motions of small-town legal work with as little effort and passion as possible. Wills and estates, real estate closings, divorces and custody were his areas of practice. His partner, Duncan Crawford, had retired several years ago, and Gibson planned to do the same very soon.

"First of all, let me say how sorry I am for your loss," he said as if reading from a script. "Your father was a fine man and a pillar of the agricultural community. I understand that you found his body yourself. That must have been terrible."

"Yes, that's correct," said Kella, ready to tell a made-up story that she had recited many times of how she discovered her father dead at the edge of the pond, leaving Damien's name out of it.

"Thank you for dropping off the paperwork. We will be acting as the solicitor for your father's estate, as you know, and you alone have been named as the executor. We have been in touch with the bank and insurance company as well as the mortgage company, and I think we have a pretty good snapshot of your father's financial position. I want to help you through this process as smoothly as possible, so I'm going to need to ask you a few personal questions if you don't mind."

"Of course," said Kella.

"Your father has left the farm property to you, as you know. Can you give me a ballpark figure of your current financial status? Your personal net worth? Do you have your own savings, investments, stocks, or bonds of any kind?"

Kella was unprepared for this line of questioning and tried to do some quick addition in her head. She had a checking account with less than ten thousand dollars in it. She had a vague idea of a life insurance policy that she had started to pay into after she got divorced. Kella had inherited her father's lackadaisical approach to money management.

"I've got about ten grand in the bank right now, I think. I get $500 a month child support from my ex-husband. I don't think there is anything else that's actually mine. Dad took care of all that, I guess."

"I wish I could tell you otherwise, Kella, but your father has left you in a very precarious financial position. He took on a large first mortgage when he and your mother divorced and then added a second mortgage when he paid off Rita."

Kella bristled at the mention of Rita. She had been Danby's live-in girlfriend for a few years. He could barely keep up with her spending habits, and when she found out the gravy train was going to have to pull into the station, she hit the road and slapped him with a lawsuit claiming her rights to a portion of his assets. Under the law, their common-law relationship had lasted over three years, and she was entitled to her greedy claim. Danby rolled over and paid up without a fight, putting him further in debt.

"Your father was currently in what we call a reverse mortgage situation, Kella. His equity in the property had been decreasing for several years, although he did make occasional payments. Were you planning to stay on the farm property?"

*Stay on the farm property?* she thought. Was there any other option? She never considered living anywhere else. Ever. She wanted to continue to run her little horse business and raise her daughter there. Maybe she could hire an assistant who could move into Danby's apartment. She could advertise to find a few more boarders to make ends meet.

"Well, yes, I want to stay on the farm. Why? Is that going to be difficult?" she asked.

"I'm going to meet with the mortgage holders and establish their position for you, but typically in these cases they will want the current mortgage dispersed. If you are to be named as the owner on title of the farm, you could take on a new mortgage, but first you would need to go through the proper channels. There would be a credit check, and they would need your financials as well as your income and expense statements for the past five years and your tax returns. Just to make sure that you could carry the payments on your own of course."

"What kind of payments are we talking about here?" asked Kella.

"With a fresh start at current rates, I think the first and second could be combined. I don't think you will qualify for prime rates from a bank, so you may be paying a slightly higher interest rate from a private lender." Mr. Gibson did some tapping on a calculator on his desk and made some notes on a legal pad.

"I'm not in the mortgage business, Kella, and I am not in a position to act as your financial advisor in any way, but I'm going to estimate that you would be looking at monthly payments of about $4,000 in order to carry the farm property on your own. Alternatively, if you sold the farm at current market value, you would probably walk away with less than $100,000 in your pocket after commissions and disbursements.

Kella felt a ringing in her ears and a tightness in her chest. *Is this really happening?* she thought. Kella thought she was going to walk out of the lawyer's office with a nice check in her hand that would ease the pain of her father's death and keep her and her daughter comfortable as she continued to operate her business. Four thousand dollars per month was going to be impossible. Most months, she barely brought that in as a gross amount. There was no way she could pay all of the farm expenses plus the mortgage.

"How much time do I have?" she asked.

"Like I said, I'm going to meet with the mortgage holders to establish their position, but it appears that they already had a prickly relationship with your father, and they will likely want a resolution to this sooner rather than later. I'll be able to stall for a while, but before too long, they will either want to see regular payments in good faith, or they will put the mortgage in a default position and issue a foreclosure on the property. In either case, this isn't something that's going to go away. I wish I had better news for you, Kella, but it is what it is."

In January 1977, Danby Major was leafing through the December 1976 issue of the *American Quarter Horse Journal*. He scanned the "Empty Saddles" obituary page, and one name jumped out at him immediately.

> Delfer, Gaylon Frederic. Passed away on or about August 30, 1976. Centennial, Nebraska. In his sixty-eighth year. Predeceased by his parents, Rueben and Elizabeth (nee Beeswater). Also predeceased by his son, James Wendell Delfer USMC (Vietnam 1974). Gaylon Delfer was a breeder and exhibitor of Quarter Horses and a life member of the AQHA. Gaylon was the proud owner of the stallion Gee Bar Beaumont. He was a generous supporter of high school sports programs and the Knapple County 4H Club. At his request, there was no funeral service. Donations in his memory may be made to the Aksarben Little Britches Rodeo and the Nebraska Quarter Horse Association Youth Scholarship Foundation.

Danby read the notice several times, checking the dates. It looked like Gaylon Delfer had died less than two weeks after he visited him. He thought again about the photo of his son, James, the barren mess that had been left of a once-proud ranch, and the pathetic man that lay on the sofa. The war in Vietnam had been over for almost two years, he thought, but there were still victims.

## 24

Kella spent the next two months in deep denial. She kept waiting for word from the lawyer that things had been settled, another bank account or some investments were discovered, there had been a mistake, or there was a life insurance policy that would save the day. No such word came.

Instead, she was rapidly depleting her meager savings trying to keep the farm afloat. She cut back on expensive supplements for her horses, put a bit less bedding in the stalls, and skimped wherever she could. Her own horses went barefoot for now, and she skipped some vaccinations and deworming.

After Danby's death, when she could have turned to Damien for comfort, she did the opposite. She kept him at arm's length. It was back to business only. While she was grieving the loss of her father, she had no affection for anyone.

Meanwhile, she tried to keep things as normal as possible for Corby. There were more and more weekends where she asked Corby's father if he could take her. She knew at least Corby would be getting spoiled by someone. She would get good meals and maybe even some new clothes if her grandmother was around.

Kella spent her alone time with her head under the covers as much as possible. Maybe it was the time of year—the cold, dark days of winter that seemed to never end. She felt no motivation for anything anymore, but like Glenn Gibson said, this wasn't going to go away.

On this particular morning, she planned to go to Watson's Feed & Farm Supply to pick up some bags of oats for the remaining horses at the farm. The Watson clan were an agricultural dynasty in the region. Several brothers had several sons, and the operations expanded from the original century-old farmstead to multiple properties and rented land. They had a large dairy cow business as well as commercial beef cattle on another property. Acres and acres of corn and soybeans and a start-up chicken farm were underway. On one property, they severed a few acres of frontage and created their own feed and farm supply store in a renovated barn, with additional metal storage buildings added on. This had become a regular hangout for local farmers, especially in the winter when there was less to do on the land. The coffee pot was always on, and the gossip filled the air on any given morning.

Kella backed the pickup truck up to the loading dock and went inside to place her order and get the paper invoice to show the man in the feed shed.

She approached the counter to place her order, and Josh Watson, the owner's son, spoke to her before she could begin to give him the list. "Kella, my dad said that if I see you, I should send you in to his office to talk to him about something."

"Okay," said Kella. "Is he in there now?"

"Yes," said Josh. "Just give me a second, and I'll tell him you're here."

Kella waited while Josh went down the narrow hallway to his dad's office. There were others behind her now in line, and they were looking impatient with the delay.

Josh came back and said, "Go on in," to Kella.

Kella pushed the door into the office of Neil Watson. Neil was a sixty-something farmer turned businessman. He was tall and fit looking for his age and had a full head of white hair. He stood up from his desk as Kella entered and extended his big baseball-glove-size hand that would be more at home on the steering wheel of a tractor than typing on a keyboard. "Hello, Kella," he said. "Thanks for coming in. I was so sorry to hear about your father. Such a loss. How are you and your daughter doing? Corrie is it?"

"It's Corby. Thank you, we're fine," said Kella, suspecting there was another agenda to this conversation.

"So, Kella, I've been noticing that you are getting further and further behind on your account here since your father passed, and we were hoping to get that straightened out as soon as we can."

"I understand, Mr. Watson," said Kella. "I just need a bit more time to get some of my father's things in order, and then I'll be able to keep current on the payments I'm sure."

"That would be great, Kella. I hate to have to ask, but did you happen to bring a check with you today?"

"Actually, I won't be able to make a payment today, but I'm only looking for ten bags of oats and five salt blocks, if that's okay. Can you just add it to my bill for now?"

Neil Watson rocked back in his office chair and set both hands flat on the desk.

"If it was just me, I could probably carry you for a bit longer since I knew your dad and so on. I don't know if you are aware, but as of January 1, we were taken over by Agrequine Industries based in Calgary, and everything needs to be done by the book in order to satisfy the corporate bookkeepers. My hands are tied, Kella."

"All right then, I do have a bit of cash on me, so I'll just pay cash for a couple bags for now," said Kella.

"Well, I'd be happy to take your cash, Kella, but I'll need to apply it to your outstanding bill. Are you completely out of oats?" said Neil.

"I've just got enough in the barn for tonight's feeding."

"Just a minute. Let me see what I can do." Neil stepped out of his office and called to Josh. There were now four or five new customers in the feed store.

"Josh, do we have any ripped bags of oats set aside right now?" he shouted.

During the loading and unloading process of feed bags, some got ripped and spilled, and instead of selling them, they patched the bags with duct tape and counted them as losses on the invoice from the manufacturer.

"I think there are two bags out there!" shouted Josh, while processing the order for his current customer.

"Can you call out to Bryan and tell him to set them aside for Kella Major?" Neil shouted down the hall. The mention of her name caused a couple of customers to turn their heads.

"Thank you," said Kella. "I hope to get this all straightened out as soon as I can."

"I hope so too," said Neil as he watched her leave.

Kella walked past the others in the feed store and straight out to her truck. Bryan was loading the two half-filled oat bags into the back of the pickup. She thanked him and drove away.

Kella felt embarrassed by the encounter with Neil Watson. No doubt her father had become an expert at stickhandling these situations, but it was new territory for her, and she hated it.

She had enough cash in her purse to buy three bags of oats, but she would need to drive to the TSC Farm Supply store in Beaverwood to get them. Hardly worth the gas to do it, but she wasn't thinking clearly anymore. At the store in Beaverwood, nobody would know her. She didn't have an account there, and she would be welcome to pay cash for any purchase. *I can't keep doing this forever,* she thought. *I'm going to need to come up with a better plan.*

In the TSC was a bulletin board with assorted flyers and

handwritten notices. A help wanted ad caught her attention. "Horse farm in need of experienced help. Feeding, mucking, and turn out. Must be available to work weekends." Kella considered the irony of getting a job on someone else's horse farm. She knew she was overqualified, but it would be less stressful to at least get a regular paycheck somewhere else rather than struggle to keep her business going herself. At the desk in the store, she placed her small order, paid for the bags, and then went out to her truck to drive it to the loading area. She didn't want to explain the two ripped bags from Watson's in the truck, so she dragged them to the passenger seat before she moved it. The boy checked her paperwork and then loaded three bags on a dolly and wheeled them to the back of the truck. As each bag landed with a thud on the truck bed, the pickup squatted a tiny bit lower. Kella looked at her cargo and realized how much more precious each bag had become than it had been just a few months earlier.

On her drive home, she looked at the two torn bags next to her. One had a hole in the lower corner where a mouse had made an entrance, and oats were now spilling onto the floormat like water out of a hose. She watched the flow of the oats and thought about how it represented her life right now. Things were slipping away, and she was losing control. She was in no way prepared to take on this much responsibility. She had managed to put off adulthood as long as possible, but with the death of her father, she had no choice. It was time for her to make some tough decisions. She wiped her tears and runny nose on the sleeve of her coat and hoped that there was not a mouse inside that bag.

Kella collected the mail from the mailbox at the end of her driveway when she arrived home. Bills for her cell phone and a bill for the oil in her furnace, a bill from Watson's Feeds, and a letter addressed to Danby from the mortgage company. She couldn't open it but would save it for her next meeting in Bonne River with Glenn Gibson.

Also in the stack of mail was the monthly local real estate publication with all the listings of homes and farms for sale in the area. She leafed through the pages and wondered if selling her farm was going to be the next step. How many of these sellers were in the same position? How many other people's dreams were over? What was the reason most people sold property? Death. Divorce. The end of an era of some description. She realized that she probably wasn't alone in her desperation.

Among the listings was a page displaying the offerings of a high school friend who was now a Realtor named Tina Giragardi. Tina's photo in the corner of her page showed her holding onto a horse. Kella knew that Tina had never owned a horse in her life and that the equine companion in the portrait was just a prop to connect her with the lucrative horse industry and position herself as their agent of choice. "Let's make the ride decisions together!" was her clever slogan.

Kella stared at Tina's phone numbers and email address for a while before reaching for her phone.

She decided to send her a simple text to get the ball rolling: "Hi Tina. This is Kella Major. I'm thinking of selling our farm. I'd like to meet with you to discuss it. Contact me at this number when you can."

Kella felt exposed and vulnerable. She felt as though an incision had been made in her torso, and she had been opened up and laid out on display—all of her flaws and imperfections, her failures and missed opportunities revealed for the judgment of others. All of these strangers snooping through her house, and while she knew that their presence was the point of the exercise, what bothered her the most was that none of them, not one, had gone out to the barn. Nobody had appreciated all the work she had done all morning. Nobody caught a whiff of the stable. Nobody poked their head into the workshop. Nobody would know about the trout or the raspberries.

Mercifully, the time frame for the event had expired, and the only car remaining next to the house was that of Kella's agent. She had greeted each arrival and proudly gloated over her latest listing. She was carrying a half a case of water back out to her car when she spotted Kella and waved her over. Kella pulled up to the nearest fence and pulled the toggle to shut off the tractor, and the knocking and wheezing of the diesel engine fell silent.

Tina Giragardi came over to the fence nearest to where Kella was sitting on the tractor. "How did it go?" asked Kella.

"Well, I've had lots of positive feedback and a few things that we can do to be better positioned for the market moving forward."

"Does anyone have any buyers in mind?" asked Kella.

"Like I explained before the open house, these things take time. Each agent will take a look at their client list and see if there is a match for anyone. In the meantime, we have some more work to do."

"What sort of work?" asked Kella.

"One of the comments that I heard over and over was regarding the staging of the home. Buyers these days are pretty savvy with all of the renovation and decorating shows on television, and most are looking for that fresh, move-in-ready feel when they step through the door. Have you thought of doing some purging or editing? Maybe have a garage sale or rent a storage unit for a while? You know, it would be really great if the bedrooms and bathrooms could get a fresh coat of paint."

Kella knew exactly what Tina was getting at. This house had been the Major home for a long, long time, and there hadn't been a whole lot of emphasis on updating the decor over the years.

"You want me to paint the bathrooms?" Kella asked. "Is that what you think buyers are looking for?"

"Its' not just the bathrooms per se, but it's just the overall feeling, the first impression. We just want to make sure we are putting our best foot forward. I know it's really hard, but maybe you could clear out some of your father's things. His apartment and the little office could really use a freshen up."

Kella had been reluctant to touch any of Danby's things since he died. She had hung up the coat that he died in right back in the mudroom where it always was. His boots still stood at the doorway as if he was going to reappear and need them again. In his apartment, she had cleaned out his fridge but not much else. It was still too painful. She needed help. Maybe professional help, but she was still having trouble finding the motivation. She just wanted to go back to the way things used to be. Back when she and her dad had their routines. Life was easy. She never realized how good she had it. There was so much that her father had done to protect her from any trouble, but now it had all landed on her lap.

"I'll see what I can do," she said to Tina.

"That's awesome," said Tina with feigned enthusiasm. "Keep me posted on the progress. The listing is online now, and you can expect to have showings at any time. I've put in the notes that you need two hours' notice, but sometimes you need to be flexible when out-of-town buyers are inspecting multiple properties. To be on the safe side, try to keep bedrooms, bathrooms, and the kitchen as tidy as possible at all times."

"What about the barn, arena, and workshop?" asked Kella.

"Sure, those too. People might want to take a look around."

Tina's cell phone beeped, and she was responding to a text while she spoke to Kella. "I've gotta dash," said Tina. "I'll let you know if I hear anything. Otherwise, remember what I said and see what you can do."

Kella watched Tina get into her car and drive out the lane. She looked toward the house and thought about all that was inside and how overwhelming it was going to be to deal with it all.

*People might want to take a look around? Really?* It made Kella furious to think that buyers would be more interested in the colors in the bathroom rather than the great sandy footing in the outdoor arena, the ventilation fans they had installed in the stable, the wheels they put on the bottom of all the gates in the paddocks to make them easier to open. Nobody was ever going to appreciate this farm the way that Kella did, and it was heartbreaking. Soon the Major Meadows sign at the end of the lane would be taken down, and someone would give the place a new name—all of its history forgotten, all of her father's hard work with nothing left to show for it.

It was so unfair to put Corby through this due to no fault of her own. First she lost her grandfather, and now she was going to lose the only home she had ever really known. The future looked like a dark gray fog for both of them.

Kella stepped on the clutch, pushed in the kill switch, and turned the key to start up the tractor. She would spend another half an hour making the final rounds around the pasture with the harrows before putting away the machinery and bringing the horses into the freshly cleaned barn. Tomorrow, the For Sale sign was going up at the end of the driveway, and life would never be the same.

# 26

Within a few weeks of the open house, Kella faced a serious dilemma. She needed to make some cash, build her business, and find new customers to teach, more horses to train, and more boarders to fill the stalls, but the real estate sign at the end of the driveway had taken all of the energy out of Major Meadows.

Like rats leaving a sinking ship, she was living in fear each day that one by one her existing clients would find somewhere else to keep their horses.

Her fears were realized when Megan Riley's mother said that she needed to have a talk with Kella before tonight's riding lesson.

Mrs. Riley left Megan to groom Boo a bit longer, and she and Kella stepped outside of the barn.

"Megan's father and I have been talking, and we think it's time for us to make a change," she said. "I know you've got a lot on your plate right now, Kella, and we think it would be in everyone's best interest if we moved Boo to a barn where Megan could have a more consistent program for the summer show season. It's nothing against you, Kella. You've been amazing."

Kella felt a lump in her throat and was frustrated that she had to fight back tears.

"I'd really appreciate it if you could stick it out with me for a while," she said. "The farm is probably not going to sell right away.

There's always a possibility that I'll be able to stay on and keep doing my business here with the new owners, or I'll try to find somewhere else to work out of. I really don't want to lose Megan and Boo. They are doing so well."

"I understand, Kella. This is really hard for us too. We've already made arrangements at Diamond Ride Equestrian Centre. Megan took a lesson there on the weekend with Stephanie Barker, and they really hit it off."

Diamond Ride Equestrian Centre was the most posh facility in the region. Stephanie Barker was the resident trainer and was highly respected as a coach and competitor. She was short-listed to compete with the Canadian Equestrian Team. Kella and Major Meadows were seriously outranked. The mention of Diamond Ride was like a punch in the stomach to Kella.

"So you'll be leaving at the end of the month?" she asked.

"Actually, Stephanie is sending a trailer to pick up Boo tomorrow morning. We will take his tack and grooming box with us tonight and leave his shipping wraps. My husband wanted me to ask if you can figure out the refund on our board for the remaining three weeks we paid for and send us a check for the balance."

Kella was scrambling to think of an excuse not to issue a refund. She would need to read the standard contract that she had the Rileys sign when Boo arrived two years ago. Her dad handled all of those details. Worse still, that money had been spent as soon as it was in Kella's bank account.

"I'll see what I can do about that," said Kella.

The conversation ended abruptly when Megan interrupted.

"Can we go now?" she asked while looking at her phone and without making eye contact with Kella.

She watched Mrs. Riley and Megan load the tack and grooming box into the back of her Cadillac Escalade while she made herself busy sweeping the barn. They drove out without a word.

Kella sat down on a hay bale and pulled out her phone. She checked Megan's Instagram account. The last three posts were of her riding another horse under Stephanie's guidance: #diamondride #diamondridegirls.

Kella read Megan's cryptic comments:

"Making a flying change."

"Diamonds are a girl's best friend."

Kella felt crushed. Cider came and sat beside her, and she scratched the back of her head while she panted, her tongue hanging out with saliva dripping from her mouth.

"What are we going to do, girl?" she asked the dog.

# 27

Corby had finished grade eight and was looking forward to her summer vacation. Traditionally, the month of July was spent at the McLaren family cottage at Sugar Maple Bay.

Kella needed the break, and it couldn't come at a better time. She knew that she was not in a mood to provide any entertainment for Corby this summer. With her away, it would give Kella a chance to clean up some things around the house and keep it presentable for showings. So far, Tina Giragardi had sent only two potential buyers. The first was a group of men from an Asian religious sect who wanted to transform the property into a spiritual retreat. Further investigation at the Duckville Town Hall told them that the current zoning prohibited such use, and they were discouraged by the red tape that they would need to cut through to change it.

The second prospect was a family with a horse-crazy teenaged daughter. They were considering a move to the country but were really looking for more of a hobby farm and not a full-time business operation. Like Tina said, this was going to take time. Perhaps more time than Kella had. She was still fielding weekly calls from the lawyer with updates on the mortgage situation. He was acting as the intermediary, but words like "foreclosure" and "default" were coming up more frequently, and Kella was terrified. If she dropped the price much lower, she would have no equity to take with her after the sale, and she needed some kind of nest egg to get a fresh start.

Kella left Corby in charge of packing her own clothes for the cottage, then went over a list of some essentials with her. Neither were too worried, as there was no doubt that Corby's grandmother would take her shopping if she needed anything else.

Reese showed up on time to take Corby up north but uncharacteristically sought out Kella in the barn for a little chat.

"Any bites on the property?" he asked.

"Unfortunately no," said Kella.

"Do you know what you want to do once it sells? Where you want to live? Where you're going to work?" he asked.

"You know what, Reese, I'm just trying to keep my head above water here," she said as she pushed a wheelbarrow out to the manure pile. "Maybe I haven't thought that far ahead just yet. Anything could happen, I guess. I'm keeping my options open."

"Okay, just keep me in the loop, will you? If you need me to take Corby more often or whatever, just let me know."

Their conversation ended when Corby and Cider came bounding into the barn. "I'm ready to go," she said.

Kella kissed her goodbye and watched the two of them drive out the lane. She stood and wondered how different life would have been if she and Reese had stayed together. They would probably have another child or two by now. Kella would be spending summers at the lake and weekends at the country club. She would have a responsible financial plan in place and a supportive husband. But that was not the life she had chosen. She was better suited to the unpredictability of the horse business, and she wouldn't trade the past ten years that she spent working side by side with her father for anything.

Corby and Reese settled into their regular driving routine. They would join the cottage-bound traffic on Hwy 400 and head north to the Muskoka region that was the jewel of Ontario. As they joined the bumper-to-bumper traffic with all the Toronto area city dwellers escaping for the lakes, rocks, trees, and fresh air, Reese decided to make some new rules. Corby had her earbuds plugged into an iPad and was completely unaware of her surroundings.

Reese tapped her on the shoulder. "How about we put away the iPad for this trip and take a look at the countryside for a change?"

"What's to see?" Corby asked. "Looks like cars and more cars."

"Take a look past the cars," her dad said. "This area is called the Holland Marsh. Look how black the soil looks. This was once just a marshy wetland, and then it was drained to create farmland. Some of the best vegetables in the country are grown right here. When they used to use horses to harvest the crops, they actually attached boards to the horse's feet to keep them from sinking into the ground."

"Dad?"

"Yes, Corby?"

"You know school ended last week, right?"

"Yes."

"Well, my brain doesn't want to learn anything new right now."

"Okay, let's just listen to some music then. I get to choose."

Reese tuned the radio to a classic rock station and began singing along to AC/DC. Corby rolled her eyes and stared out the window. She saw the selection of boats, trailers, and motorhomes for sale at all of the roadside dealers as the marketplace became more and more recreational. Campgrounds and small motels, dock builders, water toys, antique stores, and a go-cart track welcomed the weary commuters into cottage country.

After almost an hour of stop-and-go traffic, they were north of Barrie and onto Highway 11, driving through the walls of granite where the highway was carved into the exposed layer of the Canadian Shield. "See these rocks on the side of the road?" Reese said. "When I was a kid, people would get out of their cars and paint their names and all sorts of graffiti on them. Sometimes we would pass the same names or initials for years."

"Why doesn't anyone do that anymore?" Corby asked.

"I guess the Ministry of Transportation sent their crews out to paint over all of it with gray paint to match the rocks. Eventually, it just wasn't a cool thing to do."

"Did you ever paint on the rocks, Dad?"

"I didn't, but your aunt Melinda did. She was about twelve, and she wanted to paint a peace sign on a rock, so my dad stopped the car and let her out with a small can of white paint and a paintbrush. The rest of us waited in the car until she was done. She was slightly panicked and was rushing so that she wouldn't be noticed by the passing cars. I told her that if the OPP saw her, she would be arrested and go to jail.

"The next week when we were driving up to the cottage, my dad slowed the car at the exact spot where she did her paint job, but instead of painting a complete peace symbol, she left out the bottom part of it and created a perfect Mercedes Benz logo. I teased her for days at how her protest of the Gulf War became an ad for a German luxury car." Reese laughed hysterically at his story, but Corby wasn't laughing.

"Painting on rocks and ruining the environment. Not cool, Dad," Corby said. "Can we get burgers?"

There was a certain charbroiled burger place along the highway that had been a stopping point for generations. It was so popular that they had to build their own pedestrian overpass on the divided highway to accommodate southbound patrons.

"We will see what kind of wait they have. I don't want to be standing in line forever," said Reese.

He slowed down as they approached, and just like any other summer evening, the parking lot was packed, and there was a long line of people ready to order from the limited menu. "Let's wait and see what Grandma has for us when we get there," he said as a waft of grilled beef aroma blew through the car.

Later, they drove off of the main highway and onto a bumpy little road pointed to Sugar Maple Bay. The pavement turned to a gravel road at a spot where two tall pine trees and a telephone pole supported a menagerie of handmade signs pointing cottage visitors to their destinations. The McLaren sign had been painted by Reese's mother onto the blade end of a broken paddle. Other families put their own personal spin on the little signs, some with letters made of twigs, others professionally painted in an Old English font. This collection of haphazard markers always felt to Corby like a familiar beacon of her arrival in a safe and welcoming community of summer fun.

"Don't let any mosquitos in!" called Reese's mother when she heard the spring on the wooden screen door stretch open.

The four-bedroom cottage was built sometime in the late 1930s and had been passed down through the McLaren clan for generations. Outside of the main cottage was a garage/work-shop that McLaren men had been tinkering in on weekends for decades. Cans of dried-up paint, an old boat motor in need of parts that were no longer available, a stack of shutters that used to seal the windows for the winter. On a set of sawhorses was the rib cage of a cedar strip canoe that Reese and his father had been building for more than three years. A project with no deadline and no purpose other than some quality father and son time together and the dream of creating an object of beauty and function to be enjoyed by descendants to come. Wooden steps from the back door led over the smooth granite rocks to the weathered dock, and to the left was the flat-roofed boathouse that had room for a motor boat and a Jet Ski and a flat roof for sunbathers above. Flowerboxes filled with red geraniums adorned the structure, and a Canadian flag flew from a pole jutting from the front of the rooftop. Inside the cottage, a pine harvest table with long benches down each side showed the patina from years of holidays and milestones celebrated with family meals. A cork board in the kitchen held snapshots of summer fun through the ages, including photos of both Reese and his father, Corwin, both at age six, grinning toothlessly while standing on the exact same rock with the cottage in the background. Also on the wall in the living room were two small oil paintings of local landscapes painted by famed Group of Seven artist A.Y. Jackson. They were always included in the tour of the cottage for any adult visitor who would appreciate their significance as family heirlooms.

Delilah McLaren put down her knitting and greeted the pair at the door with a hug. Corby absorbed the refreshing and familiar fragrance of the family cottage. The hints of pine and cedar, the faint smell of lake water, and the musky scent of ashes in the stone fireplace. She carried her bag down the hall to her room. There was a set of bunk beds against one wall for her cousins and one single bed for her. In the room, there were ribbons on the wall that she had won in summers past in the Sugar Bay Regatta for swimming races and the father/daughter canoe race. There was a cozy quilt on the bed that had been a favorite of Reese's when he was a child, and there was a treasured but outgrown wooden rocking horse that had been hand-made by her grandfather.

Corby set her bag on top of the old trunk against the wall, lay on the bed, and pulled out her phone to text her mom that she had arrived.

Kella was enjoying the last glass of wine from a bottle that her friend Jessica had brought over. Cider perked up her ears when she heard the phone beep.

"We made it," texted Corby.

"Great. Thanks for checking in. Good night," replied Kella.

Corby joined her father and grandmother in the kitchen. "Have you two eaten?" asked Delilah.

"We almost stopped for burgers, but the line was insane as usual," answered Reese.

"I've got some leftovers in the fridge that I can warm up for you. I thought your dad was going to be here tonight, but he was golfing in some charity tournament at the club today, so he is driving up in the morning," said Delilah.

After eating, Corby curled up on the sofa with her iPad, while the adults cleaned up the dishes. After a few minutes, Reese looked in on her, and she was sound asleep.

Delilah spoke to him in a whisper. "I'm worried about Corby starting high school this fall with so much uncertainty at home. Does Kella even know where they are going to be living after she sells the farm?"

"To be honest, Mom, I'm not sure that Kella knows what she's doing from one day to the next right now. I saw her this afternoon, and she looks like the walking dead."

"Is there any interest in the farm? I can't imagine her spending any time or money to get the house presentable. She's not exactly Martha Stewart, is she," said Delilah.

"I want Corby to have the best chance for success in grade nine, but I'm concerned that whenever they finally move, it's going to be a big distraction, and she might even have to change high schools once she gets started," said Reese.

"Your father and I have been talking about that, and we would like to offer a solution. That is, if you and Kella are both agreeable to it."

"What sort of solution?" asked Reese.

"We thought that this would be the perfect time to get her

enrolled in a private boarding school. Your dad and I would be happy to pay for it of course."

"I don't know about that, Mom," said Reese. "That's a big move and a big change for Corby."

"She's going to be facing some big changes either way, Reese. Why not at least get her settled somewhere that we can be sure will be a stable environment for the next four years of high school?"

Reese paused and thought it over. "Where did you have in mind?" he asked.

"I've actually taken the liberty of speaking with the headmaster at Deercrest Academy. Your dad and I have met him a few times at some social functions around the lake. He has a cottage just across the bay."

"Deercrest Academy? Way up here?" Reese asked. "I was thinking something closer to the city."

"She would love it up here. You know what a tomboy she is. Deercrest has a huge emphasis on sports, they have an excellent reputation of attracting international students, they even have a girls hockey team, and she is certainly going to meet a much better caliber of peers than she's hanging out with in Duckville," said Delilah.

Reese knew that his mother had the best intentions, even if she was a bit of a snob.

"I think I'll need to run it past Kella before we pursue this any further, Mom."

"Well, it just so happens that tomorrow they are having an open doors event at the academy. I was thinking I could take Corby over there and see what she thinks. I won't let on that we are seriously thinking of enrolling her. I just want to see how she reacts to the place. What harm can it do? It's only thirty-five minutes from here."

"Okay, Mom. Do your thing. It can't hurt to expose her to something new," Reese said. "And I appreciate it, I really do. I just hope Kella feels the same."

"Great, it's all set then. I'll tell Corby in the morning."

# 28

Saturday morning, Kella had the barn chores done. With Corby away, it was the perfect time to do some cleaning out of Danby's apartment and office. She wondered if it would be possible to leave the emotions out of it and just go through the actions of moving objects like a robot. Her goal was to stay as detached and neutral as possible. "It's just stuff," she told herself over and over. "It's not him."

She considered calling Damien to help, but she knew that Danby would be turning over in his grave if he knew Damien was touching his things. Connie and Jessica offered several times to help, but Kella was either too proud or just not ready yet. She also knew that they would bring a couple of bottles of wine, and the work would never get done.

Instead she brought two large garbage pails to the front porch from the barn and lined each one with a new garbage bag. One bag would be for clothes that she could donate to a charity drop-off bin, and the other would be for garbage. She decided to tackle the office first. Moving his clothes was going to be harder.

Danby's office was an eclectic collection of souvenirs of his life and times. His travels and adventures, his accomplishments and failures all came down to a random assortment of objects and papers. First she tackled the piles of old issues of magazines. Stacks of

*American Quarter Horse Journals, Western Horseman* magazine, and other equine-related periodicals. He always insisted that you never know when you'll need to look something up, but that was before Google. The magazines were interesting but not worth the space it took to store them. Kella resisted the urge to crack open any magazine that made it' way to the top of a pile. Many articles from old issues caught her attention, like "The New Natural Horsemanship, Western Pleasure—How Slow Is Too Slow," "Will Shipped Semen Hurt the Backyard Breeder?" and "AQHA Incentive Fund—Show for Fun AND Profit." All publications went straight to the recycle pile, no exceptions.

Next she looked at his trophy shelves. She thought about how hard he had worked to earn Provincial and Regional High Point Awards, Grand Champion trophies and ribbons. Most of these were earned before Kella was even born. Kella witnessed the industry pass Danby by when she was a child, but old-timers would still pull her aside to tell her that her father used to be "one helluva horseman in his day."

Kella had already purged his desk of anything business and financial related for the lawyer, so all that was left was his personal letters, his cowboy poetry, scraps of papers and notes and notices, old receipts, and forms that had never been filed properly and were now of no consequence.

She bundled it up in her hands and stuffed it all into a blue recycling bag and then set it out on the porch with the piles of magazines.

Next she found some old photo albums. The oldest ones were filled with black-and-white pictures. Some had handwritten captions with names of places, dates, horses names, and long-lost relatives. A color photo of Danby in front of a pickup truck was dated August 1976, with the caption "All loaded and ready to go."

*Go where?* she wondered. These old albums she would have

to save for Corby. Maybe some night later in the summer, they could sit down together and go through them. Then she found a small album of wedding photos of Danby and her mother, Donna. Smiling for the cameras full of hopes and dreams. They drove a horse and buggy from the church to the community hall where their reception was held. Kella's mother complained that it was the most humiliating twenty minutes of the whole day but the only part that she gave Danby free rein to plan in his own way.

A more recent album had a picture of Danby holding a microphone in his hand with his reading glasses perched on his nose. He was reading some of his beloved cowboy poetry at a regional awards banquet.

Was cowboy poetry even a thing? Kella decided to look it up. A quick Google search proved that it was not only a legitimate form of literature, but it was a growing genre with gatherings of poets and musicians meeting annually, numerous online videos and recordings, and also plenty of downloads and publications available. Kella thought that maybe Danby had missed his calling. He could have been making some money with his corny poems instead of struggling with horses all these years.

Kella paused and thought about the pile of poems that she just threw out. Maybe she could find a way to publish them and start collecting royalties.

She opened her phone again and searched self-published poetry. There was good news and bad news. The good news was that it was totally possible to publish Danby's poetry in a paperback collection that would be available for purchase online. The bad news was that it would require an up-front investment of cash that she couldn't afford, and poetry was the least profitable genre of literature, with the average self-published poet never recouping their investment. Still, she was desperate and hopeful.

Kella opened the plastic bag and retrieved the stack of

handwritten poems and notes. She laid them on the desk and flattened out the wrinkles with her hand, giving the precious manuscripts a newfound respect. She picked up the first one and read it.

# Loose Horses
# by Danby Major

When you grow up on a farm, you get used to certain sounds,
  Like the squeak of an old windmill as the blades keep going 'round.
  There's a far-off moo and bellow of a baby calf and mom,
  A rusty hinge on that old door that Dad should oil some.

Still, not many wake me up before the rooster starts to crow,
  But there's one sound cuts right through my sleep that all the ranchers know.
  It's a sound unlike all others; it's not loud, just out of place,
  And it makes you bolt from bed as if a pistol starts a race.

I know you're thinking fire, and oh sure, that's trouble too,
  But if you've ever seen loose horses, then you know what they can do.
  It was their hoof beats on the laneway that first lured me from my sleep,
  And I could hear my family stirring, but nobody made a peep.

A couple snorts and blows confirmed it, and then Dad let out the call.
  I heard "loose horses," and in seconds, I was running down the hall.
  My mom and dad already were a pullin' on their coats.
  My sister went for halters. I said that I'd go get some oats.

Our strategy was sketchy in the early-morning fog.
  We had this Border collie, and he was a herding dog,
  But he was old, and even sheep would cause him some fatigue,
  We knew that twenty frisky horses would be way out of his league.

The horses were enjoying the free run all 'round the place.
   They circled through Mom's garden without slowing down their pace.
   They trotted past machinery, over mowers, wire, and harrows,
   Tipping over buckets, bales, tools, birdfeeders, and wheelbarrows.

They weren't too organized until Mom's gelding took the lead,
   And then before you knew it, they assembled a stampede.
   The open road was in their sights, but sis was just in luck.
   She could almost reach the pedals, and the keys were in Dad's truck.

I guess the kid's been watching him when he puts it in gear,
   Cuz when she passed me on the lawn, she had a grin from ear to ear.
   She seemed to know that if she beat them to the end of our long lane,
   She could stop the charge and save us all a lot of pain.

She had shifted into third, her head barely above the wheel.
   Then she ducked down, stomped the clutch, and we could hear the
   tranny squeal.
   In fourth gear, she was neck and neck with leaders of the pack.
   We stood and watched as she found fifth, and smoke blew from the stack.

She was on a mission all alone, not much that we could do except
   To wait and watch and hope and pray that they would not get through,
   'Cause if they hit the open road, well then, all bets were off,
   And we'd need to get some neighbors' help and maybe call the cops.

Sure enough, with cowgirl nerves of steel, she beat them to the gate.
   It was a tricky bit of driving when you know she's only eight.
   She turned the wheel and skidded till the truck had blocked the way,
   And they stopped up short and spun around and headed back for hay.

Two colts had stopped to grab a snack they wouldn't be denied,
   Because the grass is always greener when you're on the other side.
   For the most part, they were in formation at a slower rate,
   So we lined up, waving arms and brooms to shoo them through the gate.

Oh, the gate, yes, it was open still, proof of the escape's cause,
　But let's not be layin' blame; let's just take some time to pause.
　Nobody's hurt, the herd is back, and Dad could hardly curse.
　Sis left the truck and walked back, cuz she couldn't find reverse.


# Grandpa's Legacy
# by Danby Major

Just out there in the backyard but a million miles away
　Was the barn, the stalls, and stories of a treasured bygone day.
　He'd raised him some good horses but more important raised some kids
　Who could ride what e'rs four legged and sure 'nuf live by their wits.

'Neath all the dust and cobwebs stood a school for all life's teachin',
　And once he had them horseback, Daddy'd really get to preachin'.
　He'd say it's not all about winnin', even though they'd done their share;
　It's the preparin' that's important so keep currying that hair.

"The world is full of obstacles, like that trail class has a few.
　And showin' in the Showmanship is like a job interview.
　Sometimes it's not just speed that wins," was the first lesson learned.
　Being in the right position is how a good barrel's turned.

On the rail in Western Pleasure is where they all learned to drive,
　Gauging pace and keeping focused while adjusting every stride.
　They made good students too, and though their grades would never slip,
　All they'd memorize were patterns for the Novice Horsemanship.

His daughters preferred ribbons they won at the county fair
　To the kind that tied up packages or decorated hair.
　They could starch and iron jeans and shirts and care for boots and hats,
　And they had a heart for all God's beasts, from bulls to kitty cats.

He sure don't miss the money that he spent on entry fees.
    Every single buck was worth it since they always tried to please.
    Sure he could have drove a newer truck or cruised on fancy boats,
    But he'd rather fund their outfits and an extra scoop of oats.

Now as he looked around the stable, he could swear that he heard
    The lost laughter of his children, but it was just a chirping bird.
    He kept all their tack and brushes 'cause he always held out hope
    That they'd bring him some grandchildren who weren't 'fraid of saddle soap.
    He even kept that buckskin that had served them all those days.
    A bit arthritic, maybe blinded, but with his own land to graze.
    "If that ol' horse could talk," he'd say, "the secrets he could tell
    'Bout how to raise a teenage girl who ain't out raising hell."

Bucky was a classic Quarter Horse—speed, temperament, and more.
    And his papers boasted bloodlines back to King P234.
    Sure he's turned out in his work clothes now, long haired and wild and dirty,
    But he's earned a soft retirement; after all, he's nearly thirty.

"C'mon there, Buck," the old man called. With that, he raised his head.
    Then he turned around and jogged right in, just like he's being led.
    "Today is kinda special, pard. Could say my dream come true.
    'Cause my grandkids from the city's comin', and their gonna be ridin' you."

Soon 'nuf, the posse had arrived in a shiny SUV
    With more lights and bells and whistles than a well-trimmed Christmas tree.
    That son-in-law was not so bad, but he was raised in town,
    And it always seemed to grandpa his folks thought he'd married down.

"How come the kids aren't gettin' out and breathin' the fresh air?"
    "Don't worry, Dad. Just one more show on their DVD player."
    "Watchin' movies in the car?" he asked. "Ain't heard of such a thing.
    Why, when you girls came along for a drive, we'd talk and laugh and sing."

He couldn't see them through the tinted glass, and he started to get annoyed.
    "Come on out here and give me a hug. I want to see my girl and boy."
    Slowly the back doors opened up, and they stepped into the light,
    But they weren't so little anymore, and Grandpa got a fright.

Especially since he planned for two, but before him stood another.
    So he turned and joked to his grandson, "What happened? You get a brother?"
    "No, Dad. That's Britney's friend Tyrone. She wanted him to come.
    You see, he hangs around so much these days he's almost like a son."

Pa had to take a breath or two and think before he spoke.
    Because three pirates stood before him. This must be some kinda joke.
    They were dressed in baggy clothes with wild rags wrapped around their brows
    And more brands and tags and tattoos than your average Hereford cow.

"Hey, waddya say we go out to the barn and visit Bucky?
    I'd even bet you'll probably get to ride him if you're lucky."
    They all stood there, staring blankly like when headlights paralyze deer.
    "They can't hear you right now, Dad. They've still got iPods in their ears."

Now Pa was proud he'd been to war and fought for this great nation,
    But at this point, he held little hope for the next generation.
    *There's just something that's a missin'*, he thought, *with these kids these days.*
    *You could say that they're just being kids or going through a phase.*

*But If I don't get them horseback soon, they could be lost forever.*
    *That Buckskin could me my last hope. I guess it's now or never.*
    He finally got the herd lined out and headed for the barn.
    Then their dad said, "Don't get dirty!" and Pa just 'bout bought the farm.

"Don't get dirty! Is he kidding?" he said underneath his breath.
   "Whoever heard of someone who had been dirtied to death?"
   These kids were sick all right, but Pa knew just the cure.
   They needed to be baptized in the scent of horse manure.

Things really started to go awry when they got to the stable.
   Buck took one look, then spooked and ran as fast as he was able.
   The kids all griped about the smell. Tyrone screamed at a spider.
   Then Pa realized, *Britney's so frail she'll never make a rider.*

He saddled Buck up anyway to give a demonstration.
   The kids were watching where they stepped, and soon they lost their
   patience.
   "Can we go in?" was now their plea 'cause lunch was on the table.
   And then they asked, "Grandpa, do you have satellite or cable?"

He knew there was no hope. He'd been defeated; there was no doubt.
   He untacked Buck, then slapped him on the rump and turned him out.
   Then later, as he waved goodbye, he thanked his lucky stars
   That his girls preferred horses to boys, fast trucks, and bars.

He knew that horses give a life purpose and hopes and dreams.
   They give people something to look forward to, it seems.
   They teach kids about hard work and responsibility,
   And they make and old man feel just like a younger man, you see.

So Grandpa figured there's no point prolonging the suspense.
   He told the kids he plans on spending their inheritance.
   He bought a new truck and new horse. Left Buck knee deep in clover.
   You'll see him showing next weekend in the Fifty and Over.

# Great Day to Be a Horse
## by Danby Major

My friends and I can start our day without a care or plan,
  Except to gallop, buck, and graze and roll in warm, soft sand.
  We'll see the sunrise through the mist to dry the dew-soaked grass.
  No calendar, no clock to watch, we let the time just pass.

Our herd all knows its order, who's to follow, who's to lead.
  We all keep watch for danger though, so often there's no need.
  We are the rulers of the plains, our instincts finely tuned
  To find the water or the shade and our supply of food.

Our bodies have been built for speed; our legs are swift and strong,
  With sharpened hooves to blaze a trail and travel all day long.
  Someday they'll tame our grandchildren and harness them for toil,
  To pull a wagon, herd a cow, and then to plow the soil.

But for now we'll still taste freedom, breathing air so crisp and clean.
  Our senses keep us safe because our eyesight is so keen.
  Our ears pick up the distant sounds; our nostrils read the air.
  The wind forecasts the weather to our mane and long tail hair.

No brand will mark our hide for now; we're no man's property.
  No bit of steel will guide our mouth; no whip or spur we'll see.
  There's no sweat from a saddle leaving stains upon our back,
  Just hoofprints on the trails we trod; no footprints make a track.

No forge will heat a horseshoe to be nailed upon our feet.
  Nobody trims our whiskers or braids our mane so neat.
  We'll jump just what we need to, and not for man's own sport.
  Our races go unnoticed; we've no stopwatch to report.

You won't see us jog in circles while a human holds the rope.
  We won't wait for an announcer just to say it's time to lope.
  We'll buck just when we want to, not just when the flank strap's tight,
  And we'll sleep under the stars and not an artificial light.

No stall that's filled with bedding will be needed for our care,
  And we won't be wearing blankets to keep us from growing hair.
  No vaccination needles to keep us free of disease,
  And we'll bolt and kick and rear and spook and bite whate'r we please.

So if you saddle up a horse today and groom their tails and manes,
  Give a moment's thought to ancient blood that's flowing in their veins.
  The mustangs, Spanish Barbs, the Arabs, Appaloosas too,
  Who were the founding fathers, making pets for me and you.

Remember where they came from; what they really want and need
  Are just a little freedom, opened doors, and unsnapped lead.
  Consider it a privilege that they let us tame their mind
  And protect the last wild horses so they don't get left behind.

Kella took some time to ponder the poetry publishing possibilities. Danby would be so proud of that. She also knew that such an endeavor would take months and maybe years to reap any financial reward. The risk was too high, and she didn't have the luxury of time. Then she gave her head a shake and remembered that this was just the sort of distraction that she wasn't going to allow herself today. *Just be a robot*, she told herself. *It's just stuff. Clear it out.*

    She then thought that she would take a break from the office and take a look around in Danby's apartment. This was going to be even harder. She decided to contact a local charity that would pick up used furniture, dishes, appliances, and any household items and provide her with a charitable donation receipt for tax purposes. Not that she needed tax deductions; what she needed right now was income. She made a plan to clear out only what she was going to save and then let the charity crew in to clear out the rest. She opened cupboards and drawers in the kitchen looking for any notable keepsakes. There was a tea towel over the handle on the oven from Jamaica—a memento of one of the very few vacations that Danby had ever taken in his life.

On the walls were some small framed pictures of Kella with various ponies and horses. School photos of Corby and her hockey team pictures. In the bedroom was a plastic, hinged hat box that carried his favorite black cowboy hat. She would save that forever. She opened the box and took out the hat and examined the wear marks and sweat stains on the brim. She put it on and looked in the mirror. How he would have loved for her to wear a cowboy hat more often. Kella only wore a floppy straw cowboy hat as a fashion accessory. She wore it to the Boots and Hearts Country Music Festival and two years ago to a Luke Bryan concert; otherwise, she was more comfortable in a ball cap or riding helmet.

Kella ran her hand over the bedspread in his sparsely decorated room. She got down on her knees beside the bed and crouched to see if there was anything stored underneath. In the darkness, she could see what looked like a large, flat package.

Kella pushed the package as far as she could toward the other side and then went around to pull it out. She lifted it up and lay it flat on the bed. It was a large, hard rectangular form wrapped in plain brown paper, and it was taped together at the ends with yellowing cello tape. There was no lettering or labels on the package of any kind. Kella carefully peeled back the failing tape and folded open the brown paper wrapping. Under the brown paper were layers of newspaper. They were from the *Duckville Dispatch* Labor Day weekend edition and dated September 4, 1976.

Inside the papers was an old framed canvas that appeared to be an original oil painting. It was a painting she had never seen before.

It had never hung on the wall in their house or in his apartment. The image was two cowboys and some cattle in a snowstorm. She guessed it was almost two feet by three feet, and it was in a gold frame. She examined the signature in the bottom right corner. Frederic Remington 1904.

Kella grabbed her phone to do a search of the unknown artist to see if it was of any importance.

# 29

When Kella entered the name in the search engine on her phone, she was surprised at the number of websites dedicated to the artist.

Frederic Sackrider Remington
(October 4, 1861–December 26, 1909)
Spouse: Eva Caten (1884–1909)

Frederic Remington was an American illustrator, painter, sculptor, and writer who was known for his depictions of western subjects and scenery. He specialized in images of cowboys, American Indians, and US cavalry as well as other figures from the western United States. Although born in New York State, where he lived for most of his life, he traveled back and forth across the country many times trying to preserve the Old West as he had seen it. He was also an outdoorsman and adventurer and painted northeastern landscapes. His ink drawings, water color, and oil paintings were published by many magazines in

```
his time, including Harper's Weekly,
Colliers, and Scribner's.

His work can be seen at the Frederic
Remington Art Museum in Ogdensburg,
New York …
```

That's all she needed to read. Details of his early life, his awards and honors were of little interest right now.

Next, Kella searched for the Frederic Remington Art Museum. She had never heard of Ogdensburg but was surprised to find it on the southern shore of the St. Lawrence River and just across the international bridge from Prescott, Ontario. Her map directions showed that this would be about a five-hour drive on the 401 Highway.

The website for the museum had contact info for all the staff, so she decided to send a short email to the curator to inquire if they were able to tell her if the painting was worth anything.

```
Dear Ms. Foster,

I have found a painting among my late father's
possessions, and I need to find out its value.
It is signed by Frederic Remington and is of
two cowboys and some cows in the snow.

I would be interested in selling this item
as soon as possible, so any guidance would
be appreciated.

Kella Major
```

As it was a Saturday afternoon, Kella wasn't expecting to receive any reply to her inquiry until Monday. However, an hour later when she checked her email, there was a message from Laura Foster at the Frederic Remington Art Museum.

Dear Kella,

I would be very interested in helping you determine if what you have is a Frederic Remington original, a print, or a copy of some kind. I would need, however, to examine the actual piece in person. In the matter of value, we at the Frederic Remington Art Museum are in the business of display and education for the public as well as occasional authentication, but we are not a commercial gallery, nor can we act as an agent on your behalf, so I cannot provide you with an actual appraisal.

Please let me know if you want to visit the museum with your painting, and I would be happy to give you an unofficial opinion in order to begin the authentication process.

Very best,
Laura

Kella looked again at the route from her home to Ogdensburg, New York. If she got up early on Monday morning and left right after she fed the horses, she could be there when the museum opened at ten. Allowing a couple of hours for a meeting, she could still be home by early evening, depending on the Toronto traffic. Kella fired another email to Laura Foster.

Laura,

I'll be there shortly after ten on Monday morning, and I will bring the painting with me.

Kella

While Kella contemplated ten hours of driving with a painting by some dude that had been dead for more than a hundred years, she added up the cost of gas and hoped this wasn't going to be a wild goose chase. Kella wrapped up the painting, located her passport, and wished it was Monday already.

# 30

Corby wasn't in her room when her grandmother looked in on her first thing in the morning. Her suspicions were confirmed when she looked out toward the lake and saw Corby standing on the dock with a fishing rod in her hand. Delilah made herself a cup of coffee and walked down to the dock to take a seat in one of the red Muskoka chairs.

"Any bites?" she said to Corby.

"I caught a very small perch, and I let it go. I thought I saw a stick floating toward me, and it turned out to be a turtle swimming by with his head sticking out of the water. I didn't want to catch him on my hook, so I waited for him to get far away."

"It looks like it's going to be another beautiful day," said Delilah. "You can go swimming later if you want."

"The lake is still pretty cold," said Corby.

"Your grandfather will be here soon. I think he wants to work on the canoe with your father today. There is also a special event that I'd like to take you to."

"What sort of event?" asked Corby.

"A friend of ours is the headmaster at a private school nearby called Deercrest Academy. He has invited us to their open doors today, and he promised us a personal tour. It's supposed to be a pretty interesting place."

"We're going to a school?" asked Corby.

"Yes, but it's more than just a school. It's not like any school you've ever seen."

Corby rolled her eyes and cast her hook and worm back into the lake and then slowly cranked the reel. "Some vacation," she said too quietly for her grandmother to hear.

"I'm going to start making breakfast," said Delilah.

"Okay, I'll be there in ten minutes," said Corby.

When Delilah got back into the cottage, Reese was already sipping a cup of coffee. Wearing just an old pair of shorts, he was unshaven, his hair was tousled, and he had his laptop open on the kitchen table.

"Your father always says the insurance business never sleeps," said Delilah.

"Did you tell her?" he asked.

"Not in so many words, but she agreed to come with me."

"I don't know what that means, and I don't want to know. You can always get your way sooner or later. Just be careful. She's been through a lot. It's a tough time for a girl her age to be facing so many changes."

"I'm only doing this for her, Reese."

He didn't look up from the screen while she started to rattle some pots and pans to start breakfast.

After breakfast, Corwin McLaren arrived with great fanfare. He had his arms filled with provisions as ordered by his wife, and he also brought a box that contained a giant inflatable pink flamingo for Corby.

"Really?" said Delilah looking at the photo on the package. "I'm sure our neighbors will be thrilled to see this monstrosity tied to our dock."

"It will be fun," he said. "I couldn't decide between this one, the giant donut, or the pizza slice one."

"Excellent choice," said Reese.

Delilah steered Corwin away from the others to have a little talk about their visit to Deercrest Academy. He was looking at Corby putting the breakfast dishes in the dishwasher.

"Is she okay with it?" he asked.

"I didn't really go into a lot of details. We'll just see how she likes the place," said Delilah.

The entrance of Deerfield Academy welcomed visitors through black wrought iron gates supported by stone walls on each side. Each gate was adorned with the Deercrest emblem and a banner reading Open Doors 2019 spanned the space above.

Deercrest Academy looked more like an exclusive country club than a high school. Manicured lawns shaded by towering pine trees, slate walkways between a collection of stone and log buildings with red steel roofs, and an expansive sports field with wooden bleachers along one side.

"This is a school?" asked Corby.

"This is the place," said Delilah as she followed a young man's direction to the parking area.

Deercrest Academy had been started in 1962 on property that had once been the summer estate of a shipping magnate from Cleveland, Ohio. It consisted of more than two hundred acres of bush and cleared land, with lake access on one side and conservation land on the other side. The school was dedicated to providing the best in academics, arts, and sports with a strong emphasis on the outdoors. It was a safe and sterilized environment for the children of the rich and powerful to get an education among their own kind.

"Let's check in at the office and see if we can get our tour," said Delilah.

After running the gauntlet of greetings from staff and some select students, Delilah inquired at the reception desk if Headmaster Montgomery was available.

Moments later, he was shaking their hands and hustling them out of the office and toward the waterfront.

Sterling Montgomery was in his midfifties and spoke with a posh British accent. His claim to fame, beyond his administrative credentials, was that he was on the men's eight-man rowing team for England at two Olympic Games.

He proudly showed off the school's water sport programs. Canoeing, sailing, and rowing were part of the physical education curriculum and interschool team competition.

"I heard that you're quite the hockey player," he said to Corby. "We have both boys' and girls' hockey teams here. We don't have an arena, but we have access to the public arena in town for our games and practices. We also clear the ice on the lake for skating in the winter when it's safe."

Delilah wanted to change the subject quickly from the topic of safe ice.

"Can we see the dorms?" she asked.

The headmaster took them through the girls' dormitory building where every room was empty for the summer and left immaculately for inspection.

"There are four students to each room, as you can see," he said. "There is an adjoining bathroom for each room, and all students eat their meals in the Lodge."

The dining hall in the Lodge was a massive space featuring arcing timber frame construction supporting a wood ceiling. At one end, there was a stage, and the walls were decorated with banners from sports championships dating back to the sixties.

"We use this space for meals, assemblies, and chapel services," he said. "It's also available for private functions. We get quite a few weddings here in the summer season. Often former students hold their receptions here. We have quite a track record for pairing up brides and grooms from our student body. Must be something in the water," he joked.

"We don't want to take up any more of your time, Mr. Montgomery," said Delilah. "I'm sure you've got other families to meet."

"Let me give you some literature, the registration forms, and a tuition fee schedule back at the office before you go. We would need transcripts from the former school as well as reference letters from a teacher or principal and any other professional member of the community who knows Corby," he said.

Corby was trying to put together the pieces of what he just said, but she kept quiet.

Back in the car on the way back to the cottage, Delilah started the conversation.

"So what did you think of Deercrest?"

"It looks amazing. I can't believe it's a high school. More like a fancy camp," said Corby.

"Would you ever be interested in attending a school like that?" asked Delilah.

Corby knew that this was more than just a casual visit. She could tell by the headmaster's tour that something was up.

"Would I have to wear a uniform?" she asked.

Delilah smiled. "Only on weekdays and for chapel on Sundays," she said.

Corby was quiet for a moment and then replied, "I don't think my mother will even notice I'm gone."

# 31

Monday morning, Kella's alarm went off at four. She raced out to the barn to turn out horses into paddocks that she had already loaded with extra hay and water the night before. She quickly showered and dressed and was on the road well before five. Toronto traffic was always lighter in the middle of the summer, and there was even less than usual as she drove across the top of the city before the commuters took over the highway.

Heading east on the 401, Lake Ontario was on her right before it narrowed into the St. Lawrence River, which was the major shipping route from the Atlantic Ocean. The suburbs turned to farms, the towns to villages, and with only one quick stop at a large roadside gas station filled with fast-food options, she was making good time. Soon she saw signs directing her to the Bridge to USA. The Ogdensburg-Prescott International Bridge was a vast span across the St. Lawrence River, and the steel grid of the bridge's surface made a low roar from her tires.

She approached the customs' booth, and although there was a stop sign to wait behind until the car in front of her had exited, she was the only car at the border.

Kella had her passport ready, her radio turned down, and her sunglasses off.

"Citizenship?" the officer asked as he took her passport.

"Canadian."

"Where are you going?"

"Just into Ogdensburg."

"What are you doing there?"

"Visiting the Remington Museum," she said.

"How long will you be out of the country?"

"I'll be back this afternoon."

"Have a good day," he said as he handed back her passport.

Kella drove to the next booth, paid a toll, followed the signs, and within minutes was in downtown Ogdensburg, New York. It was a pivotal military port during the Seven Years War and the War of 1812. It's location at the mouth of the Oswegatchie River made it part of a strategic trade route for indigenous people and early settlers.

The Remington Museum was surprisingly easy to find, with numerous roadside markers guiding the way. Kella found free parking in a municipal parking lot nearby and walked to the museum with her purse slung over her shoulder and carefully carrying the painting with both hands. The Frederic Remington Art Museum was located in a redbrick mansion with black shutters and a grand porch across the front, framed by white pillars and railings. It had a more modern addition on one side that connected it to another sizeable building that was also likely a former residence. Hand-lettered signs displayed the seasonal hours and were each adorned with the Frederic Remington signature that she had found on her father's painting.

Across the street was a public library, and from the porch, one could look just one block to the north and see the port and river with assorted docks and waterfront activity. Kella heard children squealing as they jumped off of a diving board into a public pool, and beyond that the buzz of a Jet Ski engine as it left the dock.

Kella was happy to see the Open sign on the massive oak door, and she stepped inside.

The lobby of the museum had a sweeping staircase leading to upper rooms. To one side was a corridor leading to exhibits, to the other side was a small reception desk, and beyond that was a gift shop.

An elderly gentleman in a security guard uniform greeted her and encouraged her to sign the guestbook. There was a young woman at the reception table to whom Kella introduced herself, saying she had a meeting with Laura Foster.

Kella listened as the woman called Laura on her desk phone, and she noted the distinct New York accent. *How interesting that you can just drive across a bridge and hear a different dialect.*

Meanwhile, the security guard was eyeing the package with great interest.

"Do you have a painting for Ms. Foster to look at?" he asked.

"Yes, I just need to find out if it has any value. I'd like to sell it."

"Well, if it's a Remington, that won't be too hard. Good luck," he said.

Laura Foster appeared and shook Kella's hand. "I'm pleased to meet you, Kella. Let's find out what you have here. I hope you haven't driven all this way for nothing."

Laura told Kella to follow her to the Tea Room. It was a space that would afford them privacy and good lighting.

"I get quite a few of these inquiries," said Laura. "Frederic Remington has over 3,400 known paintings and drawings, so there is a lot out there. Unfortunately, some people are actually holding a print and not an original. Let's hope that's not the case here."

Laura pointed to two card tables set in the middle of the room. There was plenty of artificial and natural light provided by the floor-to-ceiling windows on the north side of the room that faced out onto a courtyard. Under the tables was a large rug with an earth-toned Navajo pattern. Kella placed her package on the table, while Laura put on a pair of white gloves. Kella wasted no time unwrapping the painting without ceremony as Laura waited for the reveal.

Kella folded back the newspapers to give Ms. Foster her first view of the canvas.

She stood silently, leaning forward and staring intently at the image, studying the texture of the brushstrokes and holding one hand with her fingers spread against her chest. *"Drifting Before the Storm,"* said Laura in hushed reverence.

# 32

Brooklyn, New York
July 1908

Frederic Remington Esq.,

I hope this letter finds you well. You may not
remember, but we were introduced by my father,
Calvin Delfer, while he was employed by Riccardo
Bertelli at Roman Bronze Works. My wife and I have
been positively inspired by your work, and our interest
in the west is such that we plan to make a go of
ranching in the state of Nebraska. It is our intent to
depart at the beginning of September for Centennial,
Nebraska, after spending two weeks with my wife's
family, the Beeswaters, in Pelham Manor.

My father insists that we would be remiss if we did
not avail ourselves of the opportunity to meet with
you again in person and gather any useful information
from you as we prepare for our journey and ranching

venture. I understand that we will be a convenient
distance from your home in New Rochelle.

Please advise if there would be a suitable time during
the last two weeks of August to visit you.

Many thanks.

Yours truly,
Rueben Delfer


Inglenuk
Chippewa Bay, NY
August 1908

Dear Mr. Delfer,

My apologies for the tardiness of my response,
but your letter arrived when I was already at my
summer home on an island on Chippewa Bay in the
middle of the St. Lawrence River, and the forwarding
of my correspondence from New Rochelle is always
challenging.

Mrs. R and I would be delighted to host you and your
bride when we return to Endion, our home in New
Rochelle. If Sunday, August 23 is suitable for you,
then we will expect you without further reply, and

we insist that you stay as our guests for dinner and overnight if necessary.

I am envious of your decision to make a go of it in the ranching business. My own attempt at sheep ranching was not a resounding success, and so I will remain in the pursuit of the arts instead. However, I can assist you with your passage, and I will pen letters of introduction for you to present wherever necessary.

Until the twenty-third.

Y———————

Frederic Remington

**Ruben and Elizabeth Delfer arrived at Endion,** the estate of Frederic and Eva Remington at 301 Webster Avenue in New Rochelle, New York, at half past three o'clock on Sunday, August 23, 1908.

The Remingtons had spent the past eighteen years on their three-acre property, which included their imposing brick home with its twin chimneys, gothic archways, and intricate gingerbread fascia. Next to the home was Frederic's studio as well as a stable and assorted outbuildings housing an assortment of livestock.

As the Delfers arrived in their four-wheeled buggy, the Remington's black-and-white hound named Sandy began barking to announce their presence.

Frederic pushed Sandy aside as he stepped to offer a hand to Elizabeth Delfer. "Welcome, welcome," he said. "You must be the Delfers."

"Indeed," said Rueben. "Ruben and Elizabeth Delfer, sir."

"It is my pleasure to meet you both," said Remington, and then he turned and shouted, "Kid, our guests have arrived."

An Indian man stepped out of the stable, took the reins of the horse, and led it away to unharness it as Eva Remington stepped out of the house.

"This is my wife, Eva, but I like to call her Missie," said Frederic.

Introductions were made all around, and the women stepped into the house.

"I've got a bully idea for you, Rueben. You must come with me to my studio to give me a hand with something."

"Of course," said Rueben. "Though I can't imagine how I could be of any help in an art studio."

Inside the studio, Rueben was overwhelmed by an impressive collection of props and paraphernalia that Frederic Remington used to add detail and authenticity to his paintings and sculptures. There were all manner of costume and weaponry, military uniforms, Indian pottery, cowboy tack, snowshoes and rugs, taxidermy mounts of various wildlife, including a moose head gazing down from the wall above the large fireplace, and natural light filtering into the cavernous space from several skylight windows in the arched ceiling. Delfer studied the easels and art supplies, bronze sculpture armature supporting wax forms in progress, and reference photos scattered on tables.

"So, how can I help?" asked Rueben.

"As soon as I saw you, I knew you would be perfect," said Remington.

"Perfect for what, sir?"

"Modeling."

"Mr. Remington. I don't know about that. I'm really not much of a—"

Remington cut him off. "Nonsense. Now step into the corner over there and get into these buckskins."

Remington produces a buckskin jacket and breeches as well as a soft hat and a red scarf.

Delfer complied while Remington placed a western saddle onto a saddle rack and arranged it at an appropriate angle.

"Now get aboard this ol' cayuse. He's a quiet mount, but I make no warranty of his soundness," said Remington with a chuckle.

He handed Rueben a holster to strap around his waist and instructed him to take the revolver in his right hand and twist to his left with the pistol drawn.

Remington unfolded the accordion bellows of his Kodak camera and methodically took photographs from various views. Then he positioned himself in a chair with a large sketchpad and went to work to quickly block in the gesture of the pose.

"This is just what I need for a sculpture that I'm considering. I need you to imagine that there is a mountain lion pouncing onto the back of your horse, and you are preparing to dispatch it before it has you for breakfast."

"Is that likely to happen in Nebraska?" asked Rueben.

"Well, maybe not so much in the plains. The lions are more in the north and the far west."

"Where did you ever get this buckskin outfit?"

"Believe it or not, that habit belonged to General George Custer himself."

"But he died over thirty years ago," said Rueben.

"True, but his widow, Elizabeth, has generously sent me some of his accoutrements for me to use."

"I can't believe I am wearing the clothes of Custer," said Rueben.

"Now just sit still and keep that gun up and pointed at the lion," said Remington.

The door to the studio opened, and the women arrived carrying glasses of tea for the men. Mrs. Delfer stepped in first, and all she could see was her husband dressed in the buckskin suit, sitting in a saddle, and pointing a pistol over his left shoulder.

"Oh my, Rueben. What on earth is going on here?" she asked.

Eva was already laughing knowingly as she set the tray with the tea on a desk. "Don't mind Frederic. He would recruit Roosevelt himself to pose as an infantry soldier if he fit the uniform."

Remington was sketching quickly. He would finish one view and then rotate ninety degrees around Rueben to capture the pose from all sides.

Eva noticed Rueben's discomfort with the awkward position. "At least give our guest some support. His arm must be positively numb," she said as she propped a homemade crutch under his elbow.

"I'm being attacked by a mountain lion, Lizzie," said Rueben.

"You better not be," she said. "You promised my mother that we would be safe in Nebraska."

"And safe you shall be," said Remington. "The west is as tame as a cocker spaniel now. The savagery is over, and any tenderfoot can make a comfortable homestead without fear of interference by man or beast. Speaking of beast, I am hungry enough to eat a mountain lion myself. How is dinner coming along, Kid?" he said to Eva.

"I'll tell you one thing about Missie here. She can turn a pigeon into a fatted goose if need be. I'm sure my girth is evidence of her gastronomic prowess," he said, laughing.

"I assure you all that it is chicken and not pigeon on tonight's menu," said Eva as she left the studio and headed back to the kitchen to check on their cook.

Elizabeth Delfer gave herself a tour of the studio while the men were busy with the sketching.

"You sure do have an amazing collection of paintings here, Mr.

Remington," she said. "Whatever will you do with all these that are leaning against this wall?"

"Those, my dear, are from my illustration days and no longer represent my current work. Some have already been published, although I almost wish they had not been. It is now my sole desire to be recognized for my fine art paintings and sculptures, and I am severing ties with the publications that have brought me to this point."

"So will you just sell these?" she asked.

"Absolutely not. Those illustrations will neither be available for purchase nor public display."

"I like this one," she said. "Does the snow blow like that in Nebraska?"

"Ah, *Drifting Before the Storm*. Indeed it does," replied Remington. "Many a herd have been lost, and nearly as many cowboys have perished in the sort of snowstorm that you see in that painting."

Elizabeth Delfer considered that foreboding statement as she studied the image. Two cowboys on horseback bracing against the blowing snow as they guide some cattle into the wind.

"I'm looking at the horse in the background, Mr. Remington. Can you tell me, why did you paint the horse blue?" she asked.

Remington didn't look up from his sketch as he answered. "Well, we know that the horse isn't actually blue, but it's an effect that I use in the shadows of the snow as well as a technique that adds depth, as a bit of blue is added to anything in the distance. You see a lot of blue horses in my nocturnal paintings also, but that is representative of the moonlight."

"It's just fascinating," said Elizabeth as she sipped her tea.

Eva returned later to invite the others to the dining room and rescue Rueben Delfer from his pose.

"I can't thank you enough," said Remington. "It may be 1910

218

before I get a chance to complete that as a bronze, but you have been very helpful. The next year is going to be a busy one for Missie and I. We are building a new home in Ridgefield, Connecticut, and we will be packing up things here next spring. I may also have to part with my beloved summer home, Inglenuk. I'm hoping to have some new works ready for more gallery shows next year. Either way, when you see the finished sculpture with the mountain lion someday, you can claim that is you in the saddle."

At dinner, Frederic entertained his guests with his tall tales of the west. Rueben enjoyed watching his young wife squirm with wide-eyed wonder as Remington's descriptions of close calls with Indians, weather, and wildlife grew more dramatic with every glass of whiskey.

"I think it would be a perfect evening for a fire outside," said Remington as he lit his pipe. "Let's gather out back, and I'll collect some kindling to get a blaze underway."

While the others arranged some chairs around a well-used fire pit, Frederic Remington downed another shot of whiskey as he made his way back to his studio. Once inside, he gathered an armful of paintings from the stack that Elizabeth had been admiring and staggered toward the fire pit.

"What on earth are you doing, Frederic?" asked Eva as she saw him arrive with the paintings. Remington didn't reply as he lit a match to the remaining tinder and coals in the pit.

"I'd like to take this opportunity to propose a toast for our guests," he said as he held another glass in his hand. "It is a night of new beginnings, fresh starts, and untold adventure. To the future!" he said as he tossed the first painting into the flames. The fire quickly ignited the mix of oils and varnish and consumed the canvas and frame. Remington threw in two more before anyone could stop him.

"Please don't, darlin'," said Eva.

"I've wanted to do this for a long time, and you know it, Missie. From now on, I am no longer just an illustrator for hire. Rueben, give me a hand in the studio. I've got a lot more of them to carry to the crematory."

Rueben reluctantly followed Remington. Frederic grabbed another armful and instructed Rueben to do the same. Rueben loaded a few more canvases under his arm, including *Drifting Before the Storm*. As he followed the artist in the darkness between the studio and the fire pit, he tossed the painting into a bush.

Remington was giddy with delight as he watched his former career go up in smoke. The women watched helplessly as the men loaded more and more art into the fire.

"I'd like to go and check on the horse if you don't mind," said Rueben. "I don't know if the flames are upsetting him."

Rueben retraced his steps toward the studio, retrieved the painting from the bushes, and hurried to where his buggy was parked. He quickly stuffed the painting under the seat and then looked in briefly at his horse tied in a standing stall in the stable before returning to the others.

By this point, the alcohol had taken its toll on Remington, and he sat slouched in a chair with his pipe dangling from his mouth and his eyes closing.

"You really must stay the night," said Eva. "Frederic wanted to write some letters of introduction for you to take with you, but it doesn't look like he is in any condition to do that now."

"We appreciate that, Mrs. Remington, but we really need to get on our way," said Rueben.

"Are you sure?" said Elizabeth to Rueben. "I'm sure we could just stay until—"

Rueben cut her off. "No, I'm sure. It's a short drive back to Pelham Manor. Mr. Remington can just send the letters to your parents' address. We must be on our way now."

As the young couple left, Remington rose to join his wife to bid them goodbye and wish them all the best in their travels and ranching endeavors.

In June 1909, the Delfers were settled into their new home on a ranch in Centennial, Nebraska, when Elizabeth gave birth to their first and only child. They named him Gaylon Frederic Delfer.

On December 26, 1909, just days after having surgery for appendicitis, artist Frederic Remington died.

He was only forty-eight years old.

# 33

In spite of the fact that Frederic Remington's career lasted less than thirty years and that he traveled back and forth across the United States, Cuba, and Europe all before the automobile, he managed to create approximately 3,400 known drawings and paintings and twenty-two cast bronze sculptures. He also wrote articles for many publications and published eight novels. Unfortunately, it is also a historic fact that he burned as many as one hundred of his paintings, including many that had already been published.

Laura Foster carefully picked up Kella's painting and turned it over. She set it down on the paper wrapping on the table as she inspected the back. The first thing she noticed was the authentic stamp on the back of the canvas from F. W. Devoe & Co., which was where Remington purchased his supplies.

The small stamp in the shape of an artist's pallet read "Prepared by F. W. Devoe & Co. New York. Manufacturers and Importers of Artist's Materials."

The canvas was stretched onto a stained wooden frame, and the corners were braced with small cast-iron brackets rather than traditional staples. The unique plates were inscribed Pat'd Feb. 13, 1883, June 16, 1885 ADS.

Curator Laura Foster immediately recognized these features

as being consistent with most paintings by Remington. Next she looked closer at the gessoed, guilt frame and found the manufacturers mark from Ashler & Stab, NY.

If Laura was excited about the discovery, she hid it well from Kella.

"Well. What do you think?" asked Kella.

"I think I have good news and bad news for you, Ms. Major," said Laura.

"First the good news. What you have here is a very nice painting that exhibits many of the characteristics that are noted on most original paintings by Frederic Remington."

"That's great, isn't it?" asked Kella.

"Unfortunately, this particular image is on the list of paintings that were burned by the artist sometime between 1906 and 1909."

"What do you mean burned?" asked Kella.

"Remington was tired of being considered an illustrator and not entirely a fine artist, and so to clearly delineate the end of one part of his career and his commitment to fine art, he burned almost one hundred known works. *Drifting Before the Storm*, unfortunately, is on the list of burned paintings."

"But isn't this real?" asked Kella. "There must be some mistake. Are you saying that this has to be a forgery or something?"

"I'm not completely at liberty to render an official opinion on its authenticity at this time, but I can tell you that there have been fakes submitted to the committee before. I'm going to be completely honest with you, Kella. I have serious reservations about this painting."

"What committee?" asked Kella.

"There is an official committee of Remington scholars who meet once each year to authenticate any new submissions that are possibly attributed to Frederic Remington. I am one of the four members of the committee. If you are interested in submitting this piece for the committee's judgment, I can tell you the procedure, but you will need to move fast. We meet in ten days."

"Do you meet here?" asked Kella.

"I wish," said Laura. "Unfortunately, the annual meeting is held at the Buffalo Bill Center of the West in Cody, Wyoming."

"Buffalo Bill?" said Kella. "You've got to be kidding."

"The deadline for submissions has passed, but I think I can pull some strings. I'm pretty sure the group is going to want to see this one."

"So, what do I have to do?" asked Kella.

"I'll print out an application for you to fill out, and you will need to ship it to Cody, Wyoming, as soon as possible along with the required fee."

"I shouldn't ship it from Canada," said Kella. "I've already got it over the border, and I don't want any delays with the Customs Department. Is there somewhere in town that I can use?"

"You can actually take it to the Frederic Remington Post Office building right down State Street," said Laura.

Laura Foster gave Kella the paperwork to complete and helped her pack up the painting properly, using archival materials that were stored in the museum.

"Thanks for all your help," said Kella.

"Good luck," said Laura.

"I'll see your painting in Wyoming. If it is authentic, you will receive an official notification signed by all four scholars. It's quite a legal procedure. I know you indicated that you would like to sell the painting, but if it is deemed to be an original and should your circumstances change, we would be honored to display it here at the Frederic Remington Art Museum for the public to enjoy."

"I'll keep that in mind," said Kella as she carried the painting out the door and toward the post office.

# 34

Kella woke up the next morning in her own bed and stared at the ceiling. The future seemed even more uncertain than it had ever been. *Is something great going to happen to me, or is something bad going to happen to me?* She tried not to think about the painting as she went about her chores, but the possibilities of a big payday were consuming all of her thoughts. She made a point of spending more time with Cider today, as she had been left alone all day yesterday. It would be nine long days until the committee would meet in Cody, Wyoming, to decide the fate of her painting. Kella wondered where the painting came from. Did her father buy it on one of his trips out west? Why was it hidden? What did he know about the painting? Who else knew? She wanted to call her mother and ask her about it. Maybe she knew where it came from. Did she know if it was real or not?

Kella decided not to tell anyone about the painting. Not now, not ever.

Kella had reached the point that she didn't want to open any mail or answer her phone unless it was one of her friends. Every day that passed that she didn't hear from a lawyer or someone she owed money to was a victory. Showings of her property had slowed down during the dog days of summer, but that would not stop the mortgage company from foreclosing on her and forcing her to leave whenever they wanted. She started to imagine life after Major Meadows. Would she try to continue her horse business working out of some other facility? Would she find a "real job," as her mother would say? Her résumé wouldn't show any genuine work experience outside of the horse business. She had never been employed by anyone other than her father, and she couldn't picture herself fitting into a nine-to-five schedule.

Kella opened her email to find a letter from the Buffalo Bill Center of the West. She was disappointed to find out that all that it said was that they had received her submission and they would be in touch. She was happy, however, to know that the painting had arrived safely. Now all she could do was wait.

Another email arrived from her ex-husband, Reese. He explained that his parents generously were offering to send Corby to Deercrest Academy to start high school in the fall. If she agreed, they would take care of all the arrangements. Kella Googled Deercrest and took a look at their website. She had heard of the place but had never seen it in person. The first thought was how much she would miss Corby. Her second thought was how proud she would be to tell people that her daughter was attending a posh private school, regardless of the circumstances.

Kella texted Corby: "Deercrest?"

"Can I?" came Corby's reply.

"Do you want to?" Kella typed.

"Yes and no," said Corby.

"I think your grandparents need you to decide. If you want to go, it's okay with me," said Kella.

Kella considered that with Corby away for school, it would reduce her living expenses a bit and give her some breathing room since things were going to be so uncertain.

"Okay, I'll do it," texted Corby.

The day of the meeting in Cody, Wyoming, came, and Kella checked her email every two minutes. She knew that Wyoming would be a couple hours behind, but when she hadn't heard anything by eight o'clock that night, she sent an email to Laura Foster.

At ten o'clock, she got a reply.

> Hello, Kella. The committee examined your painting today, but I am not able to notify you of the final decision by email. Every submission receives an opinion in writing that is signed by all committee members. The document is then sent to you by registered mail. Tomorrow morning, we are meeting to sign off on all the paperwork.
>
> Sincerely,
> Laura

Kella didn't know how much more waiting she could take. The email from Laura didn't contain the slightest hint as to what they thought about the painting. Kella began to assume that if Laura had good news, she would have said so. Since it was going to be bad news, she was going to let the registered letter do the talking. Kella was disappointed but not surprised.

The next few days passed without news. Kella went about her daily routines at the farm. She packed up more of Danby's things and filled more bags for the garbage or for donations. A crew arrived to clear most of the big items out of his apartment. She looked around at the nearly empty space with shock and sadness. Any buyers looking at the apartment would need some imagination. Kella had neither the energy nor the funds to do any deep cleaning, painting, or decorating. She would be leaving the apartment, her house, and the rest of the farm in "as is" condition.

Kella did, however, start to check her mailbox with more enthusiasm. Finally the mail contained a card from the local post office stating that there was a registered letter waiting for her, and she could pick it up during regular business hours with proper photo identification. Kella checked the time; the post office was already closed for the day but would be open at nine tomorrow.

At 9:01 a.m. the next morning, Kella walked into the small brick building that was the Duckville Post Office. She walked past the glass display cases with commemorative stamps and coins, shelves stocked with packing materials, and the bulletin board with local notices and news. Kella presented her notification card along with her driver's license to the woman behind the counter. The woman opened a file cabinet and produced the envelope, then asked Kella to sign in a ledger and on another form before handing the sealed envelope over to her.

She marched out to her truck as quickly as possible and started to tear open the envelope before closing the truck door.

To: Kella Major

Dear Ms. Major,

The Frederic Remington artwork authentication committee thanks you for your excellent submission. The painting that you provided has undergone the closest scrutiny, including forensic testing and examination by our panel of scholars, and we are pleased to inform you that we conclude unanimously that your painting is the original Frederic Remington oil painting titled *Drifting Before the Storm,* which the artist painted in 1904. We also followed typical protocol by notifying both the FBI and the RCMP to make sure that the painting had never been reported stolen, and so far they have not found anything.

Congratulations on your fortunate find. While this piece has previously been listed among works that were burned by the artist, efforts will now be made to correct any notations regarding this work, and future publications will denote that *Drifting Before the Storm* is from the collection of Kella Major, Duckville, Canada. Our staff has repackaged the artwork appropriately, and it is being returned to you by courier. Please advise when you have received it.

Also enclosed was a notarized document of authenticity to go with the painting.

Both the letter and the certificate were signed by the four committee members, including Laura Foster.

Kella sat in her truck and wanted to explode. Now what?

She grabbed her phone and sent an email to Laura Foster.

Dear Laura,

I finally got official notice about the painting. Thanks for all your help. I would be interested in selling it as soon as possible. Can you tell me what it's worth? Does your museum want to buy it? Any information you can give me would be appreciated. I don't know anything about art!

Kella

Laura Foster had been expecting a message from Kella and responded as follows:

Dear Kella,

Congratulations. I suspected from the moment you unwrapped the painting that it had to be the original, but I couldn't tell you until we were certain.

Here at the Frederic Remington Art Museum, we would welcome the addition of your painting to our collection, and we would be proud to display it prominently in the Albert P. Newell Gallery along with some of Remington's greatest paintings and sculptures. We are not in a position to purchase the painting, but if you would loan it to us for public viewing, we would be very grateful.

I am not able to give you an official appraisal of the painting's value, but I can assure you that it is significant, and collectors would appreciate it for both its visual appeal and provenance.

If you must sell the painting, I would recommend the Scottsdale Art Auction. The next date is Saturday April 4, 2020.

Please keep in touch,
Laura

Kella considered waiting eight months before selling the painting by auction. By then, her farm would be gone, she would need to find another job, and she would be broke and possibly homeless. She decided to wait for the painting to come back, and then she could decide what to do next.

# 35

It was four days before Kella received a phone call from the courier company to say that they had a package for her at their depot next to Pearson International Airport in Toronto. Due to the insured value of the package, she would need to pick it up in person and pay the shipping fees. She didn't waste any time driving to the address she was given, and once she found the correct door in the maze of warehouses, she entered and waited in line at the counter.

She was behind two other people who picked up their mysterious shipments, and she could feel a rush of excitement as she stepped up to the clerk and presented her identification.

She brought with her the certificate of authenticity and the letter from the committee that showed that she was already the owner of the painting and that it wasn't a purchase that she had made in the United States. There would be no duty or taxes owing, and Kella gladly paid the premium COD shipping charges and finally had the package back in her hands.

Unlike the cardboard and Styrofoam configuration that she had sent the painting in, now it was housed in a sturdy, wooden crate.

As she carefully carried it through the door and to her vehicle, she smiled to herself at the casual handling that she had first given the painting before she knew anything about it. Her experience lugging heavy bales of hay every day was coming in handy. Now she lay it carefully in the back of her SUV and drove home like she was carrying the crown jewels.

Once she was home, she placed it delicately on the kitchen table. She didn't even want to unwrap it for now. She would never be able to do as good a job as they had done in Wyoming, and she decided to leave it alone.

Later that evening, she started to research her options online to sell the painting. Her first search took her to the Scottsdale Art Auction, as had been suggested by Laura Foster. The upcoming auction was indeed next April, and they were accepting works by a select list of western artists. Frederic Remington, of course, was on the list. Next she looked at the results of this year's auction. At first she was slightly discouraged, as she found several smaller pieces by known artists selling for under $1,000. She continued to scan through the results and noticed in the next section many pieces were selling for hundreds of thousands of dollars.

Kella looked at the consigner's entry form on her laptop and started to fill it out. It required a photo of the painting, which she found many versions of online already. She copied and pasted a description of the image from another website.

> *Drifting Before the Storm*. Two cowboys on horseback herding cattle in snowstorm. Painted in 1904 for *Collier's* magazine. This is one of nearly one hundred paintings that the artist felt was not representative of his current work and was burned by the artist.

Kella decided to revise the description: This is one of nearly one hundred paintings that was believed to have been burned by the artist but has recently been discovered and authenticated.

With all of the fields filled on the online form, she hovered the cursor over the Submit button. Could she afford to wait until next April to get top dollar for the painting? She hesitated and decided to sleep on it and do more research tomorrow.

The next morning, she came in from the barn, poured a fresh cup of coffee, and opened her laptop. Cider curled up on the floor next to her as she began checking her emails.

Evidently, word spreads quickly in the world of western art. She received emails from two magazines seeking an interview in order to do a feature article about the newly discovered painting. *Western Art and Architecture* and *Western Art Collector* were both vying to be the first to scoop the story. Kella wanted nothing to do with the publicity at this time and sent them each a reply, denying their requests.

A third email, however, was of greater interest. She read the following.

Dear Ms. Major,

We are premium western art dealers and gallery located in Denver, Colorado. We routinely carry works by Remington, Russell, and others and broker worldwide sales of the same.

It has come to our attention that you are in possession of the Remington original *Drifting Before the Storm*. We have a very serious Remington collector arriving from Germany in a few days, and we are certain that he would be interested in making a significant offer for the piece. We would, of course, need to have the painting here for him to view. Please advise us if this is possible and if you are interested in having us broker the sale for you. We can assure you that you

```
will be receiving top market value and the
transaction will be made with the utmost
integrity, transparency, and discretion.

All the best in the west,
Arthur and Marigold DeSalle
Rocky Trails Gallery
Denver, Colorado
```

This was just what Kella had hoped for. She needed a quick and easy way to capitalize on her good fortune as soon as possible. Before replying, she looked at the Rocky Trails Gallery website. On it, she found a photo of gallery owners Arthur and Marigold DeSalle. They were an attractive couple in their late fifties, and their About Us page told the story of how they began as art collectors themselves when Arthur was in the investment banking business and had spent the past ten years full-time with the art gallery.

Kella also took a moment to check the driving route from Duckville, Ontario, to Denver, Colorado. With Corby away for another couple of weeks, she could take the time to get the painting to Denver and get the deal completed as quickly as possible. The drive would take two full days, and she could be there just in time for the German buyer to view the painting.

Kella tried to calmly put on her shrewd horse trader hat and replied to the email.

```
Dear Arthur and Marigold,

Thank you for your interest in my painting. I
have received several inquiries, and I would
consider offering it to your buyer provided
that you assure me that the expenses of my
trip to deliver the painting will be covered
by yourselves if the sale is not completed.
```

I would be delivering the painting in person, and I could be there three days from today. Please advise.

Kella Major

Within an hour, she had a reply.

Dear Kella,

We would welcome your visit in person to Rocky Trails Gallery, and we will reserve a room for you at our expense at the Brown Palace Hotel and Spa. Attached please find our standard consigner's agreement for you to fill out, sign, and send back to us in order that we can act as your exclusive representatives to facilitate the sale of your fine painting. We look forward to meeting you soon.

Arthur and Marigold

Kella reviewed the attachment quickly. She printed it out, signed it, scanned it, and sent it back.

Since she would be leaving the next day, she needed to make quick arrangements to get someone to look after the farm. She texted Damien.

"I need a huge favor," she said.

"Name it," he replied.

"Any chance you can do my barn chores and take care of Cider for the next five or six days? I need to get away."

"When?" he asked.

"Starting tomorrow," she texted.

"I guess so."

"You're the best. I owe you big-time. I'll leave all instructions on the bulletin board. X"

Next, Kella made sure that she had fifty dollars in her pocket and started driving to downtown Toronto. This time when she left her farmhouse, she locked the door—something she didn't always do. She drove an hour to the largest branch of the TD Canada Trust bank in the city. There she opened a checking account with the fifty dollars and asked the teller for a new checkbook.

Kella knew that if she suddenly had a significant deposit to her local bank in Duckville, someone would notice. In the big city, she could be anonymous. With the bank account in order, she drove home to start packing.

Kella had little fear about driving over the border with the painting since she had done it before, except this time she would be crossing the Bluewater Bridge from Sarnia, Ontario, into Port Huron, Michigan. This border was considerably busier and more sophisticated, and she didn't want to arouse any undo suspicions about the painting. She decided to place it in the back of her vehicle and put a horse blanket over it. She added a bridle and a small grooming box and prepared to tell the border guard that she was just on her way out west to look at some horses.

Early the next morning, she started the drive with the intention of driving as far as she could before she was too tired to continue. The border crossing was just as simple as it had been in Ogdensburg, New York, and by midmorning, she was on Highway 69 to Lansing and then 94 to Chicago. South of Chicago, she got onto Interstate 80, which would take her out of Illinois and across Iowa and Nebraska toward Colorado. She was going to drive farther west than she had been in her life. The one time she had driven to Chicago was ten years ago for a girls' weekend when they went to a taping of *Oprah*.

Sixteen hours of driving, and she made it through Des Moines, Iowa, and decided to stop for the night at the cheapest place possible in West Des Moines. Not far from the interstate, she found a row of motels that looked like they hadn't been updated since the 1970s. The Tropics Motel boasted free Wi-Fi and continental breakfast for $49.95. She wouldn't be checking in on Facebook from this place, but it would do.

She backed her Lexus up to the door of room number six and unloaded her luggage and the painting in the crate. She looked around to see that nobody was paying attention while she hoisted the container through the door and set it inside the room. She closed the curtains and flopped onto the bed. The walls were covered in tacky wood paneling, and a painting of a bullfighter on black velvet hung over the bed. Kella considered the irony of the two different paintings in the room. Perhaps she should take the bullfighter to the Rocky Trails Gallery too.

Even though she had been driving for sixteen hours, Kella was still wired, and it wasn't just from the coffee and five-hour energy pills she had been popping.

She peered out through the crack in the curtains and saw the neon sign from Rose's Cantina bar next door. Would she dare go in a place like that for a drink alone? *Why not?* she thought. *What's the worst thing that can happen?*

She freshened her sparse makeup in the tiny bathroom, changed into a clean T-shirt, and carefully locked the door behind her before walking to Rose's.

Inside, she felt all eyes on her as she made her way to one of the seats at the bar. The patrons were a mixture of truck drivers, blue-collar workers, and bikers, and the men outnumbered the women by a ratio of 10:1.

Behind the bar was a woman in her late sixties with bleached blonde hair and heavy blue eye makeup. She had one too many buttons undone on her blouse, and her push-up bra was working hard for tips. Through a window over the counter behind the barmaid, Kella could see activity in the kitchen beyond the heat lamps. A young cook set a plate of french fries on the stainless steel surface and called out, "Fries up, Rose." She was busy wiping the counter and moving some glasses as she looked up at Kella.

"Holy sheep shit!" Rose said.

"Sorry?" said Kella.

"Oh, honey, I swear you are the spitting image of my daughter," said Rose. "She's forty-one, and she lives in Tennessee now, but I can't believe the resemblance. You're a bit younger of course. Something about the nose."

"I get that from my dad," said Kella.

"What can I get you, sweetie?" said Rose.

"Can I get a glass of red wine and a Caesar salad with chicken please?"

"Sure, babe. I haven't seen you in here before, have I? Where are you from?"

"Actually, I'm just passing through on my way to Denver. I live just outside of Toronto."

"Canada?" said Rose. "You're a Canuck?" The cheerful smile left Rose's face as she clipped Kella's order to the counter behind her and then delivered the french fries to another customer.

*That was weird*, thought Kella.

Rose didn't say anything else as she served Kella her wine and salad, and Kella swiveled in her chair to watch two couples line dancing to "Boot Scootin' Boogie" by Brooks and Dunn.

An older man who was sitting at the other end of the bar made his way over to talk to Kella.

"Don't even think about it, Randy," said Rose, and the man retreated back to his chair.

Kella gave Rose a smile as she left cash on the counter and stood up to leave. "You take care, sugar," said Rose.

"Thanks. You too," said Kella as she left.

The next morning, Kella received a message from Marigold DeSalle at Rocky Trails Gallery:

Dear Kella,

We have reserved a room for you beginning tonight at the Brown Palace Hotel. Just check in with the doorman, and he will arrange valet parking, which we will also cover. 1750 Tremont St. Denver is the best location to put in your GPS. You can't miss it! The doorman will also take care of placing the painting in the hotel vault, and we will arrange transport to our gallery for you in the morning. Please text me when you arrive. Safe travels.

Marigold

Kella checked her GPS and anticipated a drive of nine or ten hours today to get to Denver.

Driving west on Interstate 80 through Nebraska was one of the longest, flattest, and most boring drives she had ever experienced. Miles and miles with nothing to see but cornfields.

West of North Platte, with the Rocky Mountains on the horizon, she crossed into Colorado and merged onto Interstate 76 to Denver.

At six that evening, she reached her destination, but the Brown Palace Hotel was unlike anything she had imagined. The imposing building was literally a reddish-brown color and had an air of opulence and grandeur that Kella longed for but could hardly afford. Thankfully, the DeSalles were footing the bill for her lavish accommodations.

She was greeted by the cheerful and uniformed bell captain, and as planned, when she told him who she was and mentioned Arthur and Marigold, he took charge. He commandeered a valet driver to park her car and assured her that her bags would be delivered immediately to her suite, and the crate would be placed safely in the hotel vault. She could check in with the concierge in the lobby and with the reception desk for further information about her room. "Sorry about the messy car," she said as she handed over the keys.

Kella felt like Cinderella arriving at the ball in her jeans and T-shirt as she stepped into the soaring expanse of the lobby. The marble floors, dark oak paneling, grand staircase, chandeliers, and artwork were a stark contrast to the hideous Tropics Motel that she had stayed in last night.

The Brown Palace Hotel was touted as the oldest continually operating hotel in Denver, and since it opened its doors in 1892, they had never been locked. The palatial building had accommodated the rich, famous, and influential for more than 125 years, including inventors, presidents, royalty, rock stars, and actors.

Kella sent the DeSalles a quick text to tell them that she had arrived.

At the reception desk under the vast green awning, she was welcomed like an honored guest, and after some brief paperwork was completed, she was given a key and escorted to her room.

Almost immediately, her bag arrived at her door, and as she fumbled to get her wallet out of her purse to offer a tip, the bell hop raised a hand to say, "No need. It's all taken care of."

Once alone in her room, she kicked off her shoes and did a back dive onto the bed.

*These people really know how to treat a lady,* she thought.

A text arrived from Marigold: "Glad that you arrived safely. We hope that everything is to your satisfaction. We are out with our German client tonight, but you can enjoy dinner at the hotel. The Palace Arms restaurant is excellent, or you can try the Ship Tavern Pub if you care for something more casual. Charge meals to your room please. Enjoy. We will be in touch in the morning. Grab breakfast at Ellynton's, and we will send for you at 9:30 a.m."

Kella could not believe this was happening. She was dying to check in on Facebook and share a selfie of herself in her room on Instagram. *If that snob Jane Whetstone could see me now,* she thought, but she didn't dare let anyone know where she was or what she was up to.

She treated herself to a long bath in the most gorgeous and well-appointed hotel bathroom she had ever experienced and then got dressed and put on makeup for her grand entrance into one of the hotel restaurants. From the hallway outside her room on the fifth floor, she could look over the railing and down to the cavernous lobby below. She could see people coming and going from all walks of life. Cowboys and hikers, moguls and supermodels, every person looked even more interesting than the last, and she considered inventing a fake persona for the evening to disguise her boring identity. On second thought, she realized that if she told anyone that she was a Canadian fine art collector with a rare Frederic Remington painting, and she was in town to make a deal with a German art buyer, she would fit in just fine.

After scoping out the dining choices, she took Marigold's advice and settled on the Ship Tavern. The nautical theme was done to perfection in the old-time pub with a huge ship's mast and a crow's nest dominating the center of the room. Brass accents and authentic model ships decorated the restaurant, and Kella briefly considered taking a seat at the bar at one of the cute stools with the anchors on the side. She instead opted for a table covered in a fresh blue and white gingham tablecloth surrounded by wooden captain chairs.

Kella ordered the lobster salad roll and a signature cocktail called the Palace Mule. She sipped her drink while she did some people watching from her corner table. In her mind, she concocted a scenario where she was seated at a table sharing drinks with a gathering of worldly jet-setters. She would regale them with the entire story of the Remington painting adventure, which she was wishing she could share with just about anyone. She would embellish and guild every detail and include dramatic pauses and changes in the tone of her voice to assure that she would be the center of attention. At least tomorrow she could share it with the DeSalles, and although she was dreaming of a memorable evening with exotic characters, she was drawn even more back to the sumptuous bed waiting for her upstairs. She charged the meal to her room and made her way back to the elevators. Tonight she needed to sleep, because tomorrow was going to be one of those days that she would remember for the rest of her life.

# 36

Kella checked her email first thing in the morning before leaving her room to get breakfast. Most concerning was a message from her lawyer stating that the mortgage company was preparing foreclosure proceedings and that they needed to meet to discuss next steps as soon as possible. Reese had also sent her a form to sign from Deercrest Academy, which he needed to register Corby, as Kella was the custodial parent. There was also a request for her to judge the Hunter Division this year at the Duckville Fall Fair.

All of these matters would need to wait until she got home. A text from Marigold confirmed that Kella needed to present the receipt for the vault storage of the painting at the concierge desk and meet a driver in a dark blue Range Rover at the front entrance at nine thirty.

As much as Kella would have loved to linger over breakfast at Ellynton's in the hotel, she hadn't left herself enough time for that and settled on a cup of coffee, some toast, and a fruit cup to get her through the morning.

At 9:25, she was at the front door of the hotel, and the bell captain already had her crated painting next to him at the door.

Minutes later, a shiny blue Range Rover parked in front of the hotel, and out stepped a handsome man about thirty years old.

"Kella Major?" he asked.

"Yes, I'm Kella," she said, extending a hand to shake his.

"I'm Monroe DeSalle," he said. "My parents sent me to get you." He opened the passenger door as the rear hatch opened for the bell captain to place the painting in the back.

Kella settled into the leather seat to study the young man beside her, and a breeze of cologne enveloped her when he closed the door. "It's only a few minutes to the gallery," he said. "Have you been to Denver before?"

"Never," she said. "It's really beautiful."

"Are you staying long?" he asked.

"I need to start driving home tomorrow."

"That's too bad," he said.

Kella didn't answer, as she wondered what might transpire if she could stay longer.

Monroe was dressed in dark jeans and a designer shirt with the colorful cuffs folded open. He wore a huge watch and a couple of bracelets as well as expensive-looking leather monk shoes. He was impeccably groomed and appeared affluent and spoiled. She imagined that he built those muscles between selfies in a gym mirror and he hadn't done a hard day's work in his life. Not her type in the least.

"Do you work for your parents in the gallery?" she asked.

Monroe laughed. "Not usually," he said. "I'm home from Syria, on leave between deployments right now. I work with the US Special Forces supporting Operation Inherent Resolve that's going on in Iraq."

"Seriously?" said Kella. "I never would have guessed you are military. What do you do over there?"

"Well, in the broad sense, we are working to eliminate the Islamic State, but my command is in mapping, tracking troop movements, and that sort of thing. Pretty boring stuff really."

"I doubt that," said Kella with a newfound respect and admiration for Monroe.

"Here we are," he said as he drove into the small parking lot in front of Rocky Trails Gallery.

The gallery had a facade of sawn logs with a cedar shingled roof. Over the door hung a sandblasted redwood sign with gold leaf lettering and a painted mountain scene on the top.

The front door with the door handle in the shape of a large brass paintbrush opened, and out stepped Arthur and Marigold DeSalle.

The couple appeared to be about ten years older than the photos on their website. Arthur was dressed in a pale blue button-down shirt and an ivory linen jacket. He wore starched blue jeans and black ostrich cowboy boots. Marigold wore a long denim skirt and heels with a crisp white blouse. Her abundance of silver and turquoise jewelry jingled and jangled as she walked.

"Welcome, Kella. We have really been looking forward to meeting you," said Arthur with a firm handshake. Marigold swooped in for a hug as Monroe carried the package into the gallery.

Inside, Kella had to adjust her eyes to the dark space with track lighting illuminating each individual piece of art on the walls. Oil paintings, drawings, sketches, and watercolors filled the walls and featured the anticipated cowboy and Indian themes as well as stunning mountain landscapes and wildlife images. Wooden pedestals with green felt tops supported bronze sculptures ranging from a size you could fit in your hand to grand pieces for large mantels.

Kella followed Arthur through the Master's Collection and watched him quickly input a code on a keypad to open a door into a room that was half office, half boardroom, with a felt-covered shelf that ran the entire width of one wall. The blank wall was lit from overhead.

"Take a seat," said Marigold. "Can we get you anything? Coffee, tea, Perrier?" she asked as Monroe carefully uncrated the painting.

"No, I'm fine thanks," she said.

"That must have been quite a drive," said Arthur. "We really appreciate you responding so quickly. We are on a bit of a time crunch today as you know. Our client returns to Frankfurt this evening."

"How was everything at the Palace?" asked Marigold.

Kella watched Monroe put on a pair of white gloves as he finally exhumed the painting from the packing and placed it on the shelf.

"The hotel is just wonderful," said Kella. "Everyone has been amazing."

Monroe, Arthur, and Marigold now stood in a semicircle facing the painting, and Kella stood up to join them. She never had a chance to study it in such flattering lighting. Arthur moved in closely and put on a pair of glasses from his jacket pocket.

"Not his best work," he said. "No wonder they thought he burned it."

"Oh, Arthur, you nut," said Marigold, poking him in the side.

"It's just wonderful. Do tell us how you came to own this painting, Kella."

Kella explained to the DeSalles that she had found it among her father's possessions after he passed away and that it remained a mystery to her how and when he acquired it.

"Fascinating. So let's get down to business," said Arthur. "We need to open the doors to the public at ten, and our buyer will be here by eleven, so we need to get our ducks in a row. Do you have the certificate of authenticity with you from the Buffalo Bill?"

Kella took the envelope out of her purse, opened it, and placed it on the table. Arthur studied it with his glasses on the end of his nose.

"Do you need anything else?" asked Monroe.

"No thanks, honey, that's all," said Marigold.

As Monroe left, Arthur started into a speech that seemed like it was recited directly from a script. He explained how the art broker fee worked and how the domestic art market for investors was quite volatile right now. He assured Kella that Remingtons were still strong, but he advised that waiting for the spring auction could be a gamble. Kella nodded and tried to appear as educated in these matters as possible.

"I'm sure you have a figure in mind, so if you want to tell us what that is, we can start from there," he said.

Kella was caught off guard. Her mind went back to the price of paintings she had seen in the results from this year's Scottsdale Art Auction.

She decided to start high and see what kind of reaction she got, knowing that this was free money at this point and any amount would buy her some more time with the mortgage company.

Kella swallowed hard and said, "I was thinking $500,000."

For a moment, the room was silent as Arthur and Marigold looked at each other.

"American dollars," said Kella, waiting for a response.

Marigold placed her hand over Kella's on the table. "Darling, we can do much better than that," she said.

Arthur broke in. "One thing that we pride ourselves on in this gallery is complete transparency. We have a pretty good idea of the market value of this piece, and taking into consideration our client's budget and subtracting our fees from the equation, we are prepared to get you two point eight mill."

Kella paused as she felt a chill through her body. "Do you mean two million, eight hundred thousand American bucks?"

"That's what we were thinking. That's contingent, of course, on our buyer being in agreement, but we already have him primed, and we don't anticipate any issues."

Kella didn't know whether to laugh or cry. "Can I have some

water?" she asked as she pushed her chair back from the table and put both hands on her knees.

"Of course, honey. Are you okay?" asked Marigold as Arthur quickly went to get some water.

Kella stood up, and Marigold stood up next to her. Kella moved to Marigold and wrapped her arms around her. Marigold held onto Kella with the warmth of a mother. Kella began shaking and then sobbing. "You have … no idea … what this means … to me," she said. "Thank you … thank you … so much. I … I just wish … that my father …"

Arthur returned to the room with a glass and a bottle of Perrier in his hands.

"Did I miss something?" he said, looking at the two women in an embrace.

"Kella's just feeling a bit emotional today," said Marigold.

# 37

In the early-morning hours in late July, a cool fog hung over the fields at Major Meadows before the hot sun chased it away. Kella looked out from her bedroom window at the few horses left at the farm grazing in the big pasture. She made a mug of coffee to take with her out to the barn and began going through the motions of her day with the possibility of a new reality. While the DeSalles had already confirmed that all systems were go on the painting deal, Kella was reluctant to make any changes or notify anyone about her plans until the money was in the bank. The German buyer would transfer funds to the DeSalles from a bank in Frankfurt, and then once they confirmed his deposit, they would wire Kella's share to her bank in Toronto.

Marigold promised to text Kella to keep her up to date on the process.

The painting itself would not be going back to Germany right away. Instead, it would be displayed first at the Remington museum in Ogdensburg, and it was expected to make the rounds to some other venues in the US before joining the German's collection. If the art magazines wanted to celebrate the discovery, they were welcome to do so at the assurance that Kella's name and address would never be shared. The DeSalles' reputation was built on integrity and discretion, and they would happily deflect the publicity to themselves and Rocky Trails Gallery.

Meanwhile, since the rest of the art world was unaware that the transaction had taken place, Kella continued to receive inquiries of every kind. Content that she had made the best possible deal at the time, she resisted the urge to consider other scenarios.

*Drifting Before the Storm* was a painting without comparables. It came with a great story, and that was much of the value of any artwork. While its origins were confirmed, the past 110 years of its existence remained a mystery, and its storied path from New Rochelle, New York, to Duckville, Ontario, might never be revealed.

Kella was still playing hide-and-seek with her lawyer, the mortgage company, Watson's Feed Store, the electric company, and her hay supplier. She texted Damien.

"Thanks again. Everything go okay?"

"No worries. Cider loved trailer life," he replied.

"I owe you dinner," messaged Kella.

"Sounds good."

Early in the afternoon while Kella was riding, a message came from Marigold.

"Everything should be set," she said. "Check your account and let me know when you receive transfer. Could take a couple hours."

Kella was ready for this moment, but she wasn't. She slid down off the saddle and quickly put the horse away. Then she sat outside the barn door on a bale of hay and stared at her phone. She logged in to her online bank account and checked the balance: $42.50.

A service charge had already been deducted from her original balance.

It took a lot of discipline to put the phone in her pocket and finish up the barn chores. She cleaned stalls, swept floors, wiped off tack, and put hay in the stalls. Grass needed to be cut, so she got the old riding mower out of the shed and climbed on. After a few trips up and down the laneway with the mower, she couldn't wait any longer. She parked in front of the house, turned off the engine, and checked her phone again.

This time, her bank account showed a new balance: $3,689,686.50.

The figure was shocking to read. The conversion from US dollars to Canadian dollars was something Kella hadn't officially calculated.

She abandoned the lawnmower and ran inside.

Her first call was to Tina Giragardi. She had to take the farm off the market right away. Kella explained that her father's estate had finally been settled, and she was going to keep the farm after all. Tina was disappointed but understanding. She thanked Tina profusely for all of her help and then wrote a check to her for $10,000 as a token of goodwill and put it in an envelope. She would drop it off with a note and a bottle of wine at Tina's office in a few days.

Next she called her lawyer, Glenn Gibson.

"I need to meet with you right away," she said.

"Sounds urgent," said Gibson. "I'm in the office now if you need me."

Kella immediately got in her vehicle and drove to his practice in Bonne River.

She arrived in his office out of breath and talking a mile a minute. She explained to him the entire story—how she found the painting, the trip to Ogdensburg, and the authentication in Wyoming. She told him about the DeSalles and her adventure at the Brown Palace Hotel in Denver. Then she logged in to her bank account on the phone and showed him the balance.

"I'm not making this up," she said.

Glenn Gibson leaned back in his chair and interlocked his fingers behind his head.

"Kella, I couldn't be happier for you," he said. "Let me get a figure for you that will satisfy your mortgage for the short term, and we can work out the remaining disbursements in a few weeks."

Gibson opened a file and set a calculator on his desk.

"Do you have a checkbook with you?" he asked.

"Right here," she said.

"Write a check for me for $750,000 today, and I'll take it over to bank to have it certified. Congratulations, Kella. Your father took good care of you and your daughter after all."

"He sure did," said Kella.

On the way home, Kella stopped at Watson's Feed Store.

She settled her bill and placed the largest feed order that she had made in a year and requested that it be delivered. Neil Watson held the check in his hand. "This isn't going to be a problem, is it?"

"No," said Kella. "Between you and me, my father's estate has been settled, and everything should be just fine from now on."

Kella arrived home and stepped out of her Lexus at the end of her laneway. Tina Giragardi's sign was still mounted in the grass, and Kella rocked it back and forth until it came loose from the ground. She tossed in the back of the vehicle.

She was back in the barn sweeping out the feed room to make space for a big delivery when Damien walked in.

Kella threw her arms around him.

"Wow, I wasn't expecting this kind of greeting," he said. "I was just stopping by because I saw the sign was down. Did you sell the farm?"

"I'm not selling it," she said. "Plans have changed. We are staying. I can't thank you enough for all of your help. Can you stay for dinner?"

"Before I answer that, I want you to come out to the truck and meet my new girlfriend," he said.

Kella was deflated.

Just when she was on top of the world and ready to move forward with a freedom that she had never experienced, Damien was no longer available to share the joy with her.

She followed Damien to the truck, where Cider was already jumping at the door. Evidently they had already met.

Kella walked to the open passenger window and looked in to see a border collie puppy sitting on a Navajo rug on the front seat.

"Isn't she cute?" said Damien.

"No, you are the cute one," said Kella. "Very funny. What's her name?"

"She doesn't have one yet. What do you think?"

"How about Remington?" said Kella.

"For a girl? That sounds like a male dog's name."

"Okay, then why not Remy?" The puppy perked her ears.

"I like it," said Damien. "Remy it is."

# Author's Notes

I hope that you enjoyed reading *Paint the Horse Blue* as much as I enjoyed writing it. I want to sincerely thank Laura Foster, curator of the Frederic Remington Museum in Ogdensburg, New York, for her invaluable assistance and suggestions. The painting *Drifting Before the Storm* was truly painted by Remington in 1904, but as far as anyone knows, it was indeed burned by the artist.

I also want to thank my friends Joe and Pat Carter for their help in bringing authenticity to the chapter about the AQHA World Championship Show in Louisville, Kentucky, in 1974. Pat Carter won a World Championship there in the Trail Class. Sadly, Pat passed away before this book was published. I also want to acknowledge my longtime friend Fred Knapple and the rest of the Knapple family of Nebraska for not only being a big part of my teenage years but also reminding me of some details of the Nebraska Sand Hills in the seventies. Finally, I want to thank my son, Jared Grice, for his technical help and inspiring me to continually build a legacy to make him proud.

CPSIA information can be obtained
at www.ICGtesting.com
Printed in the USA
BVHW070903230520
580088BV00001B/133

9 781480 874855